GIRLS TAKE VEGAS

JO LYONS

Boldw**oo**d

First published in 2024 as *Benidorm Cocktail Hour*. This edition published in Great Britain in 2025 by Boldwood Books Ltd.

Copyright © Jo Lyons, 2024

Cover Design by Alexandra Allden

Cover Images: Alexandra Allden and Shutterstock

The moral right of Jo Lyons to be identified as the author of this work has been asserted in accordance with the Copyright, Designs and Patents Act 1988.

Every effort has been made to obtain the necessary permissions with reference to copyright material, both illustrative and quoted. We apologise for any omissions in this respect and will be pleased to make the appropriate acknowledgements in any future edition.

A CIP catalogue record for this book is available from the British Library.

Paperback ISBN 978-1-80557-234-3

Large Print ISBN 978-1-80557-233-6

Hardback ISBN 978-1-80557-232-9

Trade Paperback ISBN 978-1-80656-102-5

Ebook ISBN 978-1-80557-235-0

Kindle ISBN 978-1-80557-236-7

Audio CD ISBN 978-1-80557-227-5

MP3 CD ISBN 978-1-80557-228-2

Digital audio download ISBN 978-1-80557-230-5

This book is printed on certified sustainable paper. Boldwood Books is dedicated to putting sustainability at the heart of our business. For more information please visit https://www.boldwoodbooks.com/about-us/sustainability/

Boldwood Books Ltd, 23 Bowerdean Street, London, SW6 3TN

www.boldwoodbooks.com

For Alice.
Friendship is everything.

1

There is no job more glamorous than being a professional singer. My limbs are aching from spending the forty-minute trip to Alicante airport hunched on top of three suitcases, squashed in the back of a minivan that whiffed of long-dead sandwiches and stale cigarettes, listening to my support band, the Dollz, bicker about the inconvenience of having to do three back-to-back one-hour shows in Las Vegas, with only two nights off to gamble our earnings away. Even though all of our expenses are paid for, and it is the trip of a lifetime, it just goes to show that they can still find something to moan about.

I stare at Matteo's last message to me. A request to

'talk' as soon as we land at Harry Reid International Airport a few miles outside of Las Vegas. He has attached a photo of me and my classical singing partner, Luke, kissing on stage last night.

I frantically message Matteo back to say that Luke kissed me. *He* kissed *me*. Not the other way around. When he doesn't reply to the message – perhaps sending it ten times in a row is a bit much – I try to phone him, but his phone is switched off. It will be in flight mode as he is flying from LA to Las Vegas to see me. To spend a full week in my adorable, witty and definitely *not* adulterous company. I shove my phone back in my pocket. Poor Matteo. Poor, poor Matteo the Magnificent. With his dreamy, kind eyes and his gorgeous face. The last thing he will want to see is Luke kissing me on stage. It was all very innocent on my side. Luke had leaned in at the end of the song, blaming an unusually strong gravitational pull, and because he had me in a vice-like grip, there wasn't much I could do about it. He has a massive unrequited crush on me that does not seem to go away no matter how much I tell him I'm in love with another man. The kiss, about as enjoyable as Lyme disease, lasted a nanosecond, and I was extremely annoyed with him. And it is only a matter of time before everyone finds out about it and gives me a hard time.

Unfortunately, to add to my woes, on arrival at Alicante airport, there has been a confirmed sighting of Luke, and we are all severely spooked. I am quietly hyperventilating while we unpack our bags and make our way through to the check-in desks. As I stand in line, I am fully aware that I am to blame for allowing this horrific love-triangle-type situation to develop.

'Which way did he go?' bellows Big Sue, making her way back from a quick sweep of the immediate area to the check-in desk, where we are trying to off-load our many, many suitcases. We are ridiculously over the weight limit. We are all dressed like cheap, down-on-their-luck Barbies and Kens because of a series of small mishaps over the costumes for my newly engaged best friends' pre-wedding celebration (it is definitely not a stag do and is infinitely more elegant and tasteful), and we are set for a week of utter mayhem unless I can get to grips with our overfilled schedule. And, somehow, in the midst of it all, convince Matteo that I have no feelings whatsoever for Luke.

Liberty points to the security area. 'He went that way.'

Big Sue puts a cupped hand to her brow, even though we are inside, screws her eyes, and sweeps her gaze around the busy terminal. 'So, that's a ten four on the security breach. We'll have to intercept the target at the gate.'

She has gone into full military mode. Also, she is dressed as Gangsta Ken and looks quite menacing with it.

'What's he playing at?' booms Big Mand, crossing the terminal back towards us. 'I hope his next shite's a hedgehog.' She is a midwife and has a lot to do with the business end of things.

'Are you sure there aren't any flights leaving today for England, Norway, Sweden...' An idea suddenly pings into my mind. 'Or Santorini? He mentioned Santorini once. Wherever that is.'

Big Sue shakes her head. 'The only two flights leaving this morning are our one to Las Vegas, and one to somewhere no one has ever heard of.'

'Why would he follow Connie all the way to Las Vegas?' says Liberty. 'Unless she has driven him to it with her micro-cheating?'

Thankfully, Tash steps in. 'I wouldn't say micro-cheating, as such. Connie barely has a grasp of the basics when it comes to dating.'

'True,' agrees Liberty. 'It's more that she's cushioning him. Keeping him dangling, as in, he's her plan B.'

'You're right,' Tash says proudly, as though I'm not

standing right in bloody front of them having a mild heart attack. She makes sure Sister Kevin, her newest love, who was wearing a nun's wimple when she recently met in Benidorm, is listening to how wise and insightful she can be when it comes to the thorny intricacies of love languages and dating terminology.

I can't quite believe what I'm hearing. Just as I'm about to protest, the whole group is suddenly interested in what golden nuggets Liberty's mood management degree can offer us.

'Connie. What exactly happened last night at Voices?' Liberty asks, turning to me.

I gulp as Ged, Liam, Sister Kevin and all five of the Dollz stare quizzically at me. 'Well, like I said. Luke and I covered for you at Voices when you all pulled out at the last minute.' I raise my eyebrows to remind them of their unprofessional behaviour and to lay the foundation that perhaps this fiasco is not entirely of my own doing. 'We did a remarkable job considering you put my new regular slot as headline act in jeopardy. Everyone was happy. We went our separate ways. There was no micro-cheating or cushioning or whatever's trending involved whatsoever.'

'And nothing occurred between you and Luke?' Liberty is talking to me but scrolling through her phone.

'No. Not especially,' I say. I'd rather block it all out. That kiss. The look in Luke's eyes. The thunderous applause and wolf whistles from the crowd.

'Nothing at all. You're sure?' Liberty is now passing her phone around the group. They are looking at it with great interest.

'Wow. Old people really love to overshare on Facebook, don't they? Who cares if their shepherd's pie is better than last week's?' Ged remarks, casually returning the phone to Liberty. 'But it's good to know they like to catalogue every single thing that happens on a night out.'

Liberty shows me the image of Luke and me kissing on stage.

'I can explain,' I say to the crowd of disappointed faces.

* * *

'You have a very simple choice to make,' says Liam, settling into his seat beside me on board this lovely Boeing 787 Dreamliner. 'You've spent a week in Benidorm, falling in love with Matteo, your love-at-first-sight, sparkles-in-your-eyes, hot, Latino music producer.'

Like I'm not aware of all that, but carry on...

'Then, when he went off to LA for work without officially confirming whether you two were *exclusive* or not,' joins in Ged as he plonks himself down next to Liam, 'you've spent the next week having your head turned by your uber-posh Norwegian singing partner, Luke.'

'Correct,' confirms Liam. 'And just because Luke's an extremely gorgeous royal figure who saved your life once and is now proposing a multimillion-dollar-Cinderella-style marriage—'

'—doesn't mean he's right for you.' Ged raises an eyebrow. 'I still don't trust him. I mean, what is he doing, following you around the globe?'

'We don't know that for certain,' I say weakly.

Ged throws his arms up. 'Seriously? There's no other explanation, Connie, love. No matter how much you want to pretend otherwise.'

He's right. The potential of Luke being on this flight has me, Ged, Liam and all the Dollz on high alert. Big Sue tried to do a sweep of the plane but was ordered back from first class by the cabin crew because we are about to take off, and they need everyone buckled into their seats. The Dollz are sitting in the rows behind us. Cherry is slumped down in her seat with her eyes closed. She still has make-up smeared down her face and a false eyelash hanging off. It has been a harrowing last few hours for her. She has still not told her husband with the receding hairline that she may be with child. She is giving off serious unexploded-device vibes. Next to her is Liberty.

'And still, none of you have the decency to consider Luke may be after *me*,' I can hear her saying. 'I'm the hottest one out of the lot of you, and yet, *oh no*, someone that posh couldn't possibly be after someone like her.'

'Get over yourself, pet. Of course someone like him would be interested in you. You're friggin' gorgeous, and you know it. He obviously has a weird thing for classical singers. That's all.' Big Sue, as usual, has worked her magic. Liberty seems temporarily pleased with this explanation.

'It would really help matters if you explained exactly what happened last night when the both of you sang together at Voices, Connie. How did you end up kissing? What did he say after? What did *you* say?' asks Big Mand from the seat behind me. She rolls her eyes as she twists around. 'And if you two could keep your tongues to yourselves for two twatting minutes, I'd be able to hear myself twatting think! It's like sitting next to a herd of cattle slurping at a water trough.'

'Excuse us for being in love!' yells Tash, lifting her

lips briefly from Sister Kevin's. She is on a mission to secure him as her baby-daddy-to-be. The cabin crew have asked her twice already to get off his lap, do up her seat belt and keep her hands to herself. 'Ignore her, Kev, she's just jealous.'

I hear someone tut loudly. I'm not going to turn around as it may encourage the spat. I only have the duration of this flight to get everyone back on good speaking terms.

My mind flies to last night. Luke definitely kissed me. Not the other way round. Enough people filmed it for the evidence to be crystal clear. Luke did all the leaning. All one inch of it. But if I'm brutally honest, the footage looks very dubious. Especially once uploaded to the World Wide Web. Put that together with the damning tabloid attention we received during our Royal Northern Sinfonia tour, on account of a royal cousin wanting to marry Luke, and the odds are beginning to stack up against me. Matteo would have every reason to be furious.

'What did Luke say?' Big Mand repeats.

She's like a dog with a bone.

'He said that he thinks he's in love with me. That he's never felt this way before, and that he would never forgive himself if he didn't at least try to win me over because all's fair in love and war.'

I can hear some murmuring before Big Mand says, 'Oh, that's quite sweet actually.'

Then Big Sue says in a slightly choked voice, 'I guess if you feel strongly enough about a person, then you would fight for them. If it's a love worth fighting for.'

There's an almighty silence as we all wonder whether she's talking about her and Big Mand, or simply reciting Cheryl Tweedy-Cole-Fernandez-Versini-almost-Payne-then-exhaustingly-all-the-way-back-to-Tweedy again.

'Yes. Yes, you would fight for them,' Ged agrees, loudly enough for the Dollz to hear over the roar of the engines. The aircraft has started to move. 'Love conquers all. It's about openness, accepting each other for who they really are, but above all, it's about forgiveness.'

This too is followed by a lengthy silence as we appreciate Ged is really talking about the awkward situation (the accidental 'outing' that no one has dared yet mention) in the case of him and Liam versus the unconfirmed lesbians. Big Mand and Big Sue, who for whatever reasons want to stay firmly in the closet, did not appreciate Ged and Liam posting a photo of the four of them with the caption 'Just had the best double date ever'.

'Well, for what it's worth,' Tash bellows, 'I think love is blind.'

We all take a beat. This overused cliché makes no sense, not in any of the previously mentioned subtexts, unless she means Sister Kevin is blind to her obvious insanity.

A lovely lady from the airline sashays over to ask us all politely to shut up during the safety announcement, adding that we're all wrong. 'Love is about respect. Respect for the cabin crew and the pilot. And respect for what to do in the event of an emergency, such as a loss in cabin pressure, or our refusal to serve you free drinks later on if you don't pipe down and listen.'

Well, that's love sorted. At least we have safely veered off the topic of me and my unrequited love triangle. While the cabin crew do their demonstration, I look down at my ill-fitting Barbie costume. We were in such a rush that we didn't have time to change. I suggest we all swap clothes.

'I'll go in the toilet with Kev,' Tash hisses through the seats, even though they have no need to swap clothes with each other. 'It's one of his BIG birthday surprises.' She pauses to allow us to let our imaginations run wild as to what they could possibly get up to in such a confined space.

'Christ alive. I'm not going in after you two then!' shouts Liberty too loudly.

'I thought you were already giving him a surprise for his BIG birthday,' Big Sue says in a less-than-impressed tone. 'Remember?'

Tash glares frostily at her.

'BIG birthday?' Sister Kevin says, smiling as he leans forward to look along the row. 'Who has a BIG birthday coming up?'

This causes a lot of eye contact. Sister Kevin's BIG birthday has been a constant bone of contention over the past few days. Now it seems it may not be as BIG as we hoped.

'Be quiet or you'll wake Cherry. She's like a ticking time bomb, that one,' Tash says, skilfully changing the topic.

As if evoking some macabre joint memory, I see panic flush their faces. Cherry and pregnancy do not get on well. For Cherry, motherhood is just one long struggle for meaning. Tash has successfully dodged the Sister Kevin BIG birthday bullet for now. I'm just thankful that when I turn back around in my seat, Ged and Liam have their headphones on and are watching the third series of *Bridgerton*. We are all avid fans of the show.

Liam lifts an earphone. He looks distraught. This

whole week has been stressful. No wonder he's showing signs of wear and tear.

'Are you okay?' I mouth.

He shakes his head sadly. 'No.'

'Everything will be fine,' I promise, reaching over Ged to give his fingers a squeeze.

'It won't,' he says with a huge sigh. 'It won't.'

'It will.' I must stay positive and strong for him. 'We'll find a way.'

'You're wasting your time,' says Ged, lifting an earphone to intercept our conversation. 'He's talking about *Bridgerton*.'

I frown, perplexed.

'I simply can't fancy Colin,' Liam says. 'Lord knows I've tried, but I can't. I just can't.' His eyes are glassy. 'How many more brothers are there?'

Ah. I shrug sympathetically because we've all been there. When you've had a taste of what I've had – Matteo the Magnificent (I promise I will stop calling him that as soon as it wears off) – then the Colins of this world are all rendered wet blankets. That reminds me. The unrequited love triangle in *Bridgerton* is not dissimilar to my own. At the thought of Luke, my heart sinks that he might sabotage my romantic trip to see Matteo. I should put a stop to it. And even though I haven't got a spontaneous bone in my body, it's time to put on my big girl pants and take action.

I take a stealthy look around. Everyone seems to be asleep or watching their screens. I quietly un-buckle my seat belt and get up.

A hand lands heavily on my shoulder.

'Not so fast.' It's Big Sue, acting like one of those undercover air marshals you see in films. 'Where do you think you're off to?'

'The toilet,' I say hesitantly.

Big Sue sees right through me. She lifts her hand to hide her lips and leans down. 'You're off to see if Luke has boarded this flight.' She regards me for a moment. 'I'll come too. You need a distraction. I'll run interference while you enter first class.' She glances down at the complex bit of kit on her wrist. 'Ren-dezvous back here at fifteen hundred hours. Capeesh?'

The outfit has possessed Big Sue. That's the only justification I can give for her talking Italian slang and acting like a mobster. And yet...

'Capeesh.' I nod back. Who am I to burst her bubble?

2

While the cabin crew are busy doing the first trolley service of free drinks in economy, we stealthily make our way to the curtained-off area hiding the haves from the have-nots. There are two cabin crew busying themselves, restocking little bottles of Prosecco and bags of nuts.

'Excuse me,' says Big Sue. 'I think I dropped my phone down here when I was boarding. Have you seen it?'

While they immediately help her search the floor for it, I nip behind the curtain into first class. But as I start looking down each row, a sixth sense crawls up my spine, stopping me in my tracks. He's here. I can feel it. I slip into an empty seat and ask myself if this confrontation is really what I need right now. What do I say to Luke? I can hardly ask him to get off the plane. Perhaps ignoring him is actually the better course of action. It might send a more confident signal that I am not interested in him. I am en route to Las Vegas to fall into the forgiving arms of my new lover Matteo the Magnificent.

'Excuse me, madam,' says an irate cabin crew member towering over me. 'You're not allowed in here.' He points to the curtain and watches while I do the walk of shame, head hanging, back down the aisle to economy.

When I reach my seat, Big Sue is quick to ascertain whether the mission was a success. 'Mission status?'

'Negative,' I say glumly. 'Well, and positive, I suppose.'

'Did you have eyes on the target?' Big Sue presses me. 'Did you get burned?'

'No,' I say. 'I didn't touch anything hot.'

'Were. You. Com. Pro. Mised?' she explains slowly, while Liberty sniggers at my ignorance.

'It was a huge flop, was it?' asks Liberty. She hasn't been fully on board with any of our covert operations to confirm the Luke situation.

'Well, excuse me for not being a former FBI agent. How am I supposed to know the language?'

Fortunately, Big Sue, who works high up in social care, is patient. 'Did you see him?'

'Not really,' I say.

'Not really? What does that mean?'

'It was more of a feeling,' I say.

Big Sue lets out an exasperated groan. 'You felt him? As in, you could feel his presence? Like a ghost?'

Liberty snorts with laughter. 'Fucking useless, Connie. Absolutely fucking useless.'

She's not entirely wrong. I had my chance, and I messed it up. I will spend the remainder of the flight brushing up on my army surveillance speak as punishment.

'I'll go,' says Liberty, springing out of her seat. 'What's the point of having pretty privilege if you don't use it? After all, you're not the only one who has unfinished business with him.'

'How long are you going to dine out on the one blooming dance you had with Luke? One sensual dance does not a relationship make,' booms Big Mand.

Before any of us can stop her, Liberty barges past me and Big Sue, straight to first class as though she owns the place, and disappears behind the curtain.

Ged is right. It's all about confidence. You've got to admire that about her.

We sit down and wait. Surely she will be ejected as quickly as I was.

We wait.

And we wait.

'She's not coming back, is she?' I say gloomily, leaning round to face Big Sue. She has lost interest and has fallen asleep. My eyes travel the row. All the Dollz are flat out. If only I didn't have so much to worry about, I'd join them.

***

After watching the curtain for three hours, and with no sign of Liberty returning, I've suddenly lost all interest in an on-board confirmation of Luke. Liberty is welcome to him, if it means he leaves me alone. Besides, Ged and Liam have been bickering on and off about everyone and everything, including what exactly Kylie Minogue means when she sings 'Padam Padam'. Their fun, last-minute getaway to Las Vegas now seems rash, in light of the amount of emotional baggage all of their guests have brought with them.

'And we'll be bright bloody yellow in all of the

photos. We'll not be able to post any on our socials. Not one!' Liam says forlornly. 'What a waste of a trip.'

'It was your idea to get the fake tan off TikTok,' Ged reminds him. 'You're always clicking the "shop now" button. How many miracle foundation sticks does one person need? And it was your idea to rush into this trip in the first place.'

'I'm impulsive. I'm spontaneous. I'm a risk-taker. That's why this relationship works,' Liam says, waving a hand around accusingly.

I feel Ged bristle in the seat next to me. 'Meaning I'm the opposite?'

'Yes,' says Liam. 'I've always been the fun one.'

It's time to intervene. Liam and Ged have morphed into two full-on bridezillas and it is exhausting. I can't take any more.

'You're both the fun ones. You're both perfectly suited to one another because you're so...' I loosen my seat belt and lean out of my seat to face them. The three of us have lived together since the beginning of university. Their relationship could be my *Mastermind* subject. And luckily for me, I already have a speech prepared. It was meant to be for the first night in Vegas, when I plan to dedicate a special song to them while I'm on stage, but now seems like a good moment to do some of it. 'You're both so passionate and adventurous. You love music and creativity in all its forms. When one of you walks into a room, the other lights up. You share a blissful, harmonious and hopeful life together, always wanting the best for each other. I have never seen a couple more in love or more deserving of one another.'

While Liam bursts into noisy tears, the nearby cabin crew rush to comfort him. 'What seems to be the problem, sir?' one of them asks, bending down to his level.

'I just love my... my... my fiancé so much!' he wails. 'And I'm just so... so... so happy.' He flings his arms around Ged.

The glamorous flight attendant straightens up. He has a sympathetic smile on his face. 'Is this your pre-moon?'

Both Liam and Ged nod vigorously. 'Yes. Yes, it is our pre-moon. And yet some people are finding that term hard to get around. In fact, it's been borderline divisive. No one has an issue with babymoon or minimoon.'

A bit unnecessary, I think.

The attendant acknowledges this complaint with pursed lips. 'I had exactly the same problem for mine. Could I get them to stop calling it a stag do? No, I couldn't.' He winks at them both. 'I'll be right back.'

He turns to me. 'Great speech, honey. Love is all about hope. Hoping for the best for each other.'

'In fact, it is probably time we did a little toast to get this pre-moon off to a good start.' I peer through the crack in the seats behind to see that the Dollz are still asleep. Sister Kevin is engrossed in watching *The Meg 2*, much to Tash's displeasure. She had wanted to binge-watch *Married at First Sight Australia* with him. When he refused, she immediately went to sleep in a huff.

'I'll order some Prosecco,' I say quietly. As chief bridesmaid-slash-best woman, it's the least I can do. I'm also hoping the Prosecco still counts as our first free drink. My poor credit card can't take much more of a battering after buying my Sinfonia costumes, booking the numerous trips in Vegas and the over-weight luggage.

'Good idea,' says Liam. 'I'd love some Prosecco.'

It's as though the word 'Prosecco' starts off a chain reaction.

'Three!' bellows Tash from behind, suddenly awake and upright. 'I'll have three. And Kev will have...'

'I'll have a beer, thanks, Connie,' says Sister Kevin politely. 'Just one beer. Because I'm only one person.'

He is met with silence.

'What?' we hear him say to Tash. 'What have I done? Why are you looking at me like that?'

Oh. My. God. My heart is in my mouth. Ged, Liam and I exchange a fearful look. Tash will go apeshit at that comment. We have learned from experience that her reaction to drink-shaming can be somewhat violent. The best thing we can do is not turn around and draw attention to it.

The frosty silence continues.

'Who's ordering Prosecco?' Cherry sits up straight. 'You know I can't have any.' She has awoken looking furious. And like she needs to take it out on someone. She brushes her flaming-red hair from her tear-stained face.

Where do I go with this?

'Does this mean she's expecting us to have a non-alcoholic pre-moon?' hisses Ged.

'We'll get our own,' says Big Mand. She and Big Sue are still clearly annoyed with Ged and Liam over the accidental outing. 'No offence, Cherry, babes, but we need a drink. Especially after what's happened.'

Ged twists in his seat to peer through the gap. 'For the love of God. Will this blame game *never end*?'

Even I gasp in surprise. This is very out of character for Ged. He has clearly snapped. But before we get to hear the rest of what he has to say, we are interrupted by the jolly flight attendant from before.

He smiles down at Ged and Liam. 'We have two complimentary seats available in first class for you.'

Liam squeals in delight. 'Oh! Thank you, you glorious man.'

The attendant blows him a flirty air kiss. This is great. It means they can drink cocktails galore and be as openly joyful as they please, without the risk of upsetting Cherry.

'Watch out,' booms Big Mand. 'Or he'll *out* you to all the passengers.'

Ged is like lightning, spinning around. 'For the last time. We did not out you and Big Sue on purpose. We'd never do that.'

The smile on the flight attendant's face drops immediately as he gasps in horror. 'You outed them? As in *out out*?'

'Yes,' interjects Big Sue in a low voice. 'And now my own family is barely speaking to me. They think I've hidden it from them on purpose. We're all very hurt.'

'Ooh. I can imagine.' He drops down to speak to Big Sue and Big Mand. He makes namaste hands. 'I see you. I hear you. Same thing happened to me. It's awful, isn't it?'

Big Mand and Big Sue nod glumly.

'Here. You have the first-class seats,' he says. 'You obviously need them more. Follow me.'

We watch open-mouthed as Big Sue and Big Mand follow him down the aisle and disappear behind the curtain.

'What the fuck just happened?' screeches Liam. 'Did they just steal our upgrades?'

'At least I won't have to see them drinking Prosecco,' says Cherry. 'And it'll be free for them in first class, whereas they take your eyes out for it here in cattle class.'

'It's okay, Cherry. I'll not drink either,' I say, fully aware of the resentment in her voice.

'Thanks, Connie, hun. I'll just have a large gin and tonic but without the lemon or the gin, because of the bay... bay... bay...' Cherry bursts into tears.

The cabin crew fly straight back over to see what the matter is.

'I'm preg... preg... preg... pregnant,' she wails. 'And it's my husband's. And he's losing his hair!' Cherry's pre-partum sobs are so loud that surrounding passengers are leaning out of their seats to see what's happening. 'And we already have two kids that we can't control.' Cherry's face is the colour of her hair, vibrant red. 'One of them eats her own poo, for God's sake!'

She gulps in air as she wipes her face with her sleeve, smearing black mascara and blue eyeliner across her cheek.

The horrified expressions on the faces of the cabin crew and the gasps from the passengers demand some swift decisive action. But Big Sue has abandoned us for first class. My head swivels around. Tash is my only hope. She has been friends with Cherry forever. She will be used to Cherry going nuclear. She will have answers, strategies, calming techniques up her sleeve because she works at a university and deals with difficult situations on a daily basis. I twist in my seat to make eye contact with Tash.

Oh no.

Tash has been frozen in time, an appalled expression stuck to her face. She is staring at Sister Kevin as though he has announced that he is single-handedly responsible for something catastrophic, like plastics in the ocean, the global warming crisis or the end of Bennifer's very short five-minute marriage.

Tash is not moving. She has powered down like a robot, staring at him in an eerie fashion. He looks worried.

This is about the Prosecco.

Before I have time to react, the cabin crew usher Cherry out of her seat and coax her gently behind the curtain. We hear her sobs subside. I wait for her to come back through. I have no clue how to handle her. Liberty has deserted her post, and Big Sue and Big Mand have also jumped ship. Tash is the only Doll left to manage this crisis. I must snap her out of it.

I bend round to see if Tash has moved. She has not. She still looks vacant. The shock has been too great for her.

Sister Kevin turns to me in panic. 'What do we do? What's going on? What did I say?'

Poor, poor man.

'How many mini bottles of Prosecco did you say you wanted?' I coax Tash. 'Was it three or four?'

There's a slight stirring movement behind her eyes.

'They might even put a straw in the bottle for you.' I'm using my nursery-nurse voice. 'You'd like that, wouldn't you? A nice little straw?'

I am literally holding my breath.

Tash blinks slowly. She is coming around. 'Excuse me,' she says, snapping out of the trance. She rises out of her seat and thumps down the aisle towards the curtain. When she reaches it, she yells at Sister Kevin, 'And you can forget about joining the mile-high club! Not on this trip, anyway.'

Literally all the passengers twist in their seats to

see who she is talking to. Sister Kevin, because of his great, unnecessary height, six foot five or something, has singled himself out as the only candidate by helpfully going the colour of a blood orange. Tash disappears behind the curtain.

'I can't believe this,' gasps Liam. 'It's outrageous! It's completely bang out of order! It's *our* pre-moon, and yet they're all living it up in first class.' He and Ged throw me a resentful stare.

My heart sinks. I can almost hear my credit card screaming at me to leave it alone. 'Do you want me to see if I can pay for an upgrade?'

'It doesn't matter,' Ged moans. 'We'll just sleep the disappointment off. Hopefully, Big Mand and Big Sue will be in a more forgiving mood when we land.'

* * *

Eventually, the pilot announces that we are making our descent into Las Vegas, the party capital of the world. He tells us the desert is hot, hot, hot. I experience a sinking feeling in the pit of my stomach as the cabin crew busy themselves for landing. There has been no sign of the Dollz since they disappeared into first class. Sister Kevin has been sitting alone behind us watching film after film about prehistoric sharks, occasionally peering through the seat with a sheepish smile whenever we turn to check on him. He still has no idea why Tash is upset with him.

'Ask him,' whispers Ged. 'Ask him how old he is.' In light of everything that has just happened, he and Liam have chosen to fixate on how old Sister Kevin might be and if the BIG birthday celebration really is BIG enough to warrant Tash's invite to join their pre-moon. And what happens to him if Tash chooses not to forgive him?

I shake my head. There is no way I am opening that can of worms. 'You ask him.'

Ged draws his lips into a tight line and glares at me. 'But you're best woman. It's your job.'

'It's my job? To ascertain the ages of everyone in the group?'

'Yes.'

'Well, I'm a little too busy right now. I have enough on, trying to sort out Cherry and her worries over possibly being pregnant with her own husband's child. I'm also trying to figure out how to heal the rift between yourselves and Big Mand and Big Sue, don't forget. Oh, and I also need to figure out what the heck I'm going to say to Matteo, in approximately thirty minutes, when I show up with Luke in tow.'

Ged huffs but I can see he takes my point. 'Okay.

We'll bench that for now. But for the record, we feel a little abandoned. I just want this to be the best pre-moon ever. For Liam.'

'I'm sure you do,' I say quietly. 'But I'm trying my best.' I lean over to check on Liam, who is fast asleep. 'I'll think of something, I promise.'

Ged squeezes my hand. 'Thank you.'

I take in his worried features and my heart melts for him. It's not often he is this vulnerable. 'Don't worry. I've got this. Everything will be okay.'

PING. The seat belt signs come on, causing Liam to prise his eyes open. Ged immediately holds his hand for landing, and I see them exchange a sleepy loving look.

Deep breaths.

Deep breaths.

I can do this. I'll tackle one issue at a time. My gaze is drawn to the window. Dry, parched, dark brown mountain ridges and vast patches of yellow earth give way to neat squares with row upon row of houses and tree-lined streets. Cars, like ants, file neatly along roads and highways as they criss-cross the land, all leading to one magnificent patch of high-rise hotels, fountains and shopping malls, their windows reflecting the sun. It really feels like we are going to land right in the middle of it. And somewhere, as we touch down and trundle past a life-size Egyptian pyramid, in the terminal up ahead, is Matteo. My heart flutters as I close my eyes and picture him. His dark moody eyes, the strong jawline peppered with stubble, the bottom lip fuller than the top, the soft dark hair that isn't too long or too short. But most of all, it's the kind look in his eyes when he talks to me, and the way he rarely smiles as though he's saving them only for me.

3

As soon as the plane lands on the tarmac and comes to a stop, the Dollz pile through the curtain full of excitement.

'What's going on?' I am flabbergasted. Surely first class is not so amazing an experience that it has the power to reverse their collective mountain of bitterness, regret and resentment in a single journey? But apparently so.

'Oh, my God,' announces Tash, reaching up to retrieve her bag from the overhead bins. 'That was so good.'

'Unbelievable,' agrees Liberty. 'Best experience ever.'

'I feel 100 per cent recharged,' adds Cherry.

Even Big Mand and Big Sue appear relaxed and refreshed. They are smiling. They keep looking at one another and giggling.

'Who would have thought it possible?' says Big Mand with an incredulous air.

Big Sue beams at her. 'I think that was the best thing I've ever seen.'

'What's going on?' Liam asks me. 'They look so... so...'

'Rejuvenated. Glowing. Peaceful,' Ged finishes for him.

I search their faces. Every single Doll has a dreamy glint in her eyes. Tash gives me a wide smile and sighs happily. 'Better than anything.'

'What? What is better than anything?' Liam demands. He and Ged are sick with envy at them all disappearing into first class, and this is not helping.

The Dollz stop dragging bags from the overhead lockers to gaze at one another. Still dressed in the mismatched Barbie and Ken outfits, with wild hair and running make-up, they are an incredible sight. They lift their arms and make a love heart sign with their hands to each other before yelling, 'Swifties forever!'

'We've just watched the whole of *The Eras Tour*,' gushes Liberty. 'It was fucking incredible.'

'Insane,' adds Big Mand. 'Mind-blowing.'

'So incredibly life-affirming and real. She makes you want to be more,' says Big Sue. 'To be brave, adventurous, risk-taking. Just more, you know?'

'And whatever else happens, you are strong enough to deal with it,' says Cherry, sounding much more like herself. 'I am so cutting a leg out of all of our bodysuits. It's such a strong look. And sequins. We need loads more of them. I am definitely in my sequin era right now.'

'Oh,' I say, taken aback. 'I'm glad you enjoyed it so much.' I inspect their eyes for signs of intoxication, but they all seem genuinely high on life. High on Taylor Swift magic. I make a mental note to watch *The Eras Tour* on the way back instead of getting stuck down an Instagram rabbit hole of watching people fold clothes. (It's simply hypnotising. Unbelievable to think I've been folding my own clothes wrongly all these years.)

Ged and Liam seem delighted that this high-octane, vibrant mood has nothing to do with being in first class and immediately start to feed off the positive energy.

Sister Kevin is the first to jump up to help Tash with her bags. 'Sorry, babe. Whatever I said or did, I'm sorry.' He has no clue what he has done but it doesn't appear to matter. Tash plonks a kiss on his lips, radiating charm.

'Me too. I can get a little sensitive around booze and how little others drink of it. But don't worry, I'm in my forgiveness era.'

At least for now, it seems as though we can disembark as a relatively happy group. While I'm packing away my phone and travel pillow, I make eye contact with Liberty. She regards me for a moment before coming over.

'He's on board,' she says simply. 'I tried to warn him off, but he wouldn't listen. He says he had no idea you were coming to Las Vegas and that he's here for work and it's just a coincidence. I mean, who would believe that? I think he's going to be trouble.' She must see my face drop. 'But don't worry. We've got your back, hun. Isn't that right, lasses?' While the Dollz shout a variety of agreements, she nods to the curtain. 'And sorry I've been such a pain but I'm totally over it now. Besides, I'm after a billionaire cowboy with a moustache and a very large Stetson. And by Stetson, I mean...' She winks at me. 'Yeehaw, baby!'

I stare back at her. She is a veritable force of nature. Strong and powerful and beautiful, and she does not care a hoot what anyone thinks of her.

'Thank you,' I say, a little awestruck. 'That means a lot.'

Liberty embraces me and turns to the boys. 'We are going to have the best freakin' time of our lives!'

Ged and Liam instantly dish out the hugs. Even Cherry allows them close. When they approach Big Mand and Big Sue, there's an awkward moment. A lump forms in my throat as I see an expression of deep remorse cross the faces of my best friends. They didn't mean to out them. They really didn't.

Big Sue takes in a sharp breath. 'I knew this day might come. It's happened sooner than I'd have liked but...' Big Mand takes her hand. 'Taylor has helped us see that if we aren't being our authentic selves... if we present a version of ourselves to the world that isn't us... then we're not really living in the moment.'

'We're not allowing ourselves to enjoy life as it could be, because it's all premeditated and fake.' Big Mand is gazing up at Big Sue with a loving expression.

'We are still so, so sorry though,' says Liam, his voice catching. 'It was unintentional, and we had no idea that you weren't a couple. You just seem so into each other. Can you ever forgive us?'

We take a beat.

'We *are* officially in our couple era,' says Big

Mand. She goes bright red as we all cheer loudly and start another round of hugging as disembarking passengers try to squeeze past us. Liam has burst into tears again and Ged is comforting him.

The flight attendant from earlier races over to see what the hullabaloo is. 'For the love of God, please get off this plane. I've never known a group of friends cause so much drama.' He is smiling from ear to ear. 'Tell you what, lovies. I'll try to upgrade you all for the return journey if you'll just go now, so we can turn the plane around for the next lot of passengers. How does that sound?'

More whooping and thankful cheering occurs. In that split second, I swear I see a flash of Luke's hair and immediately bristle. *Why has he come? Why does he think these grand gestures will work?* I search the crowd being herded towards the exit and we make immediate eye contact. Luke tries to battle against the flow of passengers, to head in my direction, but the cabin crew block his path. With a worried frown, he disappears through the door along with the last of the passengers.

'Let's go, everyone,' barks Big Sue. 'We have a pre-moon to celebrate.'

Ged and Liam are bursting with joy.

'And a BIG birthday to celebrate,' booms Sister Kevin. 'Whose birthday is it, again?'

Tash yanks him out through the door of the aircraft before we can interrogate him further.

I take a deep breath in. Matteo, here I come. This is one problem that Taylor Swift can't solve for me.

* * *

It seems like it takes forever to get off the plane, down the tunnel and through to the terminal before our phones will work. The mood has suddenly shifted to 'Let's celebrate big time'. Liberty, Big Sue, Big Mand and Cherry are doing a conga up and down the corridor towards passport control, even though the armed border control guards are not loving the display. They put a stop to proceedings when Liberty starts kicking her height and flashing too much flesh.

As we approach the massive queue for passport control, I take the opportunity to check myself over in the nearby toilets. My hands start to shake slightly as I apply lip gloss and attempt to poke my wig back into some sort of ponytail shape. I wish I'd thought to bring some make-up to swish on my face to give me courage. I close my eyes for a brief second to wonder how cross

Matteo might be with me. He might decide I am simply not worth all this hassle. I look down at my ill-fitting Barbie dress and wonder for the billionth time why we didn't swap outfits before we set off from Benidorm.

I spot the group in the queue and approach with caution. They are in incredibly high spirits. Tash is making sure none of us get anywhere near Sister Kevin to interrogate him by keeping his lips busy. We watch as she ugly snogs him, sliding her mouth back and forwards and round and round on his.

Finally, we are standing in line at passport control. They beckon our group through a separate cubicle where there are more staff than at any other cubicle. They look us up and down. With a tip of the head and a neat hand gesture, they suggest the removal of our pink Stetson hats and deeley boppers. They indicate that we must remove our wigs. They huddle in a group whispering.

'What brings you to Nevada?' an armed officer asks brusquely.

He is startled by an almighty gasp from Tash, followed by a quick explanation from Sister Kevin to reassure her that we didn't fly to the wrong country.

'Who is in charge of this group?'

I find myself being shoved forward. It's like history repeating itself.

'Bachelorette, I presume?' he asks in a disappointed tone.

'No,' I say quickly.

'OnlyFans?' He frowns, eyeing our costumes and wigs. 'Or some kind of clown cabaret?'

'Yes,' I answer quickly. 'No. I mean we're on a pre-moon spree.'

'What exactly is that, ma'am?'

'It's, well, it's like a stag do...' I hear Ged and Liam sharply inhale. 'But much better. More sophisticated. More elegant in terms of premarital celebrations.'

The guards look us over once more with a sceptical eye, shaking their heads unconvincingly. 'Then why are these two men yellow?'

Ged swallows and points to Liam. 'It's his fault.'

'No. It was TikTok's fault,' says Liam sourly.

The guard shakes his head again.

'And we're here for work,' adds Liberty, pointing to the Dollz. 'We're professional singers.'

'You are?' the guard says with surprise.

'Yes. We're working for Eddie at Talent Star,' I say confidently. 'Our agent Nancy has filled out all the necessary paperwork.'

'Eddie at Talent Star?' The guard turns to his colleagues with a knowing expression. 'We know Eddie, right, guys?' They start chuckling and murmuring

among themselves and immediately get to work ad-
ministering our ESTA papers and taking our finger-
prints in the biometric processor. It's all very high-
tech. 'Well, that's okay then. Careful how you go, guys.
Careful how you go.'

'What was all that about?' Ged whispers.

'Yeah, suspicious, no?' Big Sue adds, leaning in.
'Something smells fishy.'

'Absolutely,' agrees Ged. 'We should keep our ears
to the ground.'

Oh, my word. These two love to turn everything
into a mission.

'Roger that,' says Big Sue with a nod.

But as long as it bonds them, I don't care. The
guards authorise our stay in Las Vegas and usher us
out towards baggage reclaim. It takes a while for us to
replace our wigs and bicker about the suitcases being
too heavy, too big, too like every other suitcase.

'Mine have pink-striped ribbons tied round them
to make them stand out,' says Liam smugly. He has
already retrieved two of his cases. Whereas none of us
thought to do that and have completely forgotten
what our suitcases look like.

'Mine are black,' says Tash. 'No, grey. Mine are
grey.' She points to a huge, lumpy case dropping onto

the carousel, but just as Sister Kevin grabs it for her and heaves it off the belt, she changes her mind. 'No. Mine are dark blue. I remember now.'

Sister Kevin exhales noisily. His little suitcase is on the trolley. He recognised it immediately. This is the third hefty case that he has been instructed to take off the carousel only to put it back immediately when we've seen it belongs to someone else. Lord help anyone who ends up with a case full of our Barbie outfits.

Eventually we make it out of there with a trolley each piled high.

'Look!' yells Cherry as we make our way through the sliding doors to the arrivals hall. 'They've got slot machines in the friggin' airport. How cool is that?'

'Look at them all!' Big Sue says, pointing to the lines of bleeping one-armed bandits in amazement.

'Talk about not wasting any time,' adds Liberty, rooting around in her bag for some dollar bills. 'Let's go!'

'There's a *Friends* one!' Liam shrieks.

Like a herd of wildebeest they charge towards the slots, leaving me with their trolleys. I sweep my gaze around the busy hall and instantly spot Matteo waiting for me. My heart thuds against my chest. My instinct is to run to the nearest beauty salon for an expensive makeover. FaceTime is no substitute for how attractive he is in real life. His dark unruly hair. His athletic, toned body standing in a relaxed and casual manner. His moody expression. His dark eyes scanning the tourists flooding through the arrival gates. And, as though he senses me near, he turns swiftly in my direction.

I smile shyly. How could I ever have doubted our feelings for each other? He's trying very hard to look stern and annoyed as he waves me over. Probably forcing himself to recall that photo of Luke kissing me. I walk over slowly, trying to prolong the inevitable, but the nearer I get, the less he can keep it up. By the time I'm standing in front of him, his face has softened. He seems very pleased to see me.

'Hi,' I say quietly, almost giggling with embarrassment over how excited I am to see him.

He visibly swallows. 'Hi.' He seems equally lost for words.

'Did you get my message?' I ask.

He nods. 'All ten of them.'

'I wasn't sure if... The Wi-Fi in Spain can be... and I didn't want to use all my mobile data without knowing if... You hear these stories about data roaming charges. So, it's best to always have it switched off.' *Oh, God. When did I turn into a mobile telecoms engineer?* 'And as for attaching photos to messages. Did you know you both get charged? The sender and the recipient? It's daylight robbery.'

Thankfully, he stops me rambling on. 'Speaking of which. About that photo... Care to explain?'

Not really.

'Yeah. Sure.' I squirm under his intense gaze. I can't believe this is the first conversation we are having. 'It might have looked as though our lips were kissing but in real life they weren't. Well, they were, but it was the camera angle mostly. And the gravity of the piece we were singing. I certainly didn't tell his lips to do that. And mine didn't respond in any way, shape or form. Emotionally, I mean. Or physically for that matter. My lips wouldn't do that sort of thing. Usually.'

I've fallen down a rabbit hole.

'Are you saying that lips can somehow think and act independently of the body?' He knits his eyebrows together. 'In an existential capacity?'

He's being facetious. His mouth curves slightly. I think he's teasing me but all he's doing is making me want to kiss him.

'Let me explain.' I drag my eyes from his lips, flustered.

He holds his hands up. 'Really. Don't bother. I'm not sure my brain can take it.'

'It's to do with singing opera and the technical and emotional demands required to navigate the demanding vocal requirements. Ask me about gesticulating in multiple languages.'

He tilts his head. 'I can't. The excitement might kill me.'

I edge a little closer to him. 'You have to be an exceptional actor, is what I'm saying. To bring the characters to life.'

'And is that what is happening here?' He shows me the photo on his phone. He doesn't seem angry or upset in the slightest. He's taking it very well. His eyes glitter with amusement as he steps towards me. He is basically letting me know that we can get past this. It isn't going to be an issue. My heart is tra-la-la-ing.

'Absolutely,' I say, taking another step towards him. We stand a few inches apart, a crackle of electricity fizzing between us.

'And there's nothing else you need to tell me?'

We are dying to kiss, but we still have this awkward obstacle holding us back. The Luke situation. It's going to ruin everything. How on earth am I going to tell Matteo that Luke's here in Las Vegas? With any luck, we'll lose him on the way to the hotel and not see him at all, and he'll give up, and Matteo won't ever need to know that Luke followed me out here.

I take a deep breath, contemplating what to say. Delay the truth? Or learn from past mistakes and be honest and upfront?

Be honest. Be upfront.

And yet...

I move even closer to Matteo. I want to kiss him so badly. I want to kiss him more than I want to tell him about Luke. Much more. I reach out to take his hand and tug him towards me. I lean my head back and allow my lips to fall slightly open. I am ripe for the kissing. I couldn't make it any more obvious.

The truth can wait. 'No. Nothing,' I say huskily. I am literally yearning for him. Every fibre in my body is calling out to make physical contact with this gorgeous man.

Matteo's gaze drops to my lips. He wants me. His eyes grow even darker as he gives me an intense look. 'Not even that you brought him with you?' He nods over to somewhere behind me.

I swivel round. Through the crowds, I see Luke doing a bad job of hiding behind a pillar. Bright blond hair is poking out from a baseball cap pulled low and black sunglasses hide his eyes as he attempts to spy on us.

'Well?' says Matteo, crossing his arms as though we've got all day for me to come up with a decent answer.

4

My heart sinks. Luke is taking things far too far. I tut vociferously and roll my eyes. 'Oh, God. I swear there's nothing going on.'

Matteo regards me intently. 'Sure? That's a long way to come for nothing to be going on.'

'I'm sure,' I say, hoping to God he believes me. 'He's making up some excuse that he's here for work.'

'Good,' he says and takes a deep breath in. 'I believe you.'

I visibly sag with relief. 'That was easy.'

He gives me a sheepish look.

'What?' I ask.

He lets out a huge groan and rubs both hands down his face. 'You're not going to like this.'

'Like what?'

'My ex-girlfriend is here,' he says, wincing. 'She followed me to the airport in LA and just booked herself onto my flight.'

My jaw drops open. *How many ex-girlfriends does this man have? Is the world littered with them?*

'Which ex-girlfriend?'

'It's Birdie,' he says, exasperated as he rakes his hand through his hair. 'She's waiting in the limo. She's... well, she's a bit...' I watch him struggle with what to say next. 'She's become a bit unhinged.'

'Birdie has become unhinged? Why? How?' *What has happened between them? Did she twang her suspenders against the soft, creamy skin of her milky thighs once too often for him to resist?*

Matteo shrugs. 'She was the one who sent me the photo of you and... Luke kissing. She kind of follows you on social media. Like, obsessively. Alerts and everything. Sorry.'

Gah! I make a mental note to switch off the alerts I have set up for Birdie's social media.

It's my turn to ask the questions. Just in case he probes too deeply into what level of social media stalking is deemed unacceptable. I'd hate for him to lump me in with Birdie. 'Are you sure there's nothing going on between the two of you? I mean, she *is* French.'

Now all I can picture is Birdie lounging, topless, an arm flung above her head as she insists that Matteo does a *Titanic* on her. *'Paint me, Jack. Paint me like one of your French girls.'* Or is it draw me? Sketch me? Shag me? I'll have to do an internet search for it when we get to the hotel. But either way, in my mind's eye, Birdie has her perfect, alluringly cruel, man-stealing breasts out on full display. Perfect cherry macarons.

Matteo smiles at me. Thankfully, he seems quite unaware of the horrified fascination I have developed with his ex. 'Nothing is going on. She's claiming she's here for work purposes, too. She's meeting some new client who is huge, which puts me in rather a difficult position trying to keep her on-side, but really, it's because she's jealous. A bit like Luke, I guess.'

'Well, then. Maybe we should introduce them to each other. They seem to have a lot in common.'

Matteo squints back over to where Luke is still hiding behind the pillar. He lets out another resigned sigh. 'I'll go have a word with him.'

I watch Matteo march forcefully over to Luke. Luke appears startled. Even though Luke is taller and very expensively dressed, Matteo, in his shorts and T-shirt, has such a commanding presence and authoritative air that Luke instantly takes a step backwards. I see the two of them talking. Luke is shaking his head. Then he looks crushed. Then he hangs his head down and holds up his hands. Now he seems to be getting a second wind, trying to negotiate, but Matteo is having none of it. I realise I'm holding my breath; my whole body is tense, wondering what it is they are saying to each other. And, finally, Luke glances guiltily in my direction before Matteo marches back towards me. It's hard to tell what he's thinking. He seems neither pleased nor displeased.

But I hope this gives Luke the reality check he so obviously needs.

'I've told him to leave us alone,' Matteo says on approach.

My stomach does a flip. He's so cool under pressure. So 'no-nonsense'. So authoritative. Decisive. It's incredibly horny to witness.

'What did he say?' I manage as a wave of lust rips through me.

Matteo tips his head to the side, a frown forming on his brow as he folds his arms. I try not to focus on the small round bulges that appear, straining against the fabric of his T-shirt. I've always had a weakness for a toned bicep. Especially a tanned one.

'He said he's here for work and nothing more because he already tried proposing to you and it didn't work.'

Ah. 'It was meaningless. Such an empty gesture, as proposals of marriage go.'

'And that you threw it back in his face.'

I did indeed. 'He was being impulsive. Rash. It was all very on-the-spur-of-the-moment. It was nothing really.'

Matteo digests what I'm saying. 'He said something about the two of you staying at York's exclusive luxury five-star spa hotel. He thinks you turned him down because it wasn't a grand enough gesture.'

'Well, erm, about that... It's not that the hotel wasn't good enough, or that we were staying there *together* together. Well, we were. But in separate rooms because he lied. I forgot to tell you that part. He completely lied about the upgrade.'

'Funny, because he also said you weren't entirely truthful about not being single.'

Yes, the delay. How do I explain the delay in telling the truth?

'And because of that, he developed feelings for you.'

Gah! 'He's just needy for attention. And I never told him I was single. I just didn't tell him you and I were in a relationship... because I wasn't sure if you thought we were exclusive or not.'

Lame. Very lame.

'That's not all. He thinks you're destined to be something to each other, because he saved your life.' Matteo is giving me an incredulous look. 'Is that true? He *saved* your life?'

They sure covered an awful lot of ground in just a couple of minutes.

'Ah,' I say, embarrassed at how callous this is going to sound. 'Yes. He *did* save my life. But that debt was repaid in full by me saving him from public embarrassment.'

Matteo raises his brow.

'He got a massive boner on stage, which I hid with my skirt...' Even to my ears, it sounds relatively disproportionate when said aloud. 'But to be fair, the proposal was entirely cocaine-fuelled, and I'm pretty sure he was just after a solution to him having to make a political marriage of convenience. I thought he was proposing a fake relationship. A fake marriage.'

'Boner? Cocaine fuelled? Fake marriage?' Matteo says, his jaw hanging open.

I'm really digging myself into a hole here.

'Not me. Just him. He was very high. And drunk. Disgustingly drunk.'

'When? Where?' Matteo is beginning to look very concerned. He swivels round to see if Luke is still hiding, but he has gone.

'In York. In the hotel's private dining room.'

'He sounds very out of order, Connie. He's crossed a line. Several lines,' he says firmly.

'Yes.' I gulp. 'I just went along with it at the time because he said we needed to stay away from the press who'd been printing lies about us.'

Matteo sounds bewildered. 'Lies? What kind of lies?'

I need to stop talking. He obviously hasn't had time to read the articles. And I'm making myself sound very wishy-washy and not in control.

'Just love-triangle sort of lies. And me being after Luke's money because he's very rich. And me trying to infiltrate the House of Glucksburg because he's Norwegian royalty. And me ruining the Sinfonia's reputation by encouraging everyone to behave as though they're in a Jilly Cooper bonkbuster. That sort of thing. Just gossipy headlines.' I blow out my cheeks. When put like that, I've had to deal with quite a lot over the past couple of weeks.

Matteo rubs his face with both hands, dragging

them down his chin. He looks stern. He must think I'm batshit crazy. 'Christ. As long as you're okay?'

'I am.'

'You come with a lot of baggage, don't you?' He shakes his head. 'Come on. You can tell me all about this love triangle when we get to the hotel.'

'And Birdie?' I ask. 'What will we tell her?'

'The same thing,' he says. 'We're a couple.' He gives me an intense look as though to say, *Aren't we?*

I nod back, squeezing his hand tightly, as a goofy grin spreads across my face. *We're a bona fide couple!*

'Let's get out of here,' he says, just as a crowd of rowdy men dressed as cheerleaders sail past. 'Everyone in this place is insane.'

'Speaking of which…' I say, nodding to the Dollz and Ged and Liam. 'I'm sorry I didn't pluck up the courage to tell you earlier.'

A faint chuckle escapes from his lips. 'Ah, yes. You brought your yellow friends with you.'

I laugh. 'Don't even go there.'

'Very happy not to.' He pulls my hand and swirls me around Latino-style as I spin towards him. 'Nice wig. Nice Barbie dress.' He stares down at me. Sparks crackle between us. His eyes roam my face before his lips meet mine. The soft contact leaves me dizzy and in no doubt about how he feels as a riptide of passion engulfs us. He breaks off, slightly out of breath and disoriented. I unravel him. I can tell that he has no idea why we have such strong chemistry, but we just do. He pulls me into him, one hand at the nape of my neck, the other round my waist, as he finds my lips once more. This time I feel his tongue slide gently into my mouth, lightly caressing my tongue, joining us together. I tighten my arms around his neck and send a quick thank you prayer to the universe. After so many years of sadness, this thing we have brings me such joy, I can barely describe how other-worldly it feels.

We finally break apart, dazed. 'Ready, Cenicienta?'

My Cinderella nickname from when we first met. My heart skips a beat. I blink slowly. I am so unbelievably far from ready.

* * *

Once we have prised the Dollz, Ged and Liam away from the slot machines, we wheel our piled-high trolleys to the exit, where a huge pink limo is waiting for us. The uniformed driver is standing beside it, ready to assist.

'It's fully stocked,' says Matteo, slipping into host mode. 'I understand we have much to celebrate.'

'Yes,' says Liam bashfully. 'We're going to be married later this year. With an aquatic or an equestrian theme. We haven't exactly decided yet. Although we do want unicorns. Blue ones. With rainbow tails and pink hooves. And dolphins.'

He's rambling. He's become lost in Matteo's dark swirls for eyes. Ged digs him in the ribs.

'Thanks, Matteo,' Ged says, moving towards the limo. 'This is very kind of you.'

'No problem,' Matteo says, sounding slightly uncomfortable at the way Liam is still gazing at him. 'Er... You could probably go with seahorses as a compromise.'

Liam gasps as though Matteo has just announced the new *Strictly* line-up. Ged rolls his eyes. 'Honestly, Liam. We just spent four hours planning a *Bridgerton*-themed wedding. What's wrong with you?'

There's a big hoo-ha as we all get excited about this latest development. 'You do both love a bit of luxury,' I remind them. 'A *Bridgerton* wedding would be spectacular.'

'We are rather obsessed with made-up Regency shenanigans,' agrees Ged.

Liam, however, is frowning. 'I'm not sure any more. It's Colin. He's put me off.'

'Connie and I have upgraded your room at The

Venetian to a luxury king suite. You'll have exclusive access to your own poolside cabana, host service and private restroom,' Matteo interrupts, sounding rather like a concierge ticking off his list. 'Because apparently' – his eyes flick to mine – 'we're all now staying in the same place.'

'Okay, let's do a quick video of everyone getting in the limo,' I say, trying to rally the group before everyone demands an upgraded room with oversized soaking tubs and views over the sprawling city.

Only once we pile into the supersized limo do I notice Birdie sitting at the far end.

'*Bonjour!*' she says with a wide smile, patting the seat next to her as though she owns it. 'Come in.'

Matteo tries to hide his annoyance.

'We'll call it a business expense.' Birdie inspects her nails. 'After all, we're here for work.'

There's complete silence as we exchange confused looks while Matteo does awkward introductions.

'Birdie, I'd like you to meet Connie,' Matteo says, before listing everyone by name. A small bloom of pride flowers in my stomach at the way Matteo is going out of his way to learn their names and make sure my friends feel welcome and comfortable.

Birdie blows enthusiastic kisses at everyone but only smiles weakly at me. It's as far as you can get from the flirty persona she portrayed over the phone when she had her arm draped over my boyfriend. Moreover, everyone in the limo picks up on it and there's an instant atmosphere.

'Birdie...' says Matteo, his voice hard and uncompromising.

'We've met on the phone already.' Birdie rolls her eyes. 'Of course I'm delighted to see her again.' She fakes a smile and blows me a kiss.

'Lovely to see you too,' I say through pursed lips.

The Dollz set about ascertaining whether she is a threat, and whether she is aware that Matteo and I are an item. Ged and Liam, however, venture off on a slightly different tangent and ask if she has seen Harry Styles lately.

Oh. My. God. How embarrassing.

'Yes,' she says, sounding matter-of-fact and disappointingly far from unhinged. 'He's staying in our hotel, I believe. Or The Palazzo next door. One of them.'

Liam makes a strangled sound. 'Which one?' he presses her, trying to sound casual, but she's moved on to grilling me.

'Connie. You have just finished your classical tour? How was it? I saw some articles online.' She goes straight in for the kill, flashing up images on her phone of me and Luke. She waves her phone around so that everyone can see. 'I guess opera is very emotional. Or is that acting?' She does air quotes with her long, bony fingers.

Matteo pulls a face at her. 'Birdie,' he warns gently. 'I told you not to interfere.'

But Birdie totally ignores him and glares at me as though she's my mother demanding to know where I've been when I'm back late from the cinema. She's almost tapping her foot and folding her arms. Matteo was right. She is so unhinged.

'Don't answer that, Connie,' he says.

'Opera *is* very emotional,' I say, straight at her beautiful face. 'And yes, of course that's acting. Luke is a professional singer. There's nothing going on between us. Just like there's nothing going on between you two, I guess.' I flash pictures of her and Matteo back at her. Like a game of paparazzi snap.

Yes, I did come prepared with screenshots, but that does not make me unhinged. Just well organised and forward-thinking.

Birdie sits back with a resigned huff. 'Touché,' she says, uncrossing her long, bare legs and grabbing a bottle of fizz. 'Anyone for more shom-pan-yuh?'

Because she's French, unfortunately for me, every single word out of her mouth sounds extremely cool.

Even when said in a sulky tone. I imagine she is incredibly high-maintenance.

As the music is cranked up to ear-splitting levels, Birdie pours out flute after flute, passing them round, but when she gives me mine, she checks to see no one is looking and pours it into my lap.

'Oops,' she says, staring me straight in the eye. 'How clumsy of me.'

The liquid seeps through my dress like a sponge.

Oh, God. She really has it in for me.

I fake a cough. 'It's fine. Fine. Just an accident,' I say, grabbing a serviette to dab myself dry.

Matteo gives Birdie a hostile look but, before he can say anything, a tinkling laugh escapes from her glossy lips. 'Come on. It wasn't on purpose. As if I'd do that. Here, Connie. Let me pour you another.' She hands me the glass. 'Cheers. *À votre santé!*'

While we toast, I slide my eyes to Matteo. He rolls his upwards and gives me a half-smile. This week is already stressful enough without a psychotic ex-girlfriend on the loose.

'She is just like an attention-seeking version of Luke,' Liberty leans over to whisper in my ear. 'We should hook them up.'

I turn to her in surprise. 'Wouldn't you be upset by that? I thought you wanted him for yourself?'

She shakes her head. 'No. I'm sorry for behaving like a massive cock. I was just lonely and fed up. I can see the way you and Matteo are with each other. You've practically got sparkles coming out of your eyes. And that's the sort of relationship I want. Besides, Luke seems incredibly fixated on what he can't have. It's put me totally off him.'

'Right. Right,' I whisper back. Ever since I have known Liberty, she has relentlessly gone after men she can't have, or who other women may want. And, with the exception of Luke, she has never failed. Maybe they are too alike for it to work. Maybe she is right about Birdie. Perhaps she will make a better match for him. And they might leave Matteo and me alone to get on with our exclusive relationship. My heart flutters. Matteo is exclusively mine. I have his exclusive attention, romantically speaking. Which means his lips are exclusively mine to kiss. His manly fingers are exclusively for caressing my skin. His eyes, the exclusive way they leave me shivering with excitement and...

'For fuck's sake. Stop ogling him like a piece of meat.' Liberty snaps me to attention. 'Jesus. Poor man. He's already got one lunatic to contend with. At least try to play it cool or you'll scare him off like Birdie.'

'I wasn't ogling,' I hiss back.

I was very much ogling. I must get a grip. Unlike Birdie, who has her eyeballs locked on him like two nuclear missiles.

'Hopefully we'll not see anything of Luke while we're here, anyway,' I say. 'He has no idea where we're staying, and I'm sure Las Vegas is big enough not to bump into him.'

Liberty looks guiltily back at me.

My jaw falls open. 'Please tell me you did not tell him where we're—'

'It was an accident,' she says, cutting me off.

How could she tell Luke where we are staying? How?

'What's this about Luke?' joins in Cherry. Her eyes are wired because she's on her third full-fat Fanta and jumbo bag of Haribo. 'You told him where we are staying?' she bellows.

The excited chatter comes to an abrupt halt.

5

We pull up at The Venetian. It is enormous. It's the biggest hotel I've ever seen. There's a long line of cars waiting to drop off. There's a huge water fountain outside and lots of people walking around, waiting at the lights to cross the street. There are neon lights, hotels, and digital advertising screens as far as the eye can see. I press a button to roll down my window. I'm instantly hit with bright sunshine and a sweet-smelling heat. Notes of popcorn, aftershave, petrol fumes and pizza. I'm immediately reminded of Italy. Cherry is quick to show us the Wikipedia page.

'Friggin' hell. It's got 7,000 rooms across the two towers. It's the largest hotel in the world. It has its own river inside. An actual river with gondolas floating on it!' She gasps. 'And it's got a whole load of celebrities doing shows there!'

Ged and Liam light up instantly. 'Who? Who?'

Suddenly, everyone is swiping away on their phones, and the car is buzzing with excitement as we share photos of the hotel we are parked outside of. I steal a quick peek at Matteo, who has been quiet since Birdie spilled her drink and looked openly smug about Luke being at the same hotel. This potential new client must be very important. She really has Matteo between a rock and hard place.

'Found it. Residency. The Sphere. Venetian. Bla-hedy-blah,' murmurs Big Sue, swiping at her phone. 'Oh.' She looks up, disappointed. 'It's U2.'

There's a rumble of dissatisfaction across the limo.

'There's also the Bellagio, the Wynn, Caesar's Palace... There'll be lots of A-list singers around. I'm sure of it,' says Matteo.

'Of course there are,' joins in Birdie as though she lives here. 'Everyone knows this.'

From the window, mountains of suitcases are being slung on trolleys, hordes of staff are running to and fro, and throngs of people are going up and down the large travelators that take them up and into the hotel. The place is like a massive train station.

'It has its own shopping mall,' Cherry says, all breathy. 'And... tattoo parlour!'

There's a joint squeal of delight from the Dollz.

'No,' I say. 'Whatever you are all thinking, it's a firm no. A hard no. A definite no. We have zero time for anything that isn't on the itinerary. Including spending half a day on matching tattoos.'

I must stand my ground with them otherwise the whole week will be carnage. They glare at me like disgruntled children.

'So, before we go in,' I say to the group. 'I've put our itinerary in the Vegas group chat and added... Matteo.' I give him a shy flutter of my lashes. It feels like such an intimate gesture to add him to our group. But we're exclusive now so...

'Whoa. Why have you gone bright red, Connie?' demands Cherry, forcing a handful of jellied sweets into her mouth.

I glare at her.

She is oblivious. 'Your cheeks. Are you too hot?'

Sweet baby Jesus. 'No, I'm not hot. As I was saying, everyone needs to check their messages regularly for up—'

'Well, then, there's no need to be embarrassed, is there? You two are obviously exclusive now. Where are the rest of those candy gummies?'

My cheeks instantly flame brighter as she digs around the central bar area in the limo in search of something. Her attention span, perhaps?

'Do they have these sweets in the hotel? I need more. They're so lush.'

'Have you added Sister Kevin to the WhatsApp group?' barks Tash. 'He needs to know when we'll be singing so that he can come and watch every performance.'

Sister Kevin almost chokes on his bottle of beer as he tries to disguise his disappointment. But it is the cold, steely energy emitting from Birdie that causes the atmosphere to drop.

'I would like to see you perform,' she says, making it sound like a mild threat. 'After all, Matteo has told me how amazing you are. I need to see it for myself. Apparently, you will have me in tears.'

'Erm, thank you.' I smile weakly and carry on. There's no way I am including her in our group chat. No way on this earth. 'I've also emailed you each a copy, and I've saved it to the cloud just in case anyone loses their phone, or forgets their passwords, and I'm going to ask reception to print out copies to send to your rooms.'

They stare blankly back at me as though I've just

informed them that I've sent the itineraries by carrier pigeon.

'Has no one opened their emails?' I ask incredulously.

What's the point? Of course they haven't.

Big Sue, however, is more than pleased with this level of administrative thoroughness. 'Nice job, Big Guy. Nice job.' She is manspreading in her Gangsta Ken fluffy white coat, black vest top and medallion and appears to have drunk several bottles of beer which have given her a New York accent. She winks at me.

Big Guy? I hope to God that she will not persist with this nickname. It's wildly unsuitable on so many levels. Liberty sniggers next to me. I risk a peek at Matteo, who also appears to be fighting a smirk.

'Okay, *Big Guy*. What's the plan before we get out of the car?' Liberty all but yells. I roll my eyes at her. For her own amusement, she will make sure this new nickname sticks.

'It's not Big Guy. Never was,' I say, facing the group. 'The plan is to check in at reception, drop our bags in our rooms and meet back up to stay awake for the jet lag. Because we're in a new time zone, the internet says we should ideally try to adjust our eating and sleeping times to Las Vegas time. Which means we need to stay awake and sleep with everyone else.'

Liberty is quick to interject. 'You heard the boss. *Big Guy* is saying that we need to dump our stuff in our rooms and then start sleeping with everyone. That might be a struggle, even for me!'

The Dollz start hooting with laughter at my mistake. I feel my face burn even more. I'm clearly not very good at this leadership stuff.

Tash yawns openly. 'Sod that. I'm off to bed. And there's only one person I'm sleeping with.'

'No,' I say. 'You can't. We must stay awake, otherwise tomorrow you'll be wanting to sleep when we're supposed to be on stage.'

'I'll be in charge of keeping everyone awake,' says Big Mand. 'I'm used to shift work and staying up all night. I once stayed awake delivering babies for four days straight. I've got this, Big Guy.'

'Can everyone stop calling me Big Guy just because I'm in charge of the itinerary?' I say desperately.

Big Mand grins. 'Okay, Big Guy. Calm down.'

I give up.

'Right. Check in to your rooms. Freshen up but do not lie down on the beds. Meet at the...' I consult my notes. 'At the giant love sign in the lobby. The one everyone posts on Instagram. Apparently, you can't miss it.'

'You need to give an ETA,' adds Big Sue from behind dark sunglasses. Her head is slouched to one side, her hands resting between her legs as though she's about to start rapping. 'A specific meet time. In zero hundred hours. An MO. A ten four. Capeesh?'

Tiredness sweeps through my entire body. *What the fuck is she talking about?* I inwardly lament. 'Meet in exactly one hour from now. At the love sign. Everyone understand?'

I receive enthusiastic nods from them all. Matteo is grinning at me. It instantly boosts my spirits. I have a whole week in his company, and seven glorious days to enjoy time with my friends. I suddenly feel very lucky.

'Great. Let's have the best time ever!' I raise my glass.

The party mood very much returning, everyone clinks glasses. It's a lovely shared moment. Very mindful.

'Sorry. Can we do that cheers again because I need to get it for the video of us arriving?' I remember. It's bad enough keeping us all to schedule, never mind the responsibility of capturing it all on camera for the Netflix-level behind-the-scenes documentary that Ged and Liam seem to expect from me at the end.

'And can you send the clip to me for my socials, please?' Tash asks.

'No, sorry. This footage is restricted to our pre-moon. You can have it after *we've* posted it,' Ged says firmly, which pops the lovely ambiance instantly.

I let out a deep sigh. *When will this mood yo-yoing ever end?* I need to find a way to bring us all together. Something to unite us that's bigger than the sum of our various issues and gripes with each other.

'Is that Luke?' booms Big Mand, pointing her finger towards the front of the queue of taxis and limos waiting at the entrance. We crane our necks to peer out of the windows. 'Too late. He's gone.'

'Is that a confirmed sighting?' asks Big Sue.

I hold my breath. *Please no. Please no.*

'Copy that, ten four.'

FFS, what does that even mean?

Big Mand gives me a sympathetic half-smile. 'It's a confirmed sighting. Yes.'

My eyes fly to Matteo. He shrugs in a reassuring way. 'Don't worry. I'll take care of him if he starts any trouble.'

* * *

Finally, our limo pulls into the unloading bay at reception. At the very least, the Luke situation has momentarily distracted everyone, and has resulted in much positivity towards me, and how they all have my back. Cherry even stopped stuffing jellies in her mouth to pat my knee in a comforting way. We pile out of the limo. Me first, so I can capture the moment on camera.

Ged and Liam emerge with utter joy on their faces as they take in the grand entrance, its towering golden pillars reaching towards the sky and the breathtaking enormity of it. The paintings above us on the arched dome covering the doorway could belong in a museum. The boys are speechless as they cling to each other, exhilaration blooming from their faces. As the Dollz clamber out, a little worse for wear after all those free drinks, and Cherry, high as a bath full of cocaine with all the sugar, they stop to gaze up and around. Stunned into silence.

'This trip is going to be epic,' Liberty whispers, a huge grin on her face.

'Wild,' agrees Big Sue.

'Totally fucking awesome,' adds Big Mand.

'Un-fucking-forgettable,' coos Cherry.

'And savage,' says Tash. 'Totally and utterly savage.'

Matteo visibly gulps. I offer him a weak smile. 'In a good way. Unforgettably savage in a good way.'

Our chauffeur busies himself organising all of our luggage to go on trolleys with hotel staff. Arrival protocol, on first impression, is a well-oiled machine. The porters have our trolleys loaded within minutes and are beckoning us to follow them inside, through the world's biggest doors. I spot Matteo handing the chauffeur a hefty tip and shaking his hand before the man drives the limo away. None of us thought to do that.

The freezing cold air is the first thing to hit us as we cross the main lobby to the reception desk. It has an instant sobering effect.

'Ow. My nostrils are burning. What is that?' Tash squirms, holding her nose. 'Kev. *Kev!* What is it?'

Sister Kevin flounders, unable to answer her.

'It's the air conditioning,' says Birdie in a bored tone as though she's been here a billion times. 'Designed to keep everyone awake and gambling. Rumour has it they put ozone in it. And each hotel pumps their signature scent into the air.'

'Cool,' says Tash, changing her tune. 'I wonder if that is as good for the skin as it sounds?'

'It's good for profits,' Birdie says, marching away from us. She flicks her coral-coloured hair extensions, glancing back over her shoulder to make sure Matteo is watching her. When she sees he only has eyes for me, she scowls before pasting on a fake smile. '*Bueno. Ciao, belli. À plus tard!*'

We watch her sashaying through the busy crowd towards the queues at reception, her bright hair disappearing to the front of the line.

'Three languages in one sentence. Works with artists all over the globe. She's one crazy super-talented bitch,' says Liberty with a sparkle in her eye. 'But don't worry. Nothing will beat your Gregorian chant, Connie, babes. And you have slightly longer legs.'

'Oh. My. God. No one is going to forget that creepy snoozefest in a hurry,' says Tash, laughing. 'There are so many better ways to warm up your audience, pet.'

'I sing in five languages, I'll have you know,' I say, defending myself. 'Anyway, why are you comparing me to Birdie?'

They stare at Matteo as though he should know what lunatic conclusions they appear to be jumping to. He visibly swallows as the moment stretches awkwardly on. 'Shall we?' he says, indicating the reception desk.

'Right,' says Big Mand loudly. 'Remember the plan, everyone. You could be hanging around waiting for the lifts for up to thirty minutes so do not spend more than ten minutes in your rooms. And don't be tempted to have a nap or I will physically come and haul you out of bed. We need to stay awake. It's essential we get the proper amount of rest later tonight, ahead of the first gig. I also suggest we use this as an opportunity to swap our Barbie outfits.' Poor Big Mand. She has had to travel in a tiny dress that is splitting her in half. She pulls at the too-tight bodice. One of her bra cups has been on permanent display for the whole journey.

'Roger that, Mandeep,' says Big Sue. 'I suggest we all put our room numbers in the group chat. In case.'

Ged clears his throat. 'And the plan for the first night of the pre-moon?'

Christ Almighty. I've been so distracted by the whole Luke, Birdie, me and Matteo love quadrangle that I clean forgot we are here to enjoy ourselves. I flick through my phone's notes app. 'We are starting at the casino. Dressed in Barbie outfits. Then I have a private space booked for cocktail hour over in the, erm...' I scroll through, conscious of Matteo standing right next to me. He runs his hand discreetly up and down my spine, sending tingles ricocheting across my body. 'The exclusive Juliet Cocktail Room, for an evening of expertly crafted cock—' My voice breaks. It sounds like I'm saying cock more than is necessary. 'Erm, drinks, live music and an intoxicating blend of luxury, excitement and world-class service.'

'I hope they'll do us all a Skanky Lady cocktail,' gushes Tash.

'Can't wait!' squeals Liam. 'As long as the music isn't jazz. I find jazz very triggering.'

* * *

Minutes later we are at the front of the queue checking in. I have been surreptitiously glancing around for signs of Luke. It has somewhat taken the shine off the excitement. As has not being able to sleep on the plane. I stifle a yawn.

'Tired?' Matteo asks.

'I'll be fine. I'll have a quick shower in the room to wake up.'

Like me, he remembers the last time we were in a room together and a shower was involved. I'm undressing him with my eyes, and I just can't help it.

'Make it quick, Big Guy,' booms Big Mand at the pair of us. Matteo's eyes balloon. Big Mand is being very... How would you put it? Prescriptive. What if Matteo wants to make sweet, slow love to me? Unrushed. His fingers are at their best when they trail softly across my hot skin. When they deliver exquisite pleasure to my—

'The shower! Make the showers quick. In and out. No hair washing. No funny business.' Big Mand points directly at Tash. 'None. At. All.'

We bristle at the threatening tone. It's remarkable how alert and on top of her game she is. I can just imagine her thumping up and down the hospital corridors, barking orders and scaring mothers into giving birth on time.

* * *

Moments later, we all have the correct room key cards. We are all on the same floor, except for Ged and Liam, who have been upgraded.

'Yay!' says Liam, celebrating, waving his room key around. 'We have our own private lift. And naked butler. Living the dream!'

'And there's a travel rejuvenation pack, some oxygen pouches and bowel-cleansing shots waiting for us.' Ged is bursting with happiness.

'Thank you,' I mouth to Matteo.

We make our way to the lifts with a few hundred other people.

'It's like Piccadilly Circus in here,' remarks Big

Sue. 'There's the big love sign over there. The rendezvous point.'

'Ten minutes in the room,' Big Mand reminds us. 'Rendezvous point in an hour.'

'A lot can happen in ten minutes,' Tash says, winking at Sister Kevin, who looks shattered. Totally wiped out. He watched back-to-back gory films all the way here and is dead on his feet. He nods obediently.

When the lift arrives, we wait for it to empty and pile in. Our cases are being delivered to our rooms on the twenty-seventh floor.

'We'll be spending most of the week in lifts, by the looks of things,' moans Cherry. I'd almost forgotten she was with us. As the primary complainer of the group, she has been exceptionally quiet. She has dark circles beneath her eyes and her pillar-box-red ponytail is now sitting to the side of her head, streaks of make-up still visible on her cheeks. She, too, looks shattered. Only Liberty and Tash have a sense of energy about them. I let out a huge yawn, very much regretting my suggestion to stay awake, and quickly stop as Big Mand swoops round.

'NO!' she shouts. 'No yawning, people. We stay awake. Gottit?'

We nod unhappily.

'Come on,' murmurs Matteo in my ear as the lift eventually stops at our floor. 'I'll help you stay awake.'

We walk the twisty corridors, carpeted in luxurious, thick swirly patterns. Murals on the walls. Distant Italian music crooning through the pipes. You'd think we were in Italy.

Finally, the Dollz disappear into their rooms, leaving Matteo and me to walk to our room at the end of the long corridor. I gasp as he opens the door.

'Oh, my God. It's gorgeous!' I take in the sumptuous lavishness of the suite. The opulence of the décor, the furniture. I'm drawn to the massive bed. 'Wow.'

Matteo sounds pleased with himself. 'You like it?'

'Love it. Look at that view!' I yell, racing over to the window. The whole of Las Vegas is spread out before us. He stands behind me, his hands gentle on my shoulders.

'Good,' he says simply. 'Maybe it's best if you don't tell the Dollz that I upgraded our room.'

'Agreed,' I say, stifling yet another yawn. I want to kiss him so badly, but I can barely stay awake. I should kiss him now before I fall asleep standing up. I tilt my head back, thrusting my lips towards his. 'Thank you so much. It's beautiful. I love it.'

We take a moment to gaze at each other. This is all

so surreal. Me. Him. Las Vegas. Two months ago, I was single, miserable, unemployed and living in New-castle with all of my dreams shattered to pieces. Now, I'm a semi-professional singer working three jobs and living between two countries. And I'm in the arms of my dream man.

'I'm really sorry about Birdie,' he says, pointing to the still damp stain on my dress.

'I can handle it,' I say, pulling him to me. He gives me a grateful look as I snake my arms around his neck. 'How about we get me out of these wet things?'

Just as his lips are about to touch mine, his phone rings. He glances at the screen, his mouth forming a tight line before he answers. 'Birdie? What's up?'

Christ. It's like she was eavesdropping.

'Uh-huh.' Matteo listens intently. He steps away from me to stare out of the window, a serious expres-sion on his face. I stare at his back, the way his T-shirt hugs his taut frame. His biceps casually straining at the hems of the short sleeves. One hand in his shorts pocket, the other holding his phone to his ear. His long, lean legs standing slightly apart. Powerful is what he is. Confident. Casual. Not jet-lagged. 'Well, tell them to shove it. We're not obliged to redo any-thing.' He puts a hand over the phone to mouth, *Sorry.*

Birdie hasn't wasted any time in keeping us from doing anything we shouldn't in our rooms. I try to keep the disappointment from my face.

Matteo lowers his voice before saying, 'Hang on a moment.' I catch a subtle hint of spice and vanilla musk as he strides past me to the door. He points outside and I realise he needs to talk privately with her. My mood plummets. It's not ideal but what can I do?

'I might just have a super-quick shower,' I say quietly, heading to the bathroom. I have ten minutes before Big Mand thumps on our door to freshen up and change into my other Barbie outfit. One that hopefully fits. And this wig is so hot and sweaty. I can't believe I travelled all this way in it. My hair is a flat, tangled nest underneath. I only hope that Matteo doesn't walk in to find me looking like a tired old scarecrow. I strip off, flinging my clothes and wig to the bathroom floor, and walk into the spacious shower. There is a shelf lined with lotions of all kinds, designed to relax, energise, calm and invigorate. I pick up a heavy glass jar full of expensive-smelling green shower gel designed to revitalise. There is a matching face mask to go with it. To achieve deep penetration, it is best left on the skin for a maximum of two minutes. The Americans think of everything, don't they? I breathe in the luxurious lemon and heather smell and pump lashings of the thick gel out over my body. This could be just what I need to combat the fatigue.

I peer once more at my tired reflection, now covered in swamp algae. Just as I reach out to replace the jar on the shelf, I jump at the sound of knocking at the door.

'Are you busy, or can I come in?' Matteo says as the jar slips from my grasp to crash loudly and expensively to the shower floor. He bursts through the door. 'Connie?' His mouth gapes open as he takes in the sight before him.

I let out a blood-curdling scream in response.

'What in the name of kinky fuck is going on here?' booms a voice behind him. Big Mand is standing in the doorway with her arms folded and a huge grin on her face.

6

'I'd rather not talk about it,' I tell Liam when Matteo, Big Mand and I arrive at the meeting point quite a few minutes late.

'But you're green. Why are you now green?' he persists. It's the pot calling the kettle black because he and Ged are still bright yellow.

By the time quick-thinking Matteo had swept me up into his arms (a fireman's lift, of all things, while I was butt naked, screaming, 'Nobody look at me!' at the top of my lungs) to rescue me from the shower floor, which was covered in broken glass and slime, there was no hope of having an actual shower with water due to us not having anything to sweep up the shards of glass with. I'd had to wipe all that gel off while flicking bits of tap water at myself. While the gel smells terrific, the downside is that it stains when not rinsed off properly. I have ruined the hotel towels. All of them. Matteo didn't escape untouched either and it was like history repeating itself when he put me down, and I saw that I'd left stains all over his lovely white (I'm pretty sure designer) top. At least we've established that me and his white tops don't work well together.

Mortified, I'd hurriedly rummaged through my case, rammed my clothes and wig back on, and raced down to the meeting point. I couldn't even bear to catch sight of my green face in the lift mirror on the way down. Big Mand was no help. I thought she was going to have a heart attack from the way she kept howling with laughter every time she looked at me. Then we had to schlep all the way from the guest suites through the busy shopping mall area, which is life-size – as in massive – past hordes of people all dressed up for a night out, even though it is still technically morning, and through to reception to report the mess I'd made.

'Move over, Princess Fiona,' Liberty squawks as I approach the group at the giant love sign as per the itinerary. She can barely breathe for laughing. She is wiping tears from her eyes.

'What happened, Big Guy? Has the stag do theme changed to Shrek?' Big Sue asks. She slaps her thigh and bends over double.

The Dollz are finding my state of disarray hilarious. They fall about laughing. I take a moment. If we only had ten minutes maximum in our rooms to prevent anyone trying to have a nap and we all looked terrible on entering the hotel, how the heck do they now all look stunningly gorgeous? They are standing in front of me red-carpet ready. How? *How?*

'We're only kidding, Big Guy. You look... You look... You...' Liberty is honking hard. She looks amazing in her perfectly coiffed wig, her pristine make-up with heavy black flicky eyeliner and her outrageously short and sexy Barbie dress. She is attracting appreciative glances left, right and centre.

'Big Guy?' Cherry brays with laughter. 'That will never grow old.'

'Big Sue,' I say, standing with my hands on my hips. 'Please do something.' Surely she can appreciate that there are enough Bigs in our group already?

'Me?' she says, barely able to keep a straight face.

'You started this whole Big Guy thing.'

'Did I?'

It's no use. They are all delirious from lack of sleep. And now I'm seeing things too. An image of

Birdie sauntering towards us like an angry poltergeist.

'Are you *supposed* to be green?' she asks loudly as she reaches us, smirking.

'Are you *supposed* to be here?' I snap.

When Birdie doesn't answer, I give up and flick through today's agenda on my phone. 'If we're all here, then the first pre-moon-slash-BIG-birthday activity to help keep us awake is to head to the hotel casino via the infamous streets of Venice, for approximately two and a half hours of gambling.'

The Dollz start whooping and swishing their arms in the air. 'I love gambling so much!' yells Cherry. 'Not that I've ever done it. But how hard can it be?'

'Steady on there, sugar tits,' intervenes Big Sue. 'Stick close to me, little lady. I'll show you how it's done.' Big Sue links Cherry's arm and heads off through the crowd.

'I have something in my suitcase that might get the green off,' offers Liam. I regard his yellow face and try not to look doubtful. 'I'll go and get it.'

'I'll come too,' says Ged.

Liam huffs dramatically. 'You don't trust me with the naked butler, do you?'

'Of course I trust you,' he says quickly. 'It's him I

don't trust. Did you see the thighs on him? He could crack walnuts.'

'Honestly, Connie, you should see his—'

'Meet back here in half an hour!' I shriek. I don't need to hear all the details. 'I'll come back for you.'

As the pair of them go off into a dreamlike state, Big Mand grabs my arm and we scuttle to catch everyone else up. I hear Birdie talking to Matteo behind me as we hurry along. I hope he mentions that nobody invited her to come gambling with us. I can hear the odd word over the noise of chatter around us. Words like 'technical issues' and 'muddy frequency' and 'immediately'. I hear him tut impatiently, and a few seconds later, he touches my arm lightly.

I stop walking. Big Mand takes one look at Matteo's serious face and rushes to catch up with Big Sue and the others. Birdie hovers around us at a short distance.

'Hey, Connie. I, erm, I'm not sure how to put this but...'

Poor Matteo. Birdie is deliberately holding him to ransom over their work-in-progress with the top-secret celebrity.

'I get it,' I say softly. I stretch up onto my tiptoes to whisper in his ear. 'I think she's making stuff up to keep us apart.'

He nods agreement before I continue.

'Just play along with it while I get this lot sorted. I'm too tired to do much anyway. Why don't we meet in a couple of hours at the restaurant? I'll put it in the group chat. Make sure you lose her by then.'

I give him a kiss and receive an extra-hard appreciative hug in return. Matteo stares at me before breaking into a smile that lights up his entire face. It earns him another kiss. A slow, sensual one that I'm hoping will send a sharp message to Birdie.

When we break apart, Matteo cups my cheek. He blinks slowly, his mouth curving upwards. 'See you later, Big Guy.' He receives a disbelieving shake of the head from me.

While the two of them walk away in the opposite direction, I try to follow the group, but they have disappeared. This place is way bigger and busier than I ever imagined, but I suppose everything in America is. It's not long before I spot the entrance to The Poker Room and, opposite that, huge arched pillars into the casino area. I stand motionless as a stream of people brush past me. I take in the giant crystal chandeliers, the elaborately gold-painted ceilings with multiple frescos styled on the Sistine Chapel, which are in stark contrast to the blinking and beeping of the one-armed bandits and slot machines.

'Hey,' says an extremely handsome man. 'You lost?'

My jaw drops.

He holds up his hands before I can get my words out. 'No. I'm not him.'

I don't believe him.

'Honestly. If I were Harry Styles, wouldn't I have a British accent? I don't know if you can tell but I'm clearly Canadian.'

I swallow. I almost made a huge fool of myself. I was about to start begging him to do a meet 'n' greet with Ged and Liam. What a shame it's not him.

'I do a mean tribute act though if you'd like to come see me sometime?' He hands me a leaflet. 'The name's Barry.'

'Oh, thanks,' I say, patting my wig. 'We just might do that.' If the hunt for real celebrities comes to nothing then it will be good to have Barry Styles as a backup plan.

The loud bleeping pings and tinny music fill my ears. But it is the giant screens running all around the area showing sports, adverts for shows and sugar and fat-based products that draw my eye. It seems as though everything you need is here, available in this vast hotel. Bars and restaurants dot the casino area, breaking up the machines. Gamble. Eat. Drink. Repeat. Then suddenly there's a huge image of the Dollz and me up on the screen with an invitation to come and see us at The Cocktail Hour Lounge the following evening for an exclusive and immersive experience in global high-quality entertainment. I look from the screen down to my outfit. The two versions of me couldn't be further apart.

A loud squeal alerts me to the fact that the Dollz are watching the same screen. I crane my neck above the crowd and spot Big Sue fist-bumping the air. I race over.

'Good, you're here. We've got a situation,' says Big Sue, putting a finger to a non-existent earpiece.

Oh, God. What now?

'But I've only been gone less than a minute,' I whine. I really am so tired. I can't be doing with this level of nonsense.

'It's Kev!' shrieks Tash dramatically. 'He's...' She throws the back of her hand to her forehead. 'Gone off.'

'Gone off where?'

'Gone. Gone as in completely gone. He's not here. He's gone away.'

'They decided to split up,' says Liberty.

They've split up? Already? Tash *is* uber high-maintenance, I suppose.

'I'm sorry,' I say gently. 'Perhaps it was for the best.' The best for him. Before she traps him into fathering children with ridiculous names.

'She means she's lost him in the casino,' says Liberty, laughing. 'You lot are a disgrace. Even by my low standards.'

'They're just tired,' says Big Mand, defending Big Sue.

'Don't underestimate fatigue,' Big Sue says, momentarily thrown as exhaustion sweeps over her. 'It's a form of torture in some countries.' She lets out a huge yawn, blinking rapidly. 'Wait. Where are we?' She looks at the Italian-style shop facades and stone bridges. 'What is this place? How did I get here?' She grabs Big Mand's arm, panic in her voice.

'Are we outside? The sky? The river?' Cherry asks, confused at the optical illusion surrounding us. She points at the ceiling, which is painted and lit up just like a summer's day. We marvel at the gondolas floating past with Italian-looking gondoliers in uniforms of red trousers, blue and white striped tops, straw boater hats and jaunty red scarves. At least it is distracting them from me and my horrendous green face situation.

'We're in Italy,' says Big Mand, yawning as she

points to the canal. 'Come on, let's go. No, wait. What are we doing again? I've completely forgotten.'

'It's jet lag,' says Liberty, yawning. 'I knew we should have slept on the way over. Can everyone stop yawning, please?'

'Fatigue can kill,' Big Mand says, forcefully slamming her fist into her palm. 'I should know.'

'Should you?' *What sort of baby unit does she work in?*

She comes up to whisper loudly in my ear, 'You've reminded me of the time I once handed a baby to a first-time mother. She took one look and screamed the place down.'

Ah, that's not nice, is it? Most babies are ugly when they first come out.

Big Mand chuckles to herself. 'When she turned it to face me, I'd given her some blue roll full of afterbirth. To be fair, I'd done a seventy-two-hour shift. So...'

Big Mand sure knows how to make a point. Poor woman must have been so traumatised. 'And the baby?'

'Laundry drawer. Absolutely fine.'

Christ.

'Right. Okay. How about we get some caffeine? Strong coffees to keep us awake and alert?'

'Is nobody going to mention that I look bloody fabulous on that screen?' says Tash, gazing at herself. 'Or that my Kev is missing? Shouldn't we alert security or something? It's been hours.'

'It's not even been two minutes. Calm the fuck down, babes.' Liberty sweeps her bored gaze around our group. 'I'm off to The Poker Room. I spotted some Stetson hats earlier. Cherry, hun, come with me. Cherry?' Liberty frowns. 'Cherry?'

There's no sign of Cherry.

'Shit. Let's fan out,' says Big Sue. She still has her hand on her imaginary earpiece. 'Connie, you take the canal shopping area we just walked through. Mandeep, cover the casino slot machines while I do the crap tables. Tash? Tash? Where's Tash gone?'

Tash has disappeared at the first sign of having to help out.

'Roger that, Sue,' says Big Mand, scanning the crowded machine area, eyes screwed up. 'You do all the crap tables. I'll do the good ones.'

Liberty lets out an exasperated moan. 'For God's sake, it's craps tables. I'll do a sweep of the casino floor with you.'

'Whatever you do, stay awake!' booms Big Mand, yelling as though she's a mile away and a jumbo jet is flying overhead. She charges off and instantly trips over a roll of pink carpet on the floor. She falls heavily to the ground. It takes all of three seconds for us to realise the roll of carpet is Tash.

Big Mand shakes herself off as Big Sue hauls them both up.

Tash blinks rapidly. 'What happened?'

Liberty gets Tash up to speed. 'Cherry is AWOL.'

'Cherry is AWOL?' Tash repeats.

'Yes.'

'AWOL?' Tash says again. 'As in AWOL?'

Liberty sighs. 'Yes, Tash. As in AWOL.'

Tash springs into action. 'FUUUUUCK! FUCKETY FUUUUUUCK!' she screams, running off. We see her blonde wig disappear into the crowd. It doesn't look as though she'll be coming back.

'Where is she going?' asks Liberty.

'Anyone feel her reaction is a bit extreme?' I ask, convinced we're all severely jet-lagged.

'No shit, Sherlock,' says Liberty, laughing. 'Now, I'm going to have to find Tash *and* Cherry.'

'Uh-huh. Roger that,' says Big Sue briskly. She's gone full commando mode yet again, but at least I know the job will get done. She's very good like that. No nonsense. Never flaps in a crisis. 'Rendezvous at zero one hundred and twenty hours and forty pence,' says Big Sue, staring hard at her bare wrist.

Liberty and I take a moment to look bleakly at one another.

'I think it'll be easier to just round them all up and put them to bed,' she says.

It'll be like herding cats.

'I agree. We have the WhatsApp group. I'll drop this location in the chat,' I say. 'Everyone, meet back here when we've found Cherry and Tash. Okay?'

Big Sue snaps out of her trance. 'Roger that, Big Guy.'

'Affirmative,' agrees Big Mand, dusting herself off.

'Whatever... Big Guy,' chortles Liberty.

We separate out across the casino. I head outside and up a travelator towards the canal shopping centre. I marvel at how 'outside-like' it is. I wander past the canals where gondoliers are singing Italian opera to customers in the gondolas. Their voices carry across the water to the crowds gathering to watch and listen from the bridge that goes over it, just like the ones in Venice. Whoever owns the hotel has really committed to the replica. It's surreal. I watch a couple being serenaded as they float underneath the bridge. The singer is clearly opera trained. It instantly reminds me that Luke is here in this hotel. A sinking feeling floods my stomach. I really hope he gets the hint and backs off. Though I can't see how he'd find me anyway; this place is so huge. The chances of bumping into him must be virtually zero. A searing pain spears my head. I'm so tired. I pinch the bridge of my nose. Something is niggling at my brain. Why does that not sound plausible?

The penny drops.

The huge, massive TV screens showing adverts. Luke would only have to walk around the hotel once to see huge images of me and exactly where I'm going to be tomorrow evening.

Shitting hell.

7

I shake the thought of Luke and what he's planning to do from my head. I don't have the bandwidth for it. Half my mind is on what Birdie is up to with Matteo. The other half is on how to round up the Dollz so we can get some sleep. Just enough shut-eye to tide us over this difficult spell. Then there's Ged and Liam and cocktails tonight. Oh, God. Ged and Liam! I check my phone.

> Where are you? We are waiting by the love sign as agreed!

Ged has added an angry-face emoji.
I speedily type.

Sorry. Thought you'd fallen asleep.
Meet in casino at the pin drop.

I can see Ged typing.

No worries. Have spotted Harry
Styles walking to Palazzo. Am
trying to catch him up.

I type:

Abort, abort. Is not the real Harry
Styles. Is lookalike. Barry Styles.

He replies with a crying emoji.

I run from shop to shop, peering in windows full of merchandise for the hotel: jewellery, gifts and the most incredible selection of donuts. Then it hits me. I cast my gaze around. Bingo.

A huge sign saying IT'SUGAR in bright lights towers over a sweet shop. I race towards it and peer in through the window. Cherry is very easy to spot because she is slumped face down over a bowl of what look like jellies. Her flaming-red ponytail is bobbing up and down.

'Ma'am, you have to purchase those candies before you consume them,' a stern-faced assistant is telling her as I approach. Cherry lifts her face from the bowl. She's about to go nuclear. Her cheeks are full like a chipmunk's. Eyes wide with outrage.

'How much is it?' I ask. The assistant squints while she tots it all up. 'She's had seventy-four dollars' worth of Hershey's, two bags of Tootsie Rolls, a Swedish Fish and, oh yeah, a whole jumbo bag of gummies. And she's kinda ruined that bowl of candy for everyone. So...' She sucks in a sharp breath. 'Four hundred and twenty-five dollars should cover it, ma'am.'

'Cherry,' I say, shaking her out of the trance she appears to be in. 'Where's your money?'

'What money?'

'Your money to spend.'

Cherry suddenly starts sobbing loudly. Apparently, her thinning-haired husband doesn't trust her with the credit card any more. Not since she left the house to go buy a much-needed second-hand car, and returned days later with a new pair of boobs. The assistant has no idea what to do with this information. She looks around as though hoping for a passing psychiatrist. Or at the very least some hotel security.

'I'll pay,' I offer. I quickly swipe my credit card through the machine, wincing at the extortionately crippling amount, and escort Cherry out of the shop. 'Come on. You'll be okay,' I soothe. 'Everything will work out for the best. We'll just meet the others, and then get some rest.'

Cherry wipes her face and sniffs out a thank you. She's in a right mess. Back to how she was in Benidorm with streaks of make-up running down her face. 'I'll be fine once I start gambling. It'll take my mind off things.'

I nod. 'I'm sure it will. I'm sure it will.' I'm absolutely 100 per cent sure it won't, but she needs something to cling to.

* * *

A short while later, we have made it back to the drop spot. Big Sue is there holding Tash upright. Tash appears awake but apparently is sleeping with her eyes open while standing. 'Kinda like a horse,' says Big Sue. 'Who'da thunk it? Impressive, huh?' She lets go for a few seconds and Tash remains rigid.

I try not to look startled. Big Sue has now adopted a full-on Deep South accent.

'Great. So, we have Cherry, you, Tash, and where's Big Mand?'

Big Sue checks her pockets. 'No idea, Big Guy. No

idea. We've been compromised. Infiltrated. Burned. Whaddaya-gonna-do-abad-it?'

Effing hell.

I do some quick thinking. There's a bar area next to us that seems to double as a snack bar. It seems safe enough to leave these three there while I go in search of Liberty and Big Mand. Big Mand will be furious with Tash. She has made it very clear that we all must stay awake or we will be too shattered for Ged and Liam's BIG pre-moon spree extravaganza tonight, which would be our morning in body-clock time, and the knock-on effect will be wanting to sleep during our opening gig tomorrow night. The Venetian has a reputation for world-class performances, especially for its Cocktail Hour entertainment, and if we don't deliver, Nancy, our agent, will never book us ever again.

'Hey, what's up? What happened to meeting at the love sign?' asks Liam on approach. He is dressed in his Rollerblading Ken outfit. It is neon yellow with paint splashes all over it. 'What do you think?' he says, twirling around.

It's a very powerful statement, that's what I think. It leaves nothing to the imagination.

'I love it. It really brings out the yellow in your arms and legs,' says Cherry.

'I tried to talk him out of it,' says Ged, dressed in the Cowboy Ken outfit he travelled here in. 'Here's the stuff to take your green face away.' He hands me a small pot, which I slip into my pocket.

'Can you please babysit these three for me?' I ask them. 'I need to round up Liberty and Big Mand. Then I really think we should have a very short nap before cocktail hour. I've booked us all a table at the Minus5 bar. I think the freezing-cold atmosphere might help keep us awake.' I mentally cross my fingers and hope that the boys agree.

Ged yawns loudly. 'Absolutely fine by me.'

'Great. Please eat something,' I say, pointing to the rather unappetising weeks-old jumbo hot dogs, 'and I'll be back in five with the others.'

I put a message in the group chat to return to our bedrooms for an emergency snooze, but the Dollz are obviously not checking the WhatsApp updates. I race off deeper into the casino, weaving in and out of the slot machines, the gaming tables, the hundreds and hundreds of people. I scan the floor and instantly spot Liberty. Her blonde ponytail is swinging jauntily. Her tiny butt cheeks are poking below her teeny tiny Barbie dress as she leans over a roulette table to place a bet in the most provocative way I've ever seen. There are multiple sets of eyes on her. I smile fondly to myself. She really is a force to be reckoned with.

'Hey,' I say, fighting through a small crowd to get to her. 'How's it going?'

'Absolutely brilliant,' she squeals over her shoulder. 'I'm up all of these chips. No idea what they're worth, but this is amazing. And they keep bringing me free drinks!'

Liberty is shining with excitement. It seems a shame to pull her away. 'I, erm, kind of need your help.'

'For what?'

'Putting the others to bed. Big Sue and Tash are virtually asleep anyway, and Cherry... Well, Cherry...'

How to describe Cherry snorting jellies like a sugar-crazed buffalo?

'Pffft,' Liberty scoffs. 'They're not babies. Besides, I've just seen Cherry.'

'Have you? I literally just left her two seconds ago.'

'Yeah. Just now. She needed to borrow my Monzo card. Needed to buy something to drink. Even though I told her all the drinks here are free.'

Oh no.

'What?' asks Liberty. 'Why are you looking at me like that?'

'I... No reason. No reason. I'm sure Cherry wouldn't...'

'Ah, shit,' Liberty groans. 'She doesn't need my card to buy a drink, does she?'

I shake my head sympathetically.

Liberty hurriedly gathers up her chips and lifts the hem of her dress up like a tiny hammock. 'Quick, help me with this lot. Let's cash it in and hunt down Cherry before she spends every penny I have.' When we've scooped every last plastic chip into her dress, she bunches the material up at her pelvis like a lumpy colostomy bag.

'Big Mand can help us. She's the one in charge,' I say, whipping out my phone. 'Don't worry, Big Mand will have her tracked down in no time.' She's like a sniffer dog. I jab at my phone. Thank God for no-non-sense, shift-working, dependable midwives.

Liberty rolls her eyes.

'What?' I say, following her finger to a nearby sofa. It's Big Mand. She's collapsed, spread-eagled, with her nose in the air. She's flat out, snoring very loudly. She has the whole sofa and general area to herself. I watch her chest rise and fall with a steady rhythm. Legs akimbo. Barbie knee-length socks and sky-high sandals propped up on two coffee tables in front of her.

Blonde ponytail wig askew. Pink Barbie dress twisted round her body. Mouth gaping open.

'We'll come back for her,' says Liberty briskly. 'She's clearly not going anywhere. Let's bank this lot, go find that blinking Cherry, and get my card off her.'

'We can't leave her like that,' I say. 'Let's just wake her up and bring her with us.'

Liberty tuts. 'Okay. But don't say I didn't warn you.'

* * *

Five minutes later, I wish I'd listened. Big Mand is in a very deep sleep. I'm tugging at her arm while Liberty is slapping her face with increasing ferocity.

'It's no use,' I say, stepping back. 'We'll have to leave her here. She'll just have to sleep the jet lag off.'

At the mention of jet lag and sleep, Big Mand's eyes snap open. 'Who? Who is sleeping? How dare they!' she booms, leaping up. She has woken up swinging. She seems to have lost all sense of who and where she is. Her head swivels around as she pummels her fist into her palm ready for action. 'Where? Who? I'll take the lottuv-yuz.'

Liberty slaps her once more.

With glazed eyes, Big Mand responds by trying to karate kick Liberty in the throat.

It's like watching a scene from my worst nightmare slowly unfold. Big Mand has snapped. Thankfully, Liberty jumps out of the way, and Big Mand wallops her foot off a vintage slot machine instead. The machine roars to life and immediately sheds hundreds of coins in a blaring fanfare of music. The people around cheer and Big Mand is momentarily distracted as she picks up all of the coins.

As soon as she is finished, we set off in search of Cherry. Her vibrant crimson locks should be easy to spot but, amid the blaze of colour, it's nigh-on impossible. The good folk of Las Vegas have turned out in their gaudiest gambling clothes. The loud blinking and blooping and tringing assaults my ears as we weave in and out of tables, carousels of machines, lines of people yanking down the metal arms of the one-armed bandits, lost in concentration. Suddenly, we spot a flash of bright red.

'Quick,' yells Liberty. 'Over there!'

We bolt over to see Cherry engaged in what can only be described as a weird tug of war over a seat at a craps table. We hurry over to see what she is outraged about.

'This jerk won't let me sit down, even though I'm pregnant!' she yells when she spots us approaching.

He's very handsome as far as jerks go.

'To be fair,' he says to us, 'this is the first I'm hearing of it.' He sounds very reasonable. We look at Cherry. She looks guilty as hell. 'If you want the seat, take the seat,' he says, amused. 'There's plenty of them.'

She eyes him suspiciously. 'Which seat do *you* want?'

He starts to chuckle. 'Not sure.'

'What's going on?' Liberty asks. I see him eyeing her appreciatively up and down, a smile spreading across her face.

'Well, ma'am,' he drawls in a smooth American accent. 'Your friend here seems to be under the impression that whichever seat I choose is the lucky seat.'

We look to Cherry, who nods in agreement, lips pursed. 'It's true. Every time he wins, I lose. And it's all because of the seats.'

It makes no sense at all. Cherry is wired and wild-looking.

Liberty's face drains of colour. 'How much have you lost?'

Cherry waves the card around. 'Well, whatever was on there.'

Liberty lets out a whimper.

Cherry flings her arm in the man's direction. 'It's his fault. Blame him.'

He holds his hands up. 'No, ma'am. I think you're—'

He doesn't get to finish because Big Mand decides to intervene by grabbing the back of the chair he has just sat on.

To avoid contact, he leaps from his chair into the path of a passing waiter carrying a tray laden with drinks. The waiter, knocked off balance, fails to regain control.

Liberty does her best to jump out of the way, but the drinks, like falling dominoes, topple over to expertly drench both him and Liberty, before crashing loudly onto the carpet.

The chips Liberty was carrying are flung high into the air, showering us as they fall back down.

Amid the chaos, the teller announces that she's shutting the table and radios for housekeeping, while Liberty and the man stand staring at one another with beer and cocktails dripping down their fronts. Liberty, normally cool as a cucumber, looks shyly at him.

His whole face lights up.

Security is quick to arrive on the scene, probably alerted by Big Mand and her kung-fu attempt. They take one look at Big Mand's crazed expression and radio for backup. The waiter disappears, leaving the security guys to face us. 'What happened?'

'Me,' barks Big Mand. 'I happened.'

I'm sure one of them has a hand on a Taser gun of some sort at his waist.

Oh, God.

'Come with us, ma'am.' They step towards her. I gasp as Big Mand stretches out her palms towards them in a defensive manner. She has turned into Kung Fu Panda.

'Wait,' I cry out. 'We're the Cocktail Hour entertainment. We're here from England. We just arrived. We're all jet-lagged. We were booked by Eddie from Talent Star,' I rattle out quickly before turning to the dripping-wet guy. 'I'm so sorry about the accident. We'll pay for your clothes to be, erm, dry-cleaned and we'll pay for those free drinks we ruined.'

My credit card is literally tearing itself up in my bag. Snapping itself in two in protest.

Dripping-Wet Guy smiles good-naturedly. 'No need to pay, ma'am. But thanks.'

Liberty is staring at him open-mouthed as though

she's been hit by a bolt of lightning. He's quite attractive in an unconventional way, but it's his voice that lures us in. His accent is mesmerising. It's deep and rich and smooth like honey. Like dark, expensive manuka honey, not the Aldi honey-flavoured honey. He gives her a long, admiring look before he slowly strokes his stubbled chin.

'Okay, fellas. I think we're good,' he says to the security guys. 'I'll handle it from here.'

They instantly agree to do what he says. 'Yes, sir. Sorry about the...' One of them waves a hand at me and Big Mand.

'No problem, guys,' Dripping-Wet Guy says confidently. 'I'll sort this out. If you could get these chips cashed in, I'd appreciate it.' He turns to Liberty. 'You're staying here, I presume?'

She nods slowly.

'Credit her room. Thanks, guys.'

The security guys radio for help, which arrives instantly, and a waiter scampers around retrieving Liberty's chips that are scattered all over the floor. He checks her room key and hands it back.

Liberty is still staring at her handsome stranger.

'So, you're the Cocktail Hour entertainment, are you?'

We nod mutely. He's very sure of himself.

'Well. You've certainly been entertaining so far.'

Liberty blushes to her roots.

'Come with me,' he says in such a commanding voice that we find ourselves instantly trailing through the crowd behind him like little ducklings. I notice that Cherry has absconded once again with the card.

'What about Cherry?' I ask Liberty. For reasons unknown, we are walking in a straight line behind Dripping-Wet Guy.

'What about Cherry?' booms Big Mand from behind me. 'Has she been compromised?'

'Yes. In a way,' I explain as we walk. 'She's taken Liberty's credit card and is loose in the casino with it. Again.'

Big Mand's eyes grow wide with concern. 'We have to find her. Now!' She stops in her tracks to dart her gaze around the room. We also stop, and Dripping-Wet Guy continues for a few steps before doubling back to us.

He's so cool, he simply raises his brow casually. Even as Liberty explains, he is emitting 'I'll take care of it' vibes. They are gazing deeply at one another, clearly smitten. 'Where does this Cherry-pie like to go?' he asks her.

'She'll stick to the casino,' Liberty says quietly. I've never seen her behave like this with a man before.

Dripping-Wet Guy takes the opportunity to rake his eyes slowly down her body and even more slowly back up to meet her questioning gaze. He nods in approval. It's all very seventies, but Liberty is blooming under his appreciation of her sexy curves. 'Leave it to me,' he says when he finally finds his voice. He beckons over a waiter and explains the situation. 'They'll find her and bring her to us.'

'Where are we going?' I ask, toying with the idea of how to explain that we have abandoned our friends at the drop point and are on a very tight pre-moon spree schedule. Dripping-Wet Guy has such an aura of calm approachability about him that I almost want to blurt out all my troubles. I wonder what he'd make of my boyfriend currently being seduced by a hot Frenchwoman or that my unwanted admirer is loose about the hotel.

He simply answers, 'Follow me. I'll show you.'

8

We are helpless in the face of that American drawl and fall in behind him once more. I quickly text the group chat to say that we are on our way and that we just need to find Cherry first. I will skip over the part where we are following a stranger to God knows where, to do God knows what, all because Liberty has fallen for his dreamy accent, stubble and supremely confident manner.

Ged replies instantly with a photo of the rest of them all fast asleep in the booth. He says he will stand guard.

Dripping-Wet Guy leads us towards the canal shopping area, over the bridge where the gondolas float underneath, through the mall to a very elegant boutique. He stops outside. 'After you,' he says to Liberty.

My heart sinks as I peer inside. He couldn't have brought us anywhere more expensive. I fear for my credit card once more.

We go in, and immediately the shop assistants float over. They are extremely professional and have either seen it all before, the bargain-basement Barbie outfits, my green face and wigs, or they suspect we are sex workers on a shopping spree with our newest client.

They are quick to point us towards a range of elaborate gowns. 'How can we help?' a glamorous woman asks softly, smiling only at Dripping-Wet Guy. 'We have a great line in menswear.'

I take the opportunity to squint at one of the price tags on a slip of satin hanging nearby. I inhale a sharp breath and stealthily show Big Mand the tag. She lets out an anxious whine.

After a beat, I step towards Dripping-Wet Guy. 'I was imagining a dry-cleaner's,' I squeak, mortified. 'For your clothes. Not, erm, paying to replace them. I'm so sorry. I mustn't have made myself clear. Sorry. But we're British. Sorry. And we simply couldn't afford to...'

It's Dripping-Wet Guy's turn to be embarrassed.

'Ma'am. No. I'm the one who should apologise.' He puts his hand to his chest. 'I meant for her to choose an outfit. On me. For me to pay for it. Not you.' He is genuinely rattled. 'If that is agreeable with you.'

Liberty bites her lower lip provocatively and shifts her weight, placing her hand on her hip. 'I find that... very agreeable.'

'Christ,' murmurs Big Mand. 'Poor guy. He won't stand a chance. I hope he has deep pockets.'

For the next few minutes, we sit through what can only be described as a one-woman catwalk show. Firstly, Liberty, who has regained full use of her senses, insists on replacement underwear.

'For the love of God,' complains Big Mand. 'Put your flaps away. We've seen it all before.' But Liberty is taking no notice. It's as though there are only two people in the room. And it isn't me or Big Mand. By the time Liberty is nowhere near trying on actual clothes, and Dripping-Wet Guy is salivating, and completely dry by the looks of him, Big Mand puts her hands on her knees and heaves herself up.

'I'm going to find the others.'

'I'll come,' I say, jumping up. 'Unless you need me to stay with Libs.' I lower my voice. 'After all, Dripping-Wet Guy could be any old serial killer, couldn't he? We don't even know his name.'

Liberty is flirting up a storm as she emerges from the changing room curtain like she's on stage at Glastonbury. She runs her hands slowly down her body as though to smooth the barely-there material, outlining her curves in the skintight, violent-red thong basque she is trying on. The shop assistants are being kept very busy running back and forth, as Liberty simply can't seem to make a decision. She's leaning over Dripping-Wet Guy to pull at the bra cups as she jiggles her boobs into place. Now she is showing him the back, which consists of a silver string and nothing else. His eyes are popping out of his head. She has him eating out of her hand.

Poor man.

Liberty nods subtly towards the door to indicate we should leave her to get on with it. We silently slope away, and Dripping-Wet Guy does not even notice. As we emerge from the boutique, Cherry is being escorted towards us like a criminal, by the two burly security guards from earlier.

'Great,' I say. 'You've found her.' One of the security guards hands me the credit card. 'Thank you.'

'There's no need for this level of micromanagement,' she complains. 'I was just about to win big. Really big. Just one more throw of the dice and I'd have cleaned up.'

The security guard shakes his head behind her and shoots me a warning look. 'We'll take her from here, officer,' I say, as though he's the police.

Big Mand loops Cherry's arm, and we hurry away. 'I'll message Ged to say we're on our way back.'

* * *

'So, where's Liberty?' asks Tash an hour later. We are sitting at a booth in the Minus5 bar, the sub-zero temperature ensuring we are all attentive and wide awake after our brief nap. I was so disappointed to get back to my room, after having helped Ged and Big Mand carry Tash and Big Sue to their suites, to find Matteo was not back from his 'work' thing with Birdie and no message from him to say where he was. At least the hotel cleaners had been in to clear the glass away and I was able to have a proper shower, apply the cream that Ged gave me to get rid of the green face and spruce myself up.

Sister Kevin is sitting beside Tash. No longer missing in action. He was already in their room, waiting. Apparently, he'd been searching everywhere and hadn't thought to check his WhatsApp group messages.

Everyone looks refreshed.

'Liberty has met someone,' chips in Big Mand, and they all make an 'aaah' sound.

'Well, she has been here for almost two hours,' says Tash. 'She's a fast worker when she wants to be.'

'At least it'll take her mind off Luke,' says Big Sue. 'By the way, Connie, I'll put an APB out for him. See if he shows up. We can get his full MO.'

Big Sue is still talking like she's a fully paid-up member of the NYPD. Things are getting way too out of hand.

'No!' I squeal. 'No APB, whatever that is. To be honest, I'd almost forgotten he'd followed me here. I'm sure he'll have realised what an idiotic thing he's done, and will most probably be at the airport, heading back home on the next flight.'

She gives me an unconvincing look as our gazes are drawn to the gigantic screens that surround the entire bar and casino area. Luke's huge face is lighting up the screen. He smiles shyly at the camera with a huge bunch of red roses in his hand.

'I have an announcement,' he says. 'This is a message to the most beautiful woman on the planet. If you can hear me, "Mi Amore Mi Amore"...' He pauses to hold up the flowers to the camera. He totally looks as though he's been in hair and make-up. 'It's from a man who loves you from the bottom of his soul.' He shakes his head slowly. 'A man who hopes you can give him a chance to get his proposal right this time...'

My heart is in my mouth. *What is he doing?*

'He proposed?' barks Tash. 'He fucking proposed and you didn't think to mention it?'

'He was steaming drunk at the time,' I say in my defence.

'How else are you supposed to do it?' she says, frowning.

I watch, horrified, as the camera tilts to show Luke bending down on one knee. 'So where else than here, in the best city on the planet, Sin City' – he stops to treat everyone watching to his self-deprecating A-list-film-star smile – 'with all the other fools in love.' Cue small chuckle and wink to camera. He's so extraordinarily comfortable in the limelight. Perhaps from his decade on stages around the globe. There's no denying, the camera loves him. He leaves a beat for his words to sink in. He's probably got every woman in the place swooning by now. 'And this fool simply wants to know, will you marry him?'

There's a huge cheer around what sounds like the whole of Las Vegas. I am instantly mortified. 'Be here tomorrow, midnight... at the love sign' – he pauses dramatically – 'if your answer is yes.'

'Oh, my fucking word!' howls Cherry. 'How corny.'

'How staged,' adds Big Mand.

'How desperate,' says Liberty, walking towards us, hand in hand with Dripping-Wet Guy.

'Aw, shoot. And there's me thinking that was romantic and charming,' says Dripping-Wet Guy. 'I reckon that little show of his is guaranteed to melt hearts and have the girl of his dreams running back to him quicker than a streak of lightning.'

'I couldn't agree more.'

Oh, shit.

Matteo is standing glaring from the screen, to me, and back again. 'Well? Are you thinking of going?'

Matteo and I stand mutely while the group continue to express their opinions as to what my next course of action should be.

I blink slowly at Matteo. 'Where have you been?' I ask without answering his question.

His face immediately softens. 'Yeah. Sorry about that. Birdie insisted on phones off as we went through some sequences she wanted to change. We lost track of time. I've only just escaped from her.'

He sounds tired, and a bit fed up. Thankfully,

Luke's big, handsome face disappears from the screens. Adverts for shows and restaurants have replaced him. I pray they don't stick our Cocktail Hour advert up there, but it's not meant to be. The screen not only flashes up a life-size image of me posing while I look over my shoulder at the camera, but a loud trumpeting akin to a royal announcement blares out across the whole place. Tash lets out an excited scream. 'Connie, it's you!' It alerts the whole bar to my presence. Followed by, 'You look fucking gorgeous, pet! Doesn't she? Look at the arse on that! Who wouldn't want to marry those plums?' Which is nice but not what I need right now.

'Wait. Are you the same girl that guy wants to marry?' asks a passing waiter. 'Hey, Jeff. This is the proposal girl!' He points at me, and the bar staff all peer over. Thankfully, Jeff the bartender is busy with customers. 'Jeff! Jeff! It's the proposal girl!'

'Cool,' he says, dinging the bell. 'Free drinks for proposal girl and all her friends!'

Oh, no.

'No. I'm not proposal girl,' I protest, mortified. I feel Matteo's body tense beside me. 'I'm not going to accept. No need for free drinks.'

There's an outraged gasp from the Dollz and Ged and Liam. Luckily, my plea falls on deaf ears, and any additional attention from the people in the bar is drowned out by Tash squealing because the Dollz are up on screen. The advert guarantees a night of unforgettable singing and dancing as we promise to sweep customers off their feet if they come to see us at the Cocktail Hour club tomorrow at 6 p.m.

'Wait,' the waiter says again. 'Is that you guys up there?' He does a double take.

'We look better when we're not in our Barbie outfits,' says Cherry.

'Oh, man,' the waiter says. 'You're British. We love you guys. That accent. Are you from London? I love the Barbie vibe.'

'Well, at least some of us have made the effort,' says Liam, who has been unusually quiet. He looks sulkily at Liberty, who is without wig and wearing a gorgeous, slinky designer slip dress that is nothing short of spectacular on her. 'I thought this whole trip was supposed to be about us and our pre-moon.'

I flick my eyes to Cherry, our resident paralegal with a photographic mind and unparalleled ability to quote verbatim. Liam very famously and very recently, before we boarded the plane, ensured us that this trip *wasn't* to be all about them. She is opening her mouth ready to correct him. Likewise, Tash, who is still peddling Sister Kevin's BIG birthday even though he looks forty-three.

I mentally roll my eyes. Liam needs attention and he needs it right now.

Liberty is quick to leap in. She smiles at Liam before snuggling up to Dripping-Wet Guy who is no longer dripping wet but head to toe in a stylish cowboy outfit. He has a Stetson on his head. He has Liberty all over him. She has dressed him up to her ideal of a hot American rancher. I am surprised he is not wearing a fake moustache. He is obviously smitten, so that's all that matters.

'This is just temporary. There was an incident earlier requiring a quick change of clothes.' She tugs shyly at her man's arm. 'Everyone. I'd like you to meet Hank Junior.'

Honestly, if ever there was a cowboy with a fake name, he's got to be it.

Big Sue is first to act. 'Hank Junior? Really?' She pierces Hank with a sharp look. He instantly shrugs his shoulders in apology.

''Fraid so, ma'am. Hank's a popular name where I come from.'

'And where do you come from?' asks Big Mand. She has fully recovered from earlier, after a mammoth power nap and four cans of soda.

Hank strokes his chin as though giving it some thought. 'I guess you could say I'm from Texas originally.'

He's not giving much away.

'Hey now. Did you say you were celebrating?' he asks Liam, who nods forlornly. 'Well, I don't know about you folks, but here in Vegas, we like to do things in style.' He calls to the waiter. 'Can we please have a round of champagne? And can you bring some of that shrimp on ice and, heck, we'll have whatever these good folk want. Keep it coming. Charge it to my room. Thank you.' He flashes the waiter his key card. I see the waiter instantly redden.

'Yes, sir. Whatever they want, whenever they want it.'

There's a beat of silence as his words hit home. He's offering to buy us anything we want. When the waiter begins to take everyone's order, suddenly the party spirit is back in full swing. Liberty is gazing up at her generous cowboy with huge respect. She loves a man with a big, fat wallet. She'd probably overlook the lack of a moustache for that. He stares back down at her for approval.

That reminds me... I have my own love interest to attend to. The whole group are now suddenly very interested in Hank Junior and his generosity. I'm sure no one will notice if Matteo and I slip away for an hour.

I feel Matteo squeeze my hand. He leans down to whisper in my ear. 'Do you think...?'

'Way ahead of you. Let's go,' I say, dragging him silently away.

9

We race back to our room like giddy teenagers. The pressure has been steadily building since the airport. Waiting for the lift is agony. Then, in the lift, there are so many people. Matteo puts his hand on the small of my back, sending tingles floating up my spine. I place my hand casually on his buttock and lightly rub the hard surface. He shakes his head slowly at me as though to say there will be a major incident if I keep going. When we finally reach our floor, we have a maze of corridors to navigate. We keep stopping whenever a corridor is empty to kiss passionately against the wall, the housekeeping cart, the empty food trolleys. My hands sliding up and down his chest. His hands tangled in my hair. His erection throbbing impatiently against my thigh as our bodies collide together.

'Should we talk about what happened back there... on the screen?' I feel obliged to ask as my hands undo the buttons on his jeans as we reach our suite.

'No,' says Matteo, sliding his hand up my thigh and under my dress. 'I trust you. That's all there is to it.'

Everything in my whole being flutters. I want him. I want him down to my very bones. We crash against the door to our room and Matteo scrabbles to find his key card. He is having difficulty locating it because I have unbuttoned his jeans, and it has scrambled his brain. He is pulling down the shoulder of my dress to leave a trail of kisses down the length of my neck. It causes me to thrust myself against him even harder. He has his hand under my knee, and I'm half straddling him, my pelvis gyrating against his. I lift up his T-shirt to press my hands against the hot, taut skin of his abs, causing him to moan softly in my ear. He unzips the back of my dress and reaches a hand inside to cup a generous handful of voluptuous breast. He is squeezing it gently and groaning with desire. With a desperate swipe we are finally through. Matteo kicks the door shut, picks me up and flings me onto the king-size bed before settling his weight on top of me in the most delicious way.

His lips find mine in a feverish clash of desire. As the kiss deepens, Matteo grinds himself into me as I wrap myself round him. He tugs at my dress, eventually yanking it from my body in his rush to feel my skin against his. He pulls his T-shirt over his head to reveal that toned, athletic torso that has tormented my dreams for weeks. When he flings it to the floor and reaches round to unsnap my bra, I'm left panting for more as he skilfully peels down my bra straps. His breath is coming quick and fast as his gaze travels to my breasts. Taking the bra between his fingers, he lifts it from my body and tosses it to the floor. My breasts tumble free, much to his delight, causing my pelvis to twang when I see his pupils grow large with desire.

'Christ,' he says, his voice thick with lust as he covers one breast with the palm of his hand, rolling the soft mound, his thumb finding my nipple to tease it to a peak. I trail my hand across the swell of his bicep, over the curve of his shoulder and the dip of his collarbone to grab his hair and pull him back to me, the feel of his hot lips on mine sending electric sparks to every nerve ending in my body. I tug at his jeans, and he helps me to shrug them off.

Within seconds, we are almost naked, except for

my wig which is practically glued to my scalp, and the white stockings and suspender belt part of my Barbie costume. I fiddle with the tricky fastening.

Matteo drags his gaze down my body to the suspenders and stockings. 'Leave them on,' he instructs, a dark look in his eyes. His hand roams slowly down my leg and back up to the top, circling my inner thigh. He plucks at the strap holding the stockings. I hold my breath as his fingers move higher to trace the suspender belt across my stomach, before continuing down to my knickers, which conveniently – because I had the foresight to imagine this very scenario – have ribbon ties. Matteo pulls at one side, a lazy smile spreading across his face. 'Clever,' he says, pulling at the other side. He leans up on one elbow to gaze at me. 'You're so beautiful,' he whispers softly, his words sending sweet shivers to my very core. His breathing slows, and suddenly the tempo changes.

My heart is in my mouth as his eyes roam my body. He slowly pulls at my loosened white lace knickers and tugs the material away from my body, leaving me exposed to him. He blinks slowly. He leans down to graze my lips softly with his. He places sweet, hot kisses down my throat and across my collarbone. My nerve ends are on fire as he bends to take my nipple in his mouth, flicking his tongue to send shoots of lust through my entire body. His lips trail lazily down my stomach until I am arching under him, helpless with desire. When he shifts his weight further down the bed, and I feel his hands lifting my knees wide apart, I inhale sharply before I lose myself in the ecstasy of his expert tongue.

It isn't until my body is shaking from top to toe as waves of pleasure flood my senses that I notice the ceiling mirror. My eyes are wide with desire, my firm breasts are fully exposed, my hands are wrapped in Matteo's thick, shiny dark hair, his shoulder and back muscles moving lithely as he buries his face between my legs, the bed sheet only just covering his taut, round butt. It is incredibly erotic. I arch further into him as I reach a monumental climax and shudder against his mouth before collapsing back onto the mattress.

Matteo slides back up on the bed beside me, extremely pleased with himself. I have a ridiculous grin on my face. 'Oh. My. God. That was incredible.'

I push him back onto the pillows to straddle him. I notice he does a double take when he sees the ceiling mirror, a wicked glimmer in his eye. He flings the sheet from the bed. 'I am going to enjoy this so much.' My wig hair tumbles onto his chest, and my breasts graze against him, causing a low groan to escape his lips. He deftly rolls a condom on himself before taking my waist and helping me ease onto him. I hear a whisper of a gasp, maybe him, maybe me, before he looks up at me in wonder, sexy as fuck, as I slowly begin to grind against him. He doesn't take his eyes from mine. We're lost in this moment until eventually we can take no more. Matteo flips me round so that he's behind me, my hands flat against the headboard, his hands cupping my breasts, his body welded to mine, moving in perfect rhythm, growing like a wildfire in intensity, until we both shudder to a climax. We collapse, panting, back onto the pillows. Sparkles are shooting from our eyes.

He. Is. Magnificent.

He. Is. Incredible.

He. Is. Everything. I. Ever. Dreamed. Of.

* * *

'Where have you two been?' asks Ged with a knowing smile an hour later as Matteo and I stroll casually back to the bar. Our cheeks are flushed. Our pupils are dilated. Our skin is glowing. And everyone is exactly where we left them.

'Checking on things,' I say quickly. I mean, technically 'things' were checked. And thoroughly. Very,

very thoroughly. 'Are we still on for eating at the restaurant here?'

'Good to see that cream I gave you has given you such a glow.' He winks. 'By the way, Hank Junior has arranged a table for us at WAKUDA. It's exclusive.' He beams. 'The chef has *two* Michelin stars.'

'And it's Japanese,' adds Liam. 'We lurve Japanese food.' He gazes appreciatively at Hank Junior. I raise my eyebrows at Ged because, not so long ago, a drunk Liam famously threw some sushi at our living room wall in protest at the, and I quote, 'bland, tasteless, culinary bandwagon culture that is rice wrapped in flavourless green paper'. To be fair, he thought Ged would order in Chinese food for his birthday, as was custom, and had not reacted well to the surprise.

Hank Junior is sat in the centre of the action, his Stetson hat removed, a whiskey in front of him, Liberty close enough to be his conjoined twin, the Dollz and Sister Kevin all hanging off his dreamy American accent. 'I invite y'all to dine with me, if you care to.'

I'm just about to pull Big Sue to one side because I have a niggling feeling that Hank Junior's name is not the only fake thing about him, but I'm drowned out by the cheering.

We follow Hank Junior through the Grand Colonnade and across The Venetian casino floor, weaving in and out along the right-hand walkway, until we reach Restaurant Row. We pass by the love sculpture in the waterfall atrium. My heart sinks slightly at the thought of Luke and his ridiculous midnight proposal. We walk around the outskirts of The Palazzo casino until finally we arrive at one of Las Vegas's most critically acclaimed restaurants. What a highlight. Hank Junior approaches the maître d' with a smile and is immediately shown to a large oblong table. Staff are quick to take our drinks orders and to plonk down wooden grids, each of the nine boxes filled with tiny appetisers, sashimi and all manner of colourful seafood delicacies.

Out of nowhere, Birdie slithers in front of Hank Junior. 'I'm French,' she says by way of introduction, hand on razor-sharp hip, brightly coloured luscious coral-pink hair swept to the side, eyes bright with mischief. 'I do hope you haven't started without me?'

Matteo tightens his grip on my hand and groans into my ear. 'Fucking hell.'

'Take a seat,' invites Hank Junior, oblivious to the surrounding hostility. 'What's your poison?'

'She's not staying,' says Matteo, getting out of his seat. 'Birdie. This is a private celebration. We can talk work later.'

Birdie takes a long look at Matteo as she slides

into the booth next to Hank, causing us all to shuffle up. 'I'll have what you're having,' she says, ignoring Matteo. She curls up her lips to flash her great big white horse teeth at Hank and flicks back her hair, before she lets out a rather goose-like laugh, even though no one has said anything. She keeps it going until a slightly bewildered Hank has no option but to join in.

Liberty's jaw is on the floor. She must be fuming. She picks up a chopstick and all but stabs the table with it.

And just like that, the evening veers wildly off-track.

* * *

A few hours later, we have all eaten as much delicious and outrageously expensive Japanese food as we can manage. Hank Junior has become everyone's new favourite American and kept us all entertained with his stories of back home. I notice that he's never overly specific, but I seem to be the only one re-serving judgement. Birdie, who is throwing flutes of plonk down her neck, has stalked Matteo with her eyeballs at every available opportunity. And as soon as she launches her charm offensive on Hank, it becomes abundantly clear that she is out to make Matteo jealous.

'How is this happening?' I hiss out of the side of my mouth to Matteo as Birdie becomes the centre of attention.

He mutters back, all shell-shocked, 'She's worse than Luke.'

'She hasn't taken her eyes off you for a single minute,' I whisper. And as though to demonstrate, Birdie screws her eyes at me before fluttering her lashes at Matteo from across the table.

'This reminds me of the last time we ate food like this,' she says and continues the rest of the story in French. It's very reminiscent of when he and David Guetta were catching up on that multimillion-dollar superyacht we very nearly burned down.

Matteo's ear for languages is highly impressive but his cheeks flame as everyone around the table fails to follow.

'Remember?' says Birdie with a laugh, taking a huge slug of champagne. 'Oh God, where were we again? Some hotel in Paris, I think. It's such a funny story...'

'Seriously?' he says through clenched teeth. This is the third 'funny story' about Matteo that she has told in the last hour. Each time she is making sure we all know that they have enjoyed an intimate relationship. And each time Matteo has pretended not to hear because he has been gazing adoringly into my post-coital eyes while absent-mindedly kissing the back of my hand and stroking the base of my spine.

Matteo raises his eyebrows at me. I can see he has had enough of her.

'Sorry,' says Birdie, chuckling to herself. 'Old habits and all that.' She twists round to Hank sitting next to her and lays her hand possessively on his arm. 'I'm always overthinking things. When a French-woman gives her heart, she gives it so very complete-ly.' She flutters her lashes at him before checking that Matteo is watching. 'Isn't that right?'

'Well, pet,' says Tash, sounding annoyed. 'You really need to find yourself someone else to give that shrivelled-up heart to because that one's clearly taken.' She points a chopstick at Matteo.

Birdie feigns an innocent expression.

'And so is that one,' Big Sue joins in, pointing a chopstick at Hank.

I feel helpless as Matteo visibly swallows, clearly uncomfortable. Birdie is really laying it on thick. Fortunately, Liberty is on to her. She puts a hand on Hank's chin and rotates him to face her. She stares at him until he breaks into a wide smile.

'You sure are pretty, aintcha?' he murmurs.

Liberty, cool as anything, blinks slowly at him. She has made her point. Hank Junior doesn't take his eyes off her again.

This causes Birdie to talk about work. 'I've worked with all the biggest names in pop. They say I am a creative genius. They always ask me how I do it. But only Matteo knows my secrets, don't you?'

'And how do you do it?' asks Ged politely. Bless him. He has tried all sorts to stop Birdie and her ridiculous quest to make Matteo jealous by flirting with Hank Junior. It has been hard work.

'I never question the process. I collaborate with only the best,' she says, boring holes into Matteo. 'And when I commit, I demand the same commitment, don't I?'

I let out a silent groan. This is torture. 'It sounds to me as though you are overly clingy and controlling. The exact opposite of a creative genius. Don't you find that method stifling?'

Birdie's eyes flash at me. 'Why don't you ask the millions of fans who buy my records?'

Ah. Tit for tat. My speciality.

'I think the actual artists would say that those records belong to them. After all, they are the ones doing the singing.'

There follows a few moments of verbal ping-pong that descend very quickly into childish bickering, ending in Birdie screeching that she has known Matteo a lot longer than me.

'Who are you anyway? Some cheap karaoke singer he picked up in Benidorm? You are out of your depth, little girl,' she says, flinging down her napkin and getting to her feet. 'Matteo, I will see you tomorrow. We have much work to finish for our client. That is... if you still want to commit?'

With a hard edge in his voice, Matteo tries to placate her. 'Birdie, I think you're taking this a little too far.'

A little?

'It's a simple choice. Make the right one,' she says in a threatening tone before marching away, leaving us all gobsmacked.

10

The next morning, I am woken by a tap on the door. Throwing on a hotel bathrobe, I drag myself over to open it. Cherry is standing outside, holding a massive bouquet of flowers. 'These got delivered to my room by mistake. The hotel has you down as sharing with Liberty,' Cherry says, stomping past me into the room.

'Are you sure they're for me?' I say, sounding disappointed as I take the bouquet from her.

'I'll give you a hand arranging them.'

'You could always take them back to your room?'

Jeez, I hope she's not looking to stay for long. Matteo pulls the covers over himself. He is finding Cherry barging into our room very intrusive, by the expression on his face.

'I'm not sure we have room for them.'

My soul deflates. Matteo is watching me from the bed. The bouquet is so huge it takes both arms to carry it.

'Luke's certainly committing to this midnight proposal,' says Cherry. 'I'll give him that. There are another three bunches like this outside the door.'

Christ Almighty.

I plonk them down on the table near the window. They are exquisite. He must have paid a fortune. 'There's no note.' I let out a huge sigh. 'First the video, now enough flowers to open my own florist shop. I'm going to have to tell him to back off. We're work colleagues and nothing more. At this rate, we won't be able to sing together because he's making it too awkward. The Sinfonia will probably ask *me* to leave.'

Cherry walks over to the window and stands staring out across the city. 'That would be constructive dismissal. You'd never work again. You don't want to do that. Nice room.' She sweeps her gaze around. 'Spacious. Much better than mine. Much better.' A sorrowful expression sweeps over her pretty face. 'It reminds me of my honeymoon.'

Oh, God. Please don't kick off about our upgrade. I cross my fingers behind my back. I can see Matteo tense. He's trapped in the bed because he's naked underneath those sheets. He's pulled them up to his chin, clearly uncomfortable. I need to get Cherry out of here.

'Did you know that there are no clocks anywhere in this place? How is anyone supposed to know when to stop gambling?' she says, fussing with the flowers, her voice jittery.

By checking the time on our phones?

'I haven't been to bed yet,' she says, as though it's entirely the hotel's fault. 'Not sure it's worth the bother now.'

'But you'll be okay for the soundcheck later, though?'

Cherry looks at me blankly.

'For our performance today? You've got the costumes and the running list? You're still in charge of choreography?'

It's as though this is all news to her.

'I'm pregnant,' she says, busy flower arranging. 'How am I supposed to remember any of this stuff?'

Oh, my word.

'I have an idea,' she says suddenly, her mind jumping about. 'I think it'll put both Luke and Birdie off chasing you.'

'What is it?'

'You could play them at their own game. A sort of *matrimonium putativum*.'

I stare at her. I'd quite forgotten she's an experienced paralegal with a near-photographic memory.

'You could pretend to get married,' she clarifies. 'Send a clear message that neither of you is available. What do you think?' she says, and her eyes widen as she looks from Matteo to me.

I'd love to marry him, is what I think. But I must play it cool. I'll see how Matteo reacts to this bonkers plan first before I show a shred of interest.

Matteo regards Cherry for a few seconds. 'Seems a bit insane.'

'That's love for you. Sometimes it makes you do crazy things. But that's also why it'll work.' We watch her pluck a rose from the bouquet on her way out. 'See you later. There's something I need to do.'

When the door closes, Matteo lets out a puff of air. 'What do you think?'

'As in, do I think we should get fake married?' I say, walking back towards the bed. I suppress the urge to leap in the air with glee. 'How could we even possibly make that happen? I mean, when would we even...? Where would we...? How would we...?' I pretend to chuckle as though this is the most ridiculous suggestion anyone's ever made in the whole history of suggestions. *Gah!* I'd bloody love to bloody marry him. He's bloody gorgeous. My pulse is racing.

He arches an eyebrow. 'If only we were in a city that has a wedding chapel on every street corner,' he says dryly. 'A city renowned the world over for marrying couples on a whim, just because they've had too many margaritas.' He pretends to scratch his chin in thought. 'Such a shame.'

'Okay, smart-ass,' I say. *I am literally turning into an American.* 'What do you really think about it?'

I'm impressed he hasn't run a mile at the mere thought. I try not to ogle him as he slips from the bed. He stands naked and completely comfortable in front of me. It sends sharp pangs of longing straight to below my waist. 'I'll show you exactly what I think.'

I bite my lower lip suggestively. 'How about you show me in the shower?'

* * *

Before we meet the others for our first activity of the day – the SlotZilla zip line through Fremont Street – Matteo and I make our way down to the centre of the hotel, the canal shopping mall. We stand on the bridge, which is already quite busy with people watching the boats. I am still reeling from our shower, which began as soon as I suggested it. Matteo had slipped the bathrobe from my body and walked me over to stand naked in front of the window, where he brushed the hair from my neck and trailed kisses from my ear down to my shoulder. For a moment I was quite shocked. 'It's a mirrored window. No one can see us.' His knuckles had grazed my breasts as they snaked lazily across my stomach down towards my lady parts, leaving a wave of shivers in their wake. He rubbed his fingers gently over my sweet spot until I moaned for more, begging for release as he slipped them inside. I arched back against him with the whole city spread out before us.

'I can't control myself around you,' he said, his voice breaking and his words melting on my hot skin.

Matteo points to a gondola now, snapping me out of the delicious memory.

'There. We do it in there.'

'Do what? In where?'

'Look closely.'

My breath hitches in surprise as I home in on a couple floating underneath us in a white gondola. She is wearing a beautiful wedding dress. He is wearing a traditional tux.

'Couples can get married in the gondolas. I noticed it yesterday. Must be an alternative to the Vegas chapels.' Matteo smiles at me. 'If we did go through with it, we'd need to arrange for Luke and Birdie to be on this very bridge as we pass beneath.'

I gulp. It sounds so easy. 'Our timing would have to be perfect.'

'And we'd need some wedding clothes,' he says, pointing at the same couple floating by. 'Maybe not that fancy but...'

I nod. 'Yeah. I'm sure my credit card can make room for a cheap wedding dress. Unless we wear the bed sheets and have a toga theme going.'

Matteo smiles. 'Somehow, I don't think that will convince them.'

The boats are full of happy couples floating on the canal. Some are getting married and standing in front of wedding officiators, and some are lounging in each other's arms on a bed of elaborately coloured velvet cushions as they are serenaded with Italian opera. They all have something in common. They are extremely happy and madly in love. Suddenly, part of me really wants this to be *real*, not fake. The indecision must show on my face.

'Hey. Hey.' He reaches out to stroke my hair gently. 'If you don't like it, that's fine. We'll think of another way. It was a crazy idea anyway.'

I take a deep breath. Matteo has such a kind face. But we barely know each other. It would be madness to get married for real, then to start dating, then to get to know each other. But he is ridiculously handsome and kind and generous and funny and our sexual chemistry is off-the-charts amazing. What's the harm in having a practice run?

'Let's do it,' I say. 'Let's get fake married.' I'm sure I can squeeze in a harmless little wedding to our already overfull schedule.

* * *

We almost skip along to meet the others for breakfast, giggling like teenage girls over how to make the fake wedding a reality. There's a choice of officiators but, for a million reasons, we both agreed Elvis would be the perfect pick. And because we feel the need to act swiftly, without a multitude of strong opinions on everything from our fashion choices (no, no, no, you can't wear that) to the ceremony itself (no, babes, not there, not like that), we've decided not to involve the others in the planning, for fear it will escalate into a celebrity-style wedding with soaring costs and unmanageable expectations, until we've done it all and then we'll tell them. Plus, having to keep it secret has brought a rather exciting frisson to our relationship. We stop talking as we approach the table. The Dollz are already discussing our first performance tonight at the Cocktail Hour Lounge and Bar. No one seems remotely surprised to see Hank Junior being fed long strips of crispy bacon by Liberty. She is making him reach up to gobble at them. He seems helpless to do anything but obey.

After coffee and a pastry, Matteo makes an excuse to leave. He is going off to organise our nuptials. He is going to tell the hotel wedding organisers that we are simply 'rehearsing', ready for the real thing. We need everything except the official marriage certificate. I'm still in awe of how easy it all sounds. A shiver of excitement runs up my spine at the thought of fake-marrying Matteo. Of wearing a wedding dress. Of him taking my hand and saying lovely things. Of me gazing into his dark chocolate-coloured eyes and declaring undying love and devotion because, secretly, that is how I feel about him. It sounds ridiculous to fall so hard so quick, but it's the truth.

'So, guys,' I say, snapping back to reality. 'I've posted a new itinerary to the group chat. Basically, today is all about zip-lining for everyone, followed by poolside cabanas for Ged and Liam and Sister Kevin, while we're doing a soundcheck and getting ready. We do the show from 6 p.m. until 7.30 p.m. Dinner at 8 p.m. Maybe a nightclub at 10 p.m. for dancing and cock—'

'Speaking of cock,' interrupts Tash. 'What are you going to do about Luke at midnight?'

Good question.

'I'm not sure. I can't turn up because he'll think I'm interested. I don't want to hurt him because we have to maintain some sort of working relationship afterwards, but what else can I do?'

It's a real conundrum to which everyone seems to have an opinion.

'You're right. Don't go. Send a clear message that you're not interested. He's the one putting you under pressure. Don't feel guilty,' Big Sue says forcefully.

Tash agrees then immediately contradicts herself. 'Or you could go and make sure he gets the message that you aren't interested.'

'I don't trust him,' Ged says, wiping his lips with a napkin. 'Never have.'

'It's awful when you love someone and you can't tell them,' Big Mand says, out of nowhere. 'So I'm not surprised he's going to such extreme lengths to get your attention.'

We all take a beat of silence.

Liam coughs. 'Precisely. If you love someone, tell

them. Otherwise, you might live to regret it.' For the first time since the big fallout, Big Mand gives Liam a genuine smile.

'If your heart belongs to Matteo,' says Big Sue, 'then Luke shouldn't even be on your radar. You wouldn't put your career before the person you love, would you?'

'That's a great way of putting it,' I say, keen to get off the subject of Luke. 'Now, if you'll all check your agendas, we are meeting Matteo at reception because he has booked the pink limo to take us to SlotZilla.'

Again, no one is surprised to see Hank Junior joining us. He and Liberty stroll along, hand in hand, as though no one else exists.

Cherry walks beside me. 'I've never seen her so happy. And she is so super snatched. It's making me really emosh... emosh...' Cherry stops walking to wipe her eyes. 'Fucking hormones.' She takes in a huge breath and scowls it out. 'Okay. That's me done. I'm fine again, now.'

She is like a powder keg ready to blow. I hope hurling herself through the air on a zip line, high above thousands of shoppers and weaving in and out of giant inflatable flamingos for five blocks, will take her mind off things. I panic-booked this eleven-storey slot-machine-inspired experience, the world's largest, on the way here. And no, there wasn't time to check if anyone is scared of heights or giant dice.

Matteo is waiting at reception with an imperceptible smile on his face, which must mean he has been successful. By the time we arrive at SlotZilla, excitement levels have reached fever pitch. We glance up at the giant slot machine with showgirls and feathers at the sides, huge coins spilling from its mouth. Excited squeals come from the zip lines with people in a seated harness but then twice as high up there are four zoomlines where screaming adults are lying flat on their bellies attached to four thick steel ropes. Unfortunately, when we get there, there's a big sign saying no pregnant ladies can ride.

Cherry is only momentarily gutted. 'No worries. Connie, give me the card. I'll just go for a little wander.'

She means a little gamble. The place is slot machine central. And she is mistakenly thinking my credit card is the 'group' credit card just because most of our group expenses have been dumped on it for the purposes of this trip. I must look terrified because Liberty jumps in to rescue me. 'Take this card. It's the emergency $100 one.'

This act of kindness seems to ignite something in Hank Junior because he is giving Liberty big cow eyes as though she's just given Cherry one of her kidneys and all of her bone marrow wrapped up nicely in her vintage quilted lambskin Chanel handbag. Liberty waves off the attention, colour rising in her cheeks.

She. Is. Smitten.

As we make our way to the ride entrance, I ask Matteo how it's all gone regarding the wedding.

'It all seems very straightforward. We can do what they call the "vows renewal package". We go through the motions but without the legalities. They can fit us in the day after tomorrow. The difficult part is making sure that Luke and Birdie turn up on time to witness it.'

'Sounds simple enough,' I say, although I'd hate for him to think I've not got a conscience. 'It feels sneaky, hoodwinking them like this, but they are kind of driving us to it, aren't they?'

Matteo gives me a sympathetic smile. 'We don't have to do it,' he says, squeezing my hand. 'We could come up with a better idea.'

Gah!

'No,' I blurt. 'I want to marry you.'

Gah!

'I mean... I want to go along with the fake wedding. You're right. It'll send a clear message and guarantee they'll leave us alone.'

Matteo is not convinced. 'Sure?'

I nod. 'I just didn't want to seem too keen. In case you think I'm deranged.'

Matteo throws his head back and roars with laughter. 'Bit late for that.'

Cheeky.

On the way up, Big Sue is suddenly unsure. I see Big Mand subtly take her hand and whisper something in her ear. When she is finished, Big Sue has a smile in her eyes. They pair up and the instructors help them into their harnesses. Next up are Tash and Sister Kevin. She whispers in my ear, 'I don't think I'm pregnant any more. I think it was just the kebab I had, repeating on me.'

She must be referring to the kebab that 'repeated' all over the bathroom, up the walls and across the blinds of my flat in Benidorm. I will never unsee that.

I watch them being hurled off the ledge, all squeals of excitement. Hopefully, she's having a rethink about her ridiculous plan to conceive without Sister Kevin's consent.

Liberty and Hank Junior hold hands all the way through the harnessing process and can't stop giggling at each other. They lean towards each other for a quick snog before they are separated. The instructor pushes them off with a roll of his eyes as though he

can't bear to see anyone so happy. Although, to be fair
to him, there is a huge queue, and they do seem in a
rush to get people on the ride as quickly as possible.
Next, it's me and Matteo.

'Nervous?' he asks.

'A bit. You?'

'A bit,' he says back. 'It's a big leap.'

'It is,' I say, gulping. Our relationship has been
well and truly tested, a bit like this ride. 'Marriage is a
big leap. I mean, the wedding. The fake wedding. At
least, that's what I think. But I'm fine with it. Totally. I
mean, if it's too much too soon for you, then I totally
under—'

A smile spreads across his face. 'The ride, Cenicienta. The ride is a big leap. Not me and you.'

'Of course, the ride. But even if you didn't mean
the ride, if it's too big a step for— Aarrgghh!'

*The fucking instructor has pushed me off the fucking
ledge!*

As I hurtle through the sky, hundreds of people
far down below, a massive archway looming ahead,
the inside of a shopping mall, the outside of a shopping mall, lots of giant inflatables and what seems
like an eternity later, the zoomline slows to a halt and
I finish screaming. The first thing Matteo does when

his harness is unbuckled is grab me up into a huge hug.

'You okay? Want to go again?' he says, beaming. His hair is wild, and his cheeks are flushed. He's never looked so carefree and vibrant. His adventurous streak is infectious. In this moment, for him, I think I'd try anything.

11

By the time we walk from the bright lights of downtown Vegas, where shopfronts, billboards and hotels compete to see who can dazzle the tourists the most, and along the main strip, through throngs of showgirls with huge feathered hats, back to The Venetian, Matteo and I have put a solid plan together. The SlotZilla was so exhilarating that we went on several times and I could swear I'm now floating an inch above the pavement.

'I never figured you for an adrenaline junkie,' he says.

'Me neither,' I answer honestly. 'You bring out my inner reckless idiot.'

Matteo laughs. 'What's the most reckless thing

you've ever done?' He peers sideways at me while we walk.

You.

You are the most reckless thing I've ever done.

You stole my heart the second I met you.

We barely know each other and yet, I flew halfway round the world to see if you wanted to keep it.

My flushed face gives him all the answer he needs. He swallows.

'Why? What's the most reckless thing you've ever done?' I say, my voice breaking.

Matteo blushes. 'Same.'

I am saved by a ping from my phone.

Harry Styles was definitely here yesterday.

Liam has texted from his and Ged's private gazebo by the pool. They decided once on the SlotZilla was more than enough.

Our naked butler confirmed it. I saw
the selfie myself. He was wearing
paisley swimming shorts and an
open turquoise beach shirt with
palm trees on. Ged's already doing
a search on the internet so we can
order one.

I can't help smiling to myself. They seem to be enjoying themselves so far.

'Are the bridezillas happy?' Matteo asks.

'For now,' I say. 'If only Harry Styles would mirac-
ulously appear and have an afternoon free to cater to
their every whim, wearing nothing but an apron.'

Matteo colours even more.

'God. Please, don't think I'm hinting for you to
pull any strings. I'm absolutely not. I'd never do that.'

Matteo smiles. 'I know that. But just for the
record, I'd definitely ask. If you wanted me too.'

* * *

All too soon, it is time for the Dollz and me to take to
the stage. Cherry is complaining that her weight gain
is making the costumes uncomfortable, whereas, per-
sonally, I think it's the extreme smallness and ridicu-

lous thong backs that make the costumes uncomfortable. I'm just glad not to be in a wig or Barbie dress.

I glance down at my fabulous and sexy black second skin of a dress with sparkly tassels. It has my trademark cut-out bits to reveal my flat stomach. It lifts my boobs up like two small party balloons poking out and the Dollz have insisted we wear a selection of hot pants, glittery over-the-knee socks or boots, rhinestone bodysuits or catsuits with a leg missing, as though we'd marched into Tay Tay's wardrobe and helped ourselves. We resemble a fashion tribute to each of her tours. But she has worked miracles in bringing calm and a sense of forgiveness to the group, so it's totally worth it.

'We look unbelievably fabulous,' says Tash, admiring herself in the mirror. 'I'm not sure we've ever looked this amazing.' We all agree.

'Las Vegas certainly agrees with us,' says Big Mand, spectacular tonight in her fishnet body-stocking, glitter hot pants and crop top that accentuates her generous curves. Big Sue has braved the catsuit with leg cut out because she has legs three metres long and is stunning. They keep acting shyly around one another and giggling.

'So, we'll stick to the rehearsal plan,' I say, gathering everyone around me. 'All six of us start with the intro, then you do the next four numbers, then I'll do the next three, we do two more together and then I'll finish with a banger, and you join in for an encore. Okay?'

'I've never felt this nervous in my life,' says Liberty. 'It's this place. It's electric. Everything about it is bigger, better and brighter than anything I've ever seen.'

'And it's not because Hank Junior is in the audience?' supplies Cherry. 'Why don't you take the front position like you did at Benidorm Palace when you were showing off for Luke? Hank'll get a real eyeful.' Cherry winks at her and peeks behind the curtain. 'Did you tell him to chew on a toothpick?'

'I'm nothing if not thorough,' brags Liberty, adding that Hank Junior is also very commando beneath the cowboy jeans and chaps.

'He's sitting right at the front with Matteo and the boys.'

At the mention of Matteo, my pulse begins to race as adrenaline floods my system. 'Let's go out there and give Las Vegas the best performance ever!' I squeal as we hear the opening bars blare out of the speakers and the American host welcoming us on stage.

'Ladies and gentlemen, welcome to Cocktail

Hour. Tonight's entertainment is brought to you all the way from England, the United Kingdom of Britain.'

We troop onto the stage to loud applause, a buzzing energy filling the air, lights blinding us to the audience as we take our positions and belt out a sin-galong banger to get the crowd going even more.

Cherry has incorporated some special high-octane dance moves worthy of a Las Vegas show that seem to work wonders. The audience are whooping, cheering and joining in with us. By the time my solo section comes around, I am on fire. The lights are lowered, ready for a few power ballads to give the crowd a break. Matteo comes fully into view. The first thing I notice is that he can't take his eyes away from mine. And as though I have him under my spell, I sing so hypnotically that I can almost feel the magnetic force between us, the invisible threads that tie my feelings to his. Because of all the classical singing, I am pitch-perfect and out to impress the hell out of him and the whole of Las Vegas. I'm singing the words from the depths of my soul, and I mean every single one of them. I have to force myself to face the audience, dragging my gaze from his. And when the Dollz come back on stage I know I've outdone myself because Liberty is eye-rolling me.

'Alright, pet. We know you can sing. You don't have to go so overboard,' she jokes.

By the time our set is finished, the audience is begging for more. Instead of exiting the stage with us, Liberty runs to the front and leaps off the stage into Hank's waiting arms. She straddles him as the crowd go wild. He's dutifully wearing the Stetson hat and a ridiculously bushy fake moustache but removes the toothpick. It's all very, very cute. Last to leave the stage, I am doing one final wave to the crowd when a movement catches my eye. Luke is sitting near the back with a sad expression on his face.

OMG. What am I going to do about him? I just wish he'd go back home and forget about me. I make my mind up *not* to meet him at midnight, to make sure he understands that *nothing* will ever develop between us.

I look back at Matteo. I'm so head over heels in love with him. He smiles back at me before twisting in his seat to see who I was gawping at. He immediately frowns.

Uh oh.

Luke scrapes back his chair and holds out a hand to Birdie, who gets up with him. Birdie gives Matteo a withering look. Matteo's face is a mask, and she is clearly not pleased with the lack of reaction.

Luke smiles forlornly and walks towards me. Then he sees Matteo's face and seems to think better of it. He turns back towards Birdie, and I see her nodding at him. Birdie is in a figure-hugging, backless, peacock-blue silk dress. Luke is dressed for a night at the Proms. They make a striking couple. They are both confirmed sapiosexuals, and they both have music, a love of the limelight and being borderline obsessives in common. But the determination on Luke's face convinces me that he will not easily be rejected. And the sheer persistence of Birdie to always get her own way makes me sure she will stop at nothing until Matteo is hers. A sinking feeling swirls in my stomach as we make our way off stage.

* * *

'That was amazing,' says Liam when we make our way back to their table. 'You were all incredible.'

'What a way to make an impression on your opening night,' gushes Ged.

At least our agent Nancy will be pleased. We have another show here at The Cocktail Hour bar and one dodgy birthday favour for Eddie from Talent Star, and the rest of the time is all pre-moon shenanigans and romance, if Matteo would stop glaring at Luke.

'Who's for a spot of gambling?' asks Cherry, her face lit up. 'Connie, you'll come, won't you? I need someone to carry all my chips. I'm going on a gambling rampage. I feel so lucky tonight.'

She means she needs me to stop her remortgaging her home should she accidentally board the gambling bullet train.

'Count us in,' says Sister Kevin as he drapes an arm around Tash, pulling her close.

'Yep,' says Big Mand. 'Sue and I thought we'd try The Poker Room if anyone is interested?'

'We'd love to,' says Ged. 'If that's okay?'

He's taking a big gamble. The four of them haven't hung out since the Algar Falls outing incident.

Big Sue, Big Mand, Ged and Liam take a beat to make eye contact while I hold my breath. I cross my fingers, silently pleading with the universe. We're all as high as kites after the performance. Please let them all be friends, I beg. Then Big Mand does something we've never seen her do. She pulls Big Sue towards her and places a light kiss on her lips.

'It's up to you, hun. Do we want to hang out with our gay friends tonight?'

Big Sue is the picture of shock at first as her gaze sweeps around the group. When it lands on Big

Mand's hopeful face, she breaks into a huge grin. 'Fuck it. Why not?'

And this is probably inappropriate, but we all start clapping and whooping like Americans. Big Sue then sweeps Big Mand up into a full-on snog. At first, I'm delighted that they feel so comfortable and free, but after two minutes, it seems to be going on for an unnecessary amount of time. Big Sue has her hands tangled up in Big Mand's hair. Big Mand is helping herself to a handful of Big Sue's tiny breast. No one knows where to look except Sister Kevin, who appears mesmerised by this epic lesbian kiss.

Liberty is first to break the tension. 'I'll give the gambling a miss. Hank's invited me to dinner,' she says, besotted. 'At Caesars Palace. And he's agreed to keep his trash-tache on. I'll see you back in the room later. Maybe.'

Hank tips his hat at us. 'It was a real pleasure to meet y'all.'

We watch them walk away, Hank with his arm firmly round Liberty's waist, Liberty with her hand firmly cupping his buttock. Matteo and I immediately trade glances. I'd much rather be alone with him than gambling all night. His face tells me that he'd like the same.

I whisper in his ear, 'Do you want to, perhaps, erm...?'

'Yes,' he replies quickly. 'I do.'

Just as I'm about to make up an excuse for us to slope off, Matteo's phone pings. One roll of his eyes and I know it's Birdie. She's doing it again.

Matteo reads the text and gives me a pained look. 'I'm so sorry, Connie. It's work.'

'You mean it's Birdie,' I say tightly. 'Can't you just tell her that you're busy?'

We have the attention of the whole group, who have stopped kissing, talking and chewing on a newly opened packet of brightly coloured, toxic-looking gummies, to listen in to our private conversation.

'It's not Birdie, but it is complicated. As I've explained,' says Matteo through tight lips, 'I do have a business to run on the other side of the planet.'

The atmosphere suddenly tense, I react in the same way.

'Well then, if you *must* go, you *must* go,' I say rather dramatically.

Matteo gives me a confused look. 'Okay. I *will* go.'

We stare at one another awkwardly before he shakes his head, annoyed with me.

'See you later, I guess.'

'Maybe,' I say, my voice too high. 'Maybe.'

We watch him walk away. It has all gone horribly wrong, horribly quickly.

'Maybe?' says Ged. 'Maybe? The poor guy has to work with his deranged ex-girlfriend on the biggest project of his career. It could literally make or break him in this pathetic, fast-moving, Gen Z-obsessed industry... and you're like, "maybe"?'

Liam folds his arms. 'Did he make a fuss when you filled your room full of flowers from Luke? Or when Luke keeps upping the ante with his grand gestures? I mean, hello, that video?'

'Oh, the flowers,' says Cherry, chomping on a length of bicycle tyre made of jelly covered in sugar. 'I forgot to tell you, they're from Hank. To Liberty. Not you. You should really give her them back.'

* * *

'It's almost midnight,' says Cherry. She is on a winning streak on the slots, and I have been sitting watching her while my mind has been racing. Matteo has not been in touch since we parted ways. Why was I so defensive about him dropping everything when Birdie clicks her fingers? It probably wasn't even Birdie demanding his attention. I know that he has a business to run, and Matteo has explained all of this to me, and yet...

Cherry's words sink in. Midnight. Luke. The love sign. Time to make sure we are as far away as possible.

'Okay. I'll have to get going.'

Cherry gives me a sharp look. 'Wait just two more minutes. I can feel a big win coming on.' She is feeding dollar bills into a one-armed bandit and yanking on the arm, muttering expletives.

'I can't risk being near the love sign,' I say, turning to leave.

'But you're my lucky charm!' bellows Cherry, like an angry toddler. 'You have to stay with me.'

'One more go then I'm leaving.' I check my phone, but Matteo hasn't messaged. While Cherry switches seats, I text him to say that I'm sorry I was snippy earlier. He texts back immediately to say he's sorry too. He says he'll come and find me and asks where I am.

'YAY!' yells Cherry as the machine makes a massive tringing sound. A solitary ticket emerges while everyone around us starts cheering and clapping. 'Okay, I'm ready to cash in and go to bed now.'

I text Matteo to say we're in a queue at the Pallazo cashier's cage, cashing in Cherry's winnings, and I'll meet him back in the room.

It's two minutes to midnight as we hurry over the bridge, past The Palazzo waterfall atrium and the twelve-foot iconic art sculpture. When I see the ruby-red letters spelling out LOVE, my heart sinks. I really hope that by not turning up, Luke will finally get the message.

There are hundreds of people posing in front of the letters, taking selfies and generally milling about as though it's mid-afternoon and not midnight. The concept of time in this hotel simply does not exist. I can't see Luke anywhere.

'Perhaps he's changed his mind,' says Cherry, scanning the crowd.

'I hope so.' Then I hear it. My soul droops as the familiar notes of 'Mi Amore Mi Amore' tinkle out across the atrium. Luke emerges from behind the waterfall with a microphone in his hand and slowly walks towards a string quartet.

Fuck no.

'Quick,' I say, yanking at Cherry's arm as I battle with the urge to go and slap his face. 'Before he sees us.' He's standing with his legs three feet apart and grabbing air. Two of his mannerisms that I cannot blinking stand, and he has encouraged a huge crowd to gather. They probably think this is bona fide entertainment. Luke starts beating his heart dramatically before slinging his arm around the shoulder of an extremely embarrassed-looking guy.

'I can see why you thought he was attractive in a posh-boy sort of way,' Cherry says as I freeze on the spot. Matteo is standing right in front of us, frowning.

I need a second to think. This is dreadful. What a dreadful moment to be caught up in.

His head is tilted to one side as though assessing me. His gaze wanders past me, to the crowd and Luke. He's still singing by the quartet with his legs apart.

'It's not what you think,' I say.

Matteo's mouth curves slightly. 'It never is.'

12

I wake up exhausted and alone the following morning. Matteo and I engaged in a mammoth love-making session last night, well into the early hours. I think I just needed him to know that he's the one. The one for me. My whole body aches in the most delicious way. I was barely aware of him leaving this morning. Birdie has arranged a virtual breakfast briefing with their secret artist who is on a different time zone, to discuss the 'project', and Matteo will meet me later at the limo to go to the rollerblading disco.

I scan the room. Every surface is covered with flowers. Housekeeping have put them all in vases for us. Ged is right. Matteo has been more than understanding of the Luke situation. I ring reception and croakily explain the bouquets have been put in the wrong room, and they are only too happy to help move them back to Cherry and Liberty's. At least that might help.

After a quick shower, I squeeze into my Disco Barbie roller-skating costume. It's an amazing bright pink glitter hot pants onesie with neon-yellow leg warmers and wristbands. When there is a knock on the door, I insist on helping the concierge carry some of the vases. We walk down the endless corridors towards Liberty's room and hammer on the door. There's no answer. The concierge gives me an apologetic shrug as though it's his fault they aren't in. He knocks harder. It's way too early for them to be out already.

'Sorry, ma'am. It looks like they're not in.'

'Fine. We'll just go in and drop these off.'

He hesitates, until I explain that we are the Cocktail Hour entertainment, and these flowers are from Hank Junior, one of our admirers. The concierge gives me a bizarre nod of understanding and opens the door immediately. He breezes in and arranges them beautifully all over the suite. He even radios housekeeping to prioritise the room tidy. Tash was right about Cherry's knickers. There are what look like discarded croissants lying all over the room. Costumes, tights, bras, Barbie dresses cover every conceivable surface. What a mess! But there's no sign of either of them. The bed hasn't been slept in.

A prickle of concern crawls up my spine. I say goodbye to the concierge and knock on Tash and Sister Kevin's door. No answer. I try Big Mand and Big Sue's door. The same. No answer. I can only assume they have gone down for an early breakfast before the roller disco. I hurry back to my room to finish getting changed. When I race down to the meeting point, I'm absolutely flabbergasted to see the whole gang sitting at the designated breakfast bar tucking into bulging breakfast burritos and deluxe milkshakes loaded with whipped cream, wedges of cake and chocolate bars poking out of the top. Every single one of them is dressed in their Roller Ken and Roller Barbie outfits: eye-watering splashes of neon metallic hot pants, glitter crop tops, leg warmers, headbands, wristbands, wigs and huge knee pads. They look unbelievably cool. We are attracting much attention from the public. I quickly take lots of photos.

'Wow. I can't believe you all got up so early,' I say. 'I'm impressed.'

'We didn't,' says Cherry with a mouthful of burrito.

'We haven't been to bed yet,' says Tash, giggling. 'We're giving it a miss. Because of the jet lag.'

Makes no sense.

'And because we were all on such a winning streak, we couldn't leave,' says Big Sue. 'Mandeep won enough to pay off her entire mortgage.'

Wow.

'Yeah, but then I lost it all again,' she is quick to tell me. 'Easy come, easy go, as they say.'

I have no words. They are all wired.

'Hi,' says Birdie, appearing out of nowhere. 'Matteo sends his apologies. He cannot come skating.'

I frown with frustration. 'Why not this time?'

'Work. Clients. Organising his business,' she says abruptly. 'He is a very busy music producer.'

As if I didn't know.

She shrugs at my obvious disappointment. 'I did try to persuade him not to work. That's always the problem with him. He chooses work over everyone else. Every single time.'

Her words hang in the air. I know what she's up to. Planting seeds of doubt.

'I have a surprise for the boys.'

Liam and Ged try hard not to look excited. Their eyes keep flitting from me to Birdie.

'I have invited my friend to say hi.'

Just then a huge entourage sweeps towards us.

'*Bonjour, ma cherie*,' says Birdie, kissing her on both cheeks. 'I'd like you to meet some friends of mine. They are here celebrating their stag do.'

'It's a pre-moon,' says Liam snippily, until he sees who he is talking to.

I can't see who it is as I'm standing behind her, but watching my friends' jaws hit the floor suggests the woman is famous.

'We're not usually this yellow!' bellows Liam, his voice ten octaves higher than normal.

'He means we're huge fans,' says Ged. 'Huge, huge fans.'

The woman holds out both hands for them to grab. 'Love the outfits,' she tells the Dollz admiringly. 'Roller skating? So retro. So cool.'

Birdie leans in to tell her something none of us can hear.

'Say hi to Matteo for me,' the famous celebrity replies with a laugh. 'Catch you both later?'

The minders crowd round her and they scuttle away through the maze that is the casino floor.

'Fuck me,' says Big Sue. 'That's the way to do security detail. Did you see how many gadgets they had?'

'Who? Who was it?' I ask.

Liam, with sparkles in his eyes, carefully looks

around before mouthing the name. 'She's even more gorgeous in real life. Thank you, Birdie,' he gushes. 'Do you want to come roller skating with us?'

What?

* * *

My big fear is that they'll all suddenly crash and burn mid-roller skate and leave me with Birdie, but to be fair to them all, they are bang up for it. It isn't until twenty minutes in, and we are all merrily roller skating and rollerblading away to a selection of nineties bangers, that the true reason for Birdie wanting to tag along with us is revealed.

I'm just building up speed on the way round when I suddenly hit something and go flying to the ground.

'Oops,' says a catty voice. 'Sorry.'

Birdie hovers over me, hand on hip. I growl as she skates off. I won't make a big deal out of it. I'd hate to make things awkward for Ged and Liam. They invited her, they can entertain her. I'll take myself off for a skate on the far side, away from them all. But while I'm rolling backwards, practising some basic drills, I'm knocked sideways and thrown back down to the wooden floor.

'What the hell?' I say.

A hand reaches down to help me up. 'Sorry,' says a guy sheepishly. 'Some girl barged into me.'

He points a thumb behind him, and I spot Birdie waving slyly over her shoulder. *Mean cow.* I skate over to the benches at the side of the rink and take out my phone. There's a message from Matteo.

Why didn't you wait for me?

I immediately text back.

Because Birdie said you always put business before pleasure. Honestly, she's been a right pain. How quick can you get here?

Matteo arrives within half an hour. I spot him at the far corner gingerly stepping out onto the wooden rink. He holds on to the rail as I skate backwards towards him and do a semicircle around him before a full spin, criss-crossing my legs as I come out of it into a shuffle. I am fully showing off for his attention.

'Who knew?' he says, admiration blooming from his eyes. 'I'm impressed.'

I take his hand. 'Want a lesson?'

'Not really,' he says, laughing, jerkily trying to keep his balance. 'Happy to watch.'

I'm not taking 'no' for an answer and within a few minutes I have him rolling bubbles alongside me.

'I've never skated before,' he says. 'And now I know why.'

'I've never taught anyone to skate before.'

We have so much in common.

Soon, all the stress has left him. His face transforms when he's not thinking about work or organising events on both sides of the Atlantic with a thousand people vying for his attention. After one pop tune after another, the DJ switches the tempo and plays a real thumping romantic ballad. Suddenly all the lights dim, replaced by sparkling strobes. I take the opportunity to do a little roller-flirting, switching positions, all while holding his hand. Because he's such a skilled Latino, and moving his body to the beat is second nature, he is a complete natural, moving with me, like we're slow dancing but on skates. I bite my lip while I stare alluringly at him. I pull out all the stops and give him my best moves. Some of which haven't been used for over twelve years, but it's all coming back to me.

We swish past Ged and Liam, who haven't sat down once. They are loving this. Big Sue and Big Mand have copied our lead and are dancing together. We fly round the rink and out of the corner of my eye

I can see Sister Kevin with tissue sticking out of his nose. It's covered in blood. He gives us a wave as we pass by. Up ahead, Cherry and Tash are wobbling forward, holding on to the side of the roller rink.

Liberty is in front of us. If I thought I was good, she is Olympic standard. Poor Hank Junior doesn't stand a chance. He's gawping at her as though she's his Venus sent from above. She eases from a vertical split into a backwards spin. Her outfit is amazing. Her crop top is sparkly pink, and her cheerleading skirt of green sequins catch the disco lights as she moves. Her tiny skirt flaps up as she glides around the rink, revealing matching glittery knickers that are a mix of the two colours. It's a gold medal all round from me. She looks amazing.

'Are you okay?' she asks me as she circles around us.

'Yeah. Thanks,' I say, keen not to make a deal out of Birdie's bullying behaviour. 'Just a few bruises.'

'Birdie is such a bitch,' she says, before skating back to Hank Junior.

Matteo tilts his head quizzically at me.

'It's nothing,' I assure him. 'Nothing I can't handle.'

Just as I lean in to pretend-kiss Matteo as part of an elaborately sexy move that I've just invented in the heat of the moment, because he's looking so incredibly handsome, Birdie barges into me and Matteo like an angry bat out of hell and karate chops our hands apart.

'Mind if I cut in?' she yells, yanking at Matteo's hand as she flies past us. Birdie winks over her shoulder at me with a cruel smirk.

Matteo hardly has time to register what's happening because Cherry, who has obviously witnessed Birdie's antics, sticks her foot out to trip her up. Birdie and her cruel smirk go flying to the ground.

'Oops,' says Cherry. 'Not as fun when you're on the receiving end, is it?'

Matteo helps Birdie up and over to the side. I let out a small groan. Now she'll have every excuse to hog his attention. I see them deep in conversation. Once he helps her to a seat, he skates back over to me. He looks furious.

I gulp. I suppose it was sly of Cherry, and perhaps I shouldn't have laughed out loud, but Birdie did have it coming.

Matteo takes my hand. 'That's it. I've had enough.'

'I'm so sorry. I guess we took it a bit—'

'I've had enough of Birdie. The sooner we get married the better,' he says in a low voice.

I search his eyes, dark and determined. He rakes a

hand through his hair, and I watch it fall back onto his face. He looks harassed. Sexy, flustered and very, very hot and bothered. Matteo has finally snapped. And it suits him.

'Yes. Sure,' I say, trying to keep from leaping with joy. 'The sooner the better.'

13

The first thing Matteo and I need to do when we get back from the roller rink is go down to lunch and duck out of the afternoon's gambling so that we can go shopping. We meet the others at the designated booth in a snack café and pray that everyone is too tired from roller skating to kick up a fuss. I do feel a bit guilty but if we confessed to the fake wedding now, they'd all want to hijack the shopping trip, especially as it's for my wedding dress. Matteo and I have decided we must keep it a secret a little longer.

'I'm so sorry,' I say in a croaky voice. 'I think the extreme air conditioning in here is making my throat dry. I'm going to see if I can get something from the chemist. Maybe get some fresh air. I'll meet you back here for the show tonight. Is that okay?'

'You're the boss, Big Guy,' says Big Sue, slouching on the bench seat, her arm slung round Big Mand's shoulder.

'I'm not the boss, but if you insist, then can you take over duties for me, please? Make sure Ged and Liam have a great afternoon in the casino.'

'Don't worry about us. We're going to stay in the suite and keep Franz company,' Ged says casually.

'Franz?' I ask.

'Our naked butler. He's gorgeous,' gushes Liam. 'He's divine.'

'We'd hate for him to get lonely,' adds Ged with a slutty twinkle in his eye.

'How considerate,' I say, trying not to imagine the scene.

'I'll come with you. I could use the fresh air too,' says Cherry. 'That roller disco has really taken its toll on my pelvis. A walk will do me good. Do us good.' She hangs her head, gently rubbing her belly. 'Or maybe not a walk. Maybe we need a spa afternoon,' she suggests hopefully.

Gah!

I glance over at Matteo. He mimes a cough.

'Well, I also think I'm coming down with something. A bug. I'd hate for you to catch it.' I fake a cough and put a hand to my throat. 'Perhaps one of the others could spa with you?'

She eyes me closely.

She'll know I'm lying. I am the picture of good health. I'm glowing with endorphins because I'm bursting with happiness. I'm effervescent with excitement and having a terrible time trying to hide it. I'm sure it's written all over my face. I can feel my cheeks flame as Cherry continues staring at me.

I swallow loudly.

'Yeah, you look a bit swollen. You must be coming down with something.'

Once Cherry confirms that my face is puffy, the Dollz are quick to agree. Apparently, I look drained and lacking iron.

'Yeah,' says Tash, eyeing me up and down. 'You're definitely retaining water. Must be all the travelling. You might want to pick up something to help you deflate.'

Matteo stifles a snigger. I can't even look him in the eye.

* * *

We make our way from the hotel to the outside. The heat hits me in the nicest way. I realise how cold the hotel is in comparison.

'God, it's so bright out here,' I say, shielding my eyes. 'How long have I been inside?' It feels like weeks, not days.

'So, we have a choice of about fifty different wedding boutiques,' Matteo says, glancing up from his phone with a smile. 'And hundreds of wedding vendors for the other stuff.'

'Other stuff?'

'You know, like do you want a bouquet to hold on the gondola? A wedding ring?'

Oh. I forget he's fresh out of doing all of this with his cheating ex-fiancée. I wonder how he feels about wasting yet more money on a wedding that's not going anywhere.

'Seems a bit, erm, excessive for a fake wedding,' I say, trying to squash my nerves down. 'Is there a place that does everything on the cheap? I only have half a day free. And, erm, I only have so much left on my credit card.' The heat rises up from my neck. 'Because I've had to put so much Barbie—'

'Hey,' he says gently. 'Please. I agreed to this. I'm happy to pay for all of it.' He lifts my chin up. 'It's no problem. If that's okay with you? I don't want to seem... un-Dutch about it.'

I nod. My credit card will love Matteo until the end of time for this.

'Good. I'll do a search for quickie weddings.'

While he scrolls, I take the opportunity to imagine for a tiny second that this is real. My heart skips a beat. It would be so unlike me to do something so reckless as to get married in Las Vegas. My dad would kill me, for one thing. Never mind what Ged and Liam would make of me not including them in every minute detail beforehand. The fallout would be catastrophic. Whatever we do, however we do it, it must be done swiftly to quash any romantic feelings that Birdie and Luke may still have, but without destroying our working relationships with them. Then Matteo and I are free to get on with our romantic break and laugh all of this madness off. We can finish the gigs for Nancy, and we can do all of the crazy premoon activities that still remain on the list.

'I think Macy's is this way.' Matteo is studying his phone for directions. 'They have a whole floor dedicated to quickie weddings and tux hire.'

I take a deep breath. 'We're really doing this, are we?'

'We really are.' Matteo sweeps me towards him in an unusual public display of affection. 'We have to put a stop to Birdie and Luke.'

I couldn't agree more. They are becoming obsessed.

* * *

We walk the ten minutes to Macy's talking about Matteo's many work commitments. He has left an events manager in charge in Spain, but they have been ringing him every single day.

'I'm sorry my work is keeping me from you,' he says.

'I'm sorry my work and my duties as best woman are keeping me from *you*.'

'It's so good to see you though,' Matteo says almost shyly.

'I'm glad I came.'

'Me too.'

My heart is singing a high C note right now. It's smashing imaginary wine glasses across Las Vegas as Matteo cups my face, his mouth hovering over mine before he kisses me. Our lips slide tenderly together for a sweet, loving moment. I open my eyes to see him looking at me in the most caring way and I know he feels the same.

No sooner do we step foot in the bridal department of the iconic Macy's store than a personal shopper pounces on us.

'Do you have an appointment?'

I shake my head.

'Follow me,' she instructs, eyeing us up and down. She frogmarches us over to a fitting room. 'Wait here. We're very busy today. Half the city is getting married.'

Within minutes, someone is ushering us to sit on the chaise longue and they are placing two flutes of champagne on the table.

'Is this usual?' I hiss to him, taking a sip. It's delicious.

He shrugs, clinking my glass. 'We should get married more often.'

A flamboyant assistant breezes in. 'What theme are we having?'

Matteo and I look blankly at each other.

'Classic, retro, celebrity, trashy-chic, vintage, zombie?'

'Unplanned and spontaneous,' I say. 'But fun and quirky. We're in the music business.'

Her eyes light up. 'Leave it with me.'

I'd rather not, but it seems rude to decline the offer of help, and I don't know what the etiquette in America is. Within minutes, she returns with a lot of white garments slung over her arm. They do not look like traditional wedding dresses.

She ushers me into the changing room, walking into it with me. The fitting room is huge. 'Try all of these on.' She points to the pile of underwear on her arm. 'We must build the outfit from the bottom up.' She flings the garments onto little hooks on the wall before rather dramatically stepping outside and swishing the curtain shut.

I pick up the first one. It is an elaborate system of lace, ribbons and whalebone. It is a bridal basque. It's next-level sexy. Luckily for me, it is no different to the costumes the Dollz have me wearing on stage half the time, so I climb into it easily.

'It's nice,' I yell through the curtain. 'But maybe a bit much?'

I have nice underwear in my suitcase. I don't need pricey, see-through, baby-doll nighties and hold-up stockings.

'Let's see it,' she says brusquely, sounding like a head teacher from Poland or Latvia or somewhere, and I find I'm instantly doing as I'm told. There really is no need for this level of attention to detail. But as soon as I emerge from the changing room and lock eyes with Matteo sitting a few feet away on the sofa, it's as though I'm channelling my inner Liberty when she did her one-woman catwalk for Hank Junior.

His eyes widen as he almost spills his drink. I watch him recover himself as I do a little twirl for him. The sheer fabric is leaving little to the imagination. The high cut of the legs is super flattering. My waist is snatched. It's like a second skin.

'What do you think?' the assistant asks him.

He coughs, putting his drink down on the coffee table. 'Nice.'

She tuts. 'Next one, please.' As I disappear behind the curtain, I hear her explaining to Matteo, 'We must find the correct underwear so that the dress sits comfortably.'

Makes sense.

'But essentially, we must find out what your tastes are. The wedding night is the foundation stone to a healthy sex life. What drives your passions? What are your tastes?'

I hear Matteo coughing again. This must be excruciating for him. Who knew shopping for a couple of rentals would be this intrusive?

However, I am very keen for her to get to the bottom of Matteo's passions and tastes. And I am willing to try on every goddamn piece of underwear in the whole store to find out.

'You like white virginal? Full-length Victorian blushing bride nightgown? Showgirl? Been around the block and knows what she wants, *Fifty Shades* type? Cheerleader? Farm girl? City executive boss lady? Skater girl? Gothic vampire queen? What's your type?'

She's really bullying him, but to his credit he doesn't answer her. He hasn't caved as quickly as me. I fling open the curtain.

Matteo's eyes scoot across my body before he stares respectfully into the space above my head. 'Yes. That's very nice too.'

'I'm not sure about the feathers or the satin French knickers or...' I say, hesitantly, '...the frilly stockings.'

Matteo is very much a stockings kind of guy.

The assistant looks from me to Matteo and back again. She purses her lips and screws her eyes, thinking, assessing what kind of sex life we have. *How can she possibly comprehend, just by observing us for a few moments, the explosive, off-the-charts chemistry that we have the moment the bedroom door is closed? How?* She taps her chin with her finger before gasping lightly. 'I have it!' She races off, leaving us for a moment.

I wander slowly over to him. I sneak a peek around to make sure we are alone before straddling him on the sofa.

Matteo visibly swallows. His eyes drop to my breasts which, thanks to this balcony bra, are practically poking his eyes out. His hands automatically reach for my waist as I tease him by grinding against him. He lets out a low moan, closing his eyes.

'Enjoying the show?' I say huskily.

He gives me a piercing look. 'Any more of this and there won't be a show. We'll need to go back to the hotel.' His breathing is coming thick and fast. I place my lips on his and just as the kiss deepens, I climb off him, leaving him wanting more. His eyes are wide with lust and mischief.

The assistant scurries back in. 'I have it!' She waves a hand in Matteo's direction. 'I know what he likes.' She gives me a slip of the softest material I've ever felt, smiling like a wise old cougar.

'I'm sure I don't need to buy new underwear,' I say. 'I have—'

'Trust me.' She all but shoves me behind the curtain.

Once I've put the underwear on, I glimpse myself in the full-length mirror and gasp.

'Told you,' she says, poking a head round the curtain with a wink. 'Perhaps keep it a surprise for the wedding night?'

I nod. I look insanely hot. It shapes, it lifts, it fits like a glove, and it is unbelievably sexy. I must have it. I must. I've never wanted anything more in my life.

I hear her explain to Matteo that we have our foundation garments and that now we will be trying on dresses. She needs to have an idea of his taste and mine before the real selection process can begin.

Good Lord. I poke my head out to see Matteo is nodding along patiently from a standing position. His phone is in his hand. He's probably trying to keep tabs on his business and avoid Birdie. The first dress I'm handed is a real fairy-princess number. It's hideous.

I walk out holding up the many toile skirts and twirl for him. He breaks into a smile. 'Perhaps if I was Prince Charming and this was a cartoon.'

The assistant clicks her tongue and ushers me back in to help me take it off. She yells through to him, 'What are weddings like where you grew up? Traditional or modern?'

'A mix,' he says. 'In Spain, weddings are all about

good food, music, the many, many traditions... and family.'

'And which is more important to you?'

We listen to Matteo take a beat.

'Family.'

The assistant smiles. 'You've got yourself a good one there. He'll make a fine husband.'

I can feel my cheeks burn. If only she knew this was all a charade. She'd be furious. She flicks through a rack of dresses and hands me another.

'This is the one for you.' She bustles out and I can hear her grilling Matteo further. 'What sort of life will you have together?'

Christ Almighty. She's so nosy. I wish she'd just disappear and let us browse the dresses in peace.

'Erm...' He hesitates. Probably, like me, wondering how truthful to be about this web of lies. 'Connie is an amazing singer-songwriter. I guess we'll be travelling the world. Maybe base ourselves in Spain, but work between there and LA when she's not touring.'

I feel a bloom of pride that he could even think that. Even if none of it is true.

'You have a place in LA?'

What did I say? She's a professional nosy parker.

'Yes. I live there. Or, at least, I used to. We'll see.'

'You seem familiar. Like a movie star.'

Oh, my God. I know nothing about him or his work history. I should really ask him for his CV before we get hitched. I will the nosy parker assistant to keep badgering him for information.

'Are you successful?'

Good question. It's so hard to tell if he's stinking rich or just financially comfortable, because he's not in the slightest bit showy like Luke, who reeks of old money just by looking at him. My mind shoots back to Matteo and his battered old-lady scooter.

'Depends on who you ask.'

'Do you love what you do?'

'I make music with a range of artists. It can be crazy and unpredictable. But yes, I love it.'

'Love can make a man do crazy things,' she says. 'You must really love your bride to travel across the world for her.'

Gah! She's going too far! The L bomb. We've only just gone exclusive. Matteo must be cringing. I wait for his reply, but none comes. Now I feel terrible. He's being forced into a corner and interrogated.

'How long have you been together?' she probes.

'Long enough.'

Clever.

'When you know, you know,' she says. 'Am I right?'

'I guess so.'

Polite yet non-committal.

'You want children?'

I whip open the curtain, ready to rescue him.

'You don't have to... answer any questions,' I say, but Matteo is laughing.

'Yes,' he says. 'I think we settled on... was it seven or eight kids...?' Then his jaw drops as he takes me in. His eyes travel the length of my body.

'What do you think?' I ask, feeling nervous. This all feels incredibly real. I look stunning. There's no other way to describe it.

He visibly swallows, his eyes not leaving mine. Dark swirls of emotion.

'We'll take it,' we say in unison to the assistant.

She smiles enigmatically as though to say, of course you will. 'Now, sir, you next.'

* * *

A short while later, Matteo and I are carrying oversized wedding bags with huge wedding ring images on them. They will be very difficult to hide.

'I still can't believe you refused to try on under-wear and wedding suits for the assistant. She wasn't pleased,' I say with a laugh. This whole morning has me giddy.

'I can't believe you let her bully you so easily into it.'

He's right. 'I basically did everything she told me to do,' I say. 'What does that say about me?'

Matteo stops walking. 'It says that you are respectful and polite and very, very easily persuaded. It's adorable.'

When the assistant tried to boss him around, he just said a flat, 'No thanks,' in such an authoritative tone that that was the end of it.

'Well, you're...' I struggle to think of anything negative. He's gorgeous, manly, decisive and incredibly generous and thoughtful.

'What next? Rings?'

I nod. 'If you're sure? But please, I feel really guilty at how much this is all beginning to cost. Can we get some joke rings from somewhere?'

He rolls his eyes. 'No time. Let's just buy them now.' He points to the jewellery department up ahead. It is conveniently placed near the wedding boutique. As soon as I spot the classic gold wedding bands, slightly rounded, very simple and chic, I know that's what I want. The assistant gets a his 'n' hers tray out. She takes out a large ring with lots of smaller loops on and quickly sizes our wedding fingers. Within seconds, she hands Matteo a very elegant platinum and gold wedding band and he tries to put it on. It's way too small. The assistant giggles and nods her head towards me.

Oh, gosh. She wants Matteo to put it on me. To give him credit, he takes it all in his stride. He gives me a cheeky smile. I give him one back.

After all, it's only a bit of fun. As far as he's concerned. Whereas my heart is beating off the scale. Blood is swooshing through my veins like a white-water rapid. This is the stuff of dreams. Quite literally, because I have dreamt about him every night since we met.

'Where did you propose?' the assistant asks him.

Matteo's smile drops.

'You didn't propose yet?' the assistant says.

Matteo shakes his head slowly. I try not to turn into a pile of mush as he takes my hand very gently and slips the ring onto my finger. He fixes me with those dark swirls, and I feel myself literally melt. 'Connie. Will you marry me?'

My whole being is suddenly flooded with every emotion known to humankind. Tears prick at my eyes.

I love him.

I do.

I love him.

In this moment, all I want to do is tell my mother how much I love him. I wish she could see how happy I am. I wish she could see how happy he makes me. I wish she was around so that she could get to know him. I wish with my entire soul that this was real.

'Yes,' I say, my voice breaking. 'I'll marry you.'

And without warning, I burst into tears.

14

The assistant instantly recoils, disappointed. With the atmosphere well and truly awkward, she hesitates over boxing up the gorgeous wedding rings. 'Are they happy tears to be marrying your one true love, or do you want to see something more expensive perhaps?' she asks hopefully, handing me a box of tissues, oblivious to making things worse.

'I'm so sorry,' I say, mortified. What a show I've made of myself. 'I'm not sure what happened. It must be the jet lag,' I say, pulling the tissue from the box to wipe at the stray tears collecting in the corners of my eyes.

Jet lag, my hairy backside. I know fine well what happened. I got swept up in the moment. I'm allowing my brain to fantasise that all of this is real and that Matteo feels the same way. This magnificent, hunk of spunk who lives part-time in LA, who is already incredibly successful and sexy, and who knows what he wants from life.

Matteo is clearly bewildered by my outburst as he puts his arm around me. 'Okay. That's settled. We are not going through with this. Not if it's going to upset you this much.'

Ouch. He really doesn't feel the same way. How could he? We barely know each other. I sniff up my tears. How am I going to convince him I'm emotionally stable enough to go through with it?

'I'm not upset. I promise. I think it's a great idea. Really. I do.'

He seems unconvinced. 'Are you sure?'

'One hundred per cent.' I lean over to kiss him on the cheek. 'I have overactive tear ducts, that's all.'

Matteo gives me a thoughtful look. He has mopped up more of my tears than he probably cares to mention.

The assistant is speedily wrapping up the rings, a smile plastered to her face, and puts the sale through the register before we can change our minds.

Matteo waves his card at the machine as she

hands me the bag and wishes us a life of blissful happiness.

'This is the only guaranteed way to get Birdie and Luke off our backs. Lord knows what grand gesture he'll come up with next, now that the midnight proposal didn't work,' I babble as we walk towards the lift. 'Besides, we've already bought the dress and... Argh!' I grab his arm and yank him down behind a rack of coats, putting a finger to my lips.

'What? Who did you see?' he whispers. He follows my lead, and we peer through the coats.

There, walking out of the lift, hand in hand, completely loved-up and carefree, are Big Mand and Big Sue, dressed in brightly coloured tropical-print matching sarongs. Big Sue is wearing her blue, green and pink birds of paradise wrapped around her waist with a vibrant green bra top while Big Mand has hers tied around her neck, flowing gently to the ground. It has been a long while since I last saw Big Sue out of khakis. They stop in front of the jewellery counter, where Matteo and I were mopping up my tears only a few moments ago. They keep smiling at each other while they browse the trays of rings. After a few moments, Big Sue places a hand gently on the back of her girlfriend's neck and plants a light kiss on her lips.

Big Mand responds by gently rubbing Big Sue's left buttock.

Big Sue trails her fingers casually up and down Big Mand's back while the assistant tries to get them to touch something other than each other. Big Sue is pointing at her toes. The assistant pulls out a tray of shining gold and platinum toe rings. Wedding toe rings. *Who knew?* Next, Big Sue is down on one knee, fitting a toe ring to Big Mand's foot as she flicks off her slider and lifts her leg. It's all very romantic until Big Sue slides her hand up Big Mand's leg and forgets to stop.

Matteo nudges me, alarmed. 'What?' I mouth silently. He nods repeatedly to the other side of the department store, over to the dresses where we were earlier.

I peep over and put my hand to my mouth to muffle a gasp. Tash and Sister Kevin are hiding behind a rack of white princess-style wedding dresses, their faces peeking through the billowing netting and silks. Their eyes are glued to Big Sue and Big Mand as their public display of affection carries on way past what is acceptable. I see Tash whispering something into Kev's ear and he gives her a sheepish shrug.

When the women finally finish kissing and draw apart, the assistant is beaming and hurriedly indicates the engagement rings for *fingers* section. This has Big Mand squealing with delight. They are so engrossed in the trays of rings, holding hands and giggling, that they don't notice Tash spying on them with a euphoric expression on her face. Nor do they hear the ping of the lift, and Liberty and Hank Junior emerging, their arms wrapped around each other's waists. They, too, are acting like loved-up teens, giggling and stroking each other.

Liberty points to the cowboy and cowgirl *Gettin' Hitched* section full of white Stetsons, rhinestones and elaborately fringed wedding attire. They stop dead in their tracks as soon as Liberty recognises Big Sue and Big Mand from behind. She silently pulls Hank Junior by the arm and steps backwards into the lift, jabbing frantically at the buttons until the doors slide closed.

'What are we seeing? What is going on?' Matteo hisses. 'Why is everyone hiding from each other? Why are they all in the wedding department?'

Never mind that. Why aren't they all sticking to the schedule? They should all be keeping Ged and Liam company in the casino while I'm ill in bed. Pity I won't be able to call them out on it. Matteo and I are stuck hiding in the coats until the others clear out. Tash seems settled into the wedding dress rack for the long haul. While we wait, I whisper to him, 'Thank you so much for all of these beautiful things.'

Matteo blinks slowly, a pained look momentarily sweeping over his face as he wipes some smudged mascara from my cheek. 'It seems a ridiculous thing to do. Pretending to get married just to put our unwanted admirers off. What are we thinking?'

Oh no.

'It's not ridiculous. Well, it is. Totally ridiculous.' *How to explain?* His eyes are darker than ever but something about him brings me peace. A strange confidence around him that I've not known before.

A smile tugs at his mouth as he side-eyes me. 'Okay, but if you have any regrets, we cancel the whole thing. Deal?'

I nod. 'Deal. Although at this rate, we'll still be stuck in this store until the end of the trip.'

'Tell me. What's going on with the Dollz?' he whispers.

'Good question.' I snuggle into him and prepare to spill all the gossip. 'Tash is toying with the idea of conceiving a child named Elvis while she's here. Big Mand and Big Sue are clearly enjoying their new relationship as a couple. And Liberty... Well, Liberty is Liberty. Who knows what is going on there. Today, she's into huge murderer's moustaches and toothpicks. Yesterday, it was classical opera singers. To-morrow, it'll be something else. She likes to take charge.'

Matteo seems pensive before he whispers, 'That's the same as Birdie. Things ended between us years ago, but she seems annoyed that it was me who ended it rather than her.'

'I think Luke is kind of being pressured into an arranged marriage and I think he sees me as a way out.' I can't help raising a tiny smile. 'Like a fake marriage to get out of a fake marriage. Who would be that crazy?'

'Who knew you'd be in such high demand for fake marriages? Is this two proposals in as many weeks?'

I nod.

He's so nice it's making me swoon. 'What? Why are you looking at me like that?'

I'm undressing him with my eyes.

'I'm, erm...' I pause.

A small puff of air escapes his lips. 'Disgraceful. I know exactly what you're doing.'

I give him an innocent flick of my lashes and lick my top lip slowly. 'Whatever do you mean?'

His eyes rake over my face and dip down to my boobs. 'I can assure you. I'm doing exactly the same.'

* * *

Eventually, after much keeping our hands to ourselves, Big Mand and Big Sue move away from the jewellery section empty-handed and drift off to the bridal bikinis section for *Beach Weddings*. I see the assistant who accosted us earlier make a beeline for them. Meanwhile, Tash and Sister Kevin are making a run for the stairs. I notice she has bags. Lots of large white paper bags.

Once we think the coast is clear, Matteo and I make a run for it too. He jabs at the buttons on the lift while I do a continuous sweep to make sure we aren't spotted. We fall into the lift slightly out of breath and immediately burst out laughing.

'Oh my God,' says Matteo, trying not to laugh. 'Nothing is ever straightforward with you, is it?'

'I have no idea what you mean.'

'Since you burst into my life it's been one crazy thing after another. And it doesn't seem to make a difference what side of the planet we're on.'

His eyes are twinkling.

'Your point?'

He steps towards me. His breathing still ragged. 'My point is that I've not had this much fun with anyone, ever.'

Oh.

'That can't be true,' I say, suddenly feeling shy. *What about the French girls? His cheating ex-fiancée? The supermodels and professors with Nobel prizes?*

He reaches for me. 'It's true.' A spark of electricity shoots through me the moment he touches my arm, causing my lips to part and every fibre of my being to scream at him to kiss me. He strokes his thumb over my lower lip and rips his gaze from it to look me dead in the eye. 'I've never felt this way about anyone before.'

I couldn't have scripted this moment any better myself. I reach for him, placing my hand at the back of his neck, and gently pull him down. Our lips slide perfectly together, creating blooms of lust with every slow and deliberate touch. Only a crowd of people waiting to pile in alerts us that the lift doors have opened and we have reached the ground floor. We spring apart and race out of the store onto the street, bags swinging, hands clasped tightly together and a lightness in our step.

'How long have we got until you do the next show?' he says huskily.

'How long do you need?' I answer, twirling my hair and batting my lashes. I bite my bottom lip for good measure. I want him. I want him real good.

He visibly swallows, clearly unravelled. 'Taxi!' he yells, thrusting out an arm at the oncoming traffic.

Ged messages while we are in the cab to say that he and Liam have spent the entire afternoon out and about because they have heard Harry Styles is doing a secret show somewhere in the centre of Las Vegas. They have narrowed their search to twenty-seven hotels in the vicinity. They are suggesting that we all go to Tao nightclub at The Venetian after our show, as any celebrity worth their salt shows their face there. He's suggesting a Barbie-costume-and-wig-free night.

What a relief.

At least Ged and Liam weren't sneaking around Macy's wedding department like the rest of us. I can't help wondering what the Dollz are up to. Surely we can't all be doing quickie Las Vegas weddings while we are here?

When Matteo and I eventually go down to meet the Dollz at the Cocktail Hour bar (we are wearing identical soppy grins), Ged and Liam are sitting dressed in denim hot pants, cowboy boots and too-tight T-shirts with *Cowboys do it better* emblazoned across their chests.

'Someone has made a full and suspicious recovery,' Ged says, eyeing me up and down. 'Feeling okay now?'

'Yes, thanks,' I say, feigning a cough. 'I think it's this mad, freezing air con they have.'

'And what did everyone else get up to this afternoon?' he asks the group.

We are all rattled by this question. Except Cherry. Cherry has the haunted look of someone who has gambled for thirty-six hours straight, on a diet of sugar and adrenaline. 'I don't know what happened,' she's saying. 'One minute I was losing every penny I had and the next, I'd won a lovely ankle bracelet and a cuddly toy from the vending machine. Such good karma.'

'You put money in a vending machine. That's why you got those things,' explains Big Mand. 'Who left Cherry alone this afternoon? Christ knows how much she has spent.'

They all glance guiltily at each other. Apparently, they all thought Cherry was with Liberty. I wonder how this is going to go, seeing as they were all in Macy's.

'Well, I was in bed ill,' I say, to start the lies off. 'I thought Cherry was with all of you.'

Liberty is quick to follow. 'I was with Hank Junior.

We were...' She eyes Big Sue to call her bluff. 'We were in The Poker Room all afternoon. Where were you? I didn't see you in there.'

Big Sue is swift to reply. 'We left. We were doing the slots over in The Palazzo, weren't we, Mandeep?'

Big Mand is beaming at her. Probably remembering one of the many huge snogs they now seem to be enjoying in front of the entire city. 'Yes. The Palazzo, that's right.'

Tash is keen to establish her whereabouts even though no one has asked. 'I was in my room giving Kev a blow job.'

Nobody is even slightly interested in pursuing this line of enquiry.

'Dressed as a maid.'

There's really no need for her to embellish the lie. I can see they all believe her.

'He was pretending to be a billionaire,' Tash says, inspecting her nails.

Fortunately, it is time to go on stage.

'Okay,' says Cherry. 'Let's get this show over with.'

'He was stuffing money down my bra while pretending to buy stocks and shares. He bought Microsoft for a trillion dollars and came almost immediately. It was very erotic.'

Tash is over-egging the pudding. I'm willing her to stop talking, otherwise she'll arouse suspicion.

'And that's the visual you're leaving us with, is it?' asks Big Mand. 'Seconds before we go on stage, you want us to picture Sister Kevin coming hard to the sound of himself buying an imaginary company with imaginary money on an imaginary NASDAQ?'

Tash, the picture of innocence, winks at her. 'It works for me. We can't all have our lovers on stage with us.'

Big Mand blushes just in time for us to be introduced on stage. Halfway through the intro, it's hard to know where not to look. Sister Kevin has come dressed as a market trader looking like he did indeed get a blow job. He is making googly eyes at Tash.

Something is off about the entire performance. Cherry is first to miss her cue because, in all honesty, she may as well be asleep behind that exhausted expression. Big Mand seems suddenly self-conscious in front of Big Sue. She misses her cue several times because she has lost focus. Liberty is constantly searching for Hank Junior in the audience, and I'm fixated on Matteo because he's magnificent.

We finish our set to a lukewarm response. We have not brought the energy tonight. And none of us seem bothered. Our minds are clearly elsewhere. As soon as we get off stage, I'm trying to think up an excuse to get out of clubbing, so that Matteo and I can sneak away. Matteo has not been able to keep his eyes off me all night. He didn't even check his phone, even though I could see it constantly lighting up with messages on the table in front of him.

He is prioritising me. He is making sure I know that I have his full attention. A smile is hovering over that delicious mouth of his while his eyes are telling me that I am the hottest babe he's ever met. I run my gaze subtly over him. Everything about him is purposeful and confident.

'So, we're all up for clubbing at Tao?' Liam asks excitedly as we approach the table. 'It's actually one of our bucket-list items. We've never been so excited, have we, Ged? Any chance we can do the Hot Garbage routine when we get there?'

Cherry yawns loudly. 'Sure, babes. Sure.'

'Roger that,' confirms Big Sue, looping her arm around Big Mand, who is gazing adoringly at her.

Tash sits on Sister Kevin's lap and wiggles her bottom suggestively. 'Just try and stop us.'

It seems the Dollz are feeling guilty over abandoning their posts this afternoon. This could be an ideal opportunity for me to put in for an early night, on account of that *cold* I have.

'Great performance,' Matteo says as I stand in front of him. 'You must be... tired.'

Excellent. Matteo and I have become telepathically attuned. He is also trying to get out of the pre-moon shenanigans.

'I am *tired*,' I say, biting my bottom lip. I flick my hair over my shoulder and shift my weight, hand on hip, chest slightly thrusting forwards. This costume I'm wearing leaves very little to the imagination. I'm all legs and boobs. The black plastic bra top draws attention away from my flat stomach and very low-sitting matching hot pants, over fishnet tights and leopard-print high-heeled boots.

'*Too* tired?' he says, getting my drift. He must be recalling our energetic session this afternoon. That ceiling mirror really has been something of a revolution.

'Never *too* tired,' I answer, twirling a strand of hair and looking coquettishly away. I hope to God we are not talking at cross purposes.

'Christ. Get a room, you two,' says Ged in a bored tone. 'At least you've made a full recovery and you're not *too* TIRED for tonight.' His arched eyebrows are set determinedly in my direction. 'Time to party. Let's go.'

Matteo's eyes are glittering with mischief as he shrugs in defeat.

15

The following morning, Matteo and I go over the schedule while we sit up in bed. We have been up since the crack of dawn to finalise the paperwork, confirm the booking for the gondola, choose a small flower arrangement for me to carry, and reserve a restaurant table for tonight. Something special as it's our wedding night. Even though none of it is real, we thought it might be nice anyway. And in light of all the sneaking around and the Dollz with all their drama and Ged and Liam wanting to spend every spare moment celebrity hunting, we've made the grown-up decision that it might be best to just keep our quickie fake wedding to ourselves and get it over with without any of them knowing or us hijacking everyone else's time.

'What time are we meeting everyone to "do" the High Roller?' Matteo asks me. He has a loved-up glaze to his eyes and his voice is oozing pure manuka honey. I have placed a giant pillow between us. It's all we can do to keep focused.

I flick through the schedule. 'I have a Happy Hour Cabin booked for an hour and a half's time. They should all be finishing breakfast by now. Then once we get back to the hotel the plan is to lose them in the casino. Sneak back here to get ready. Go down to reception to meet our officiator, get married in the gondola, and float under the bridge at precisely 3 p.m. All while the others are busy in the casino over in The Palazzo.'

'And we'll keep floating back and forth until we are sure that Birdie and Luke have seen us. I arranged for Birdie to meet with a potential client at the bridge. Did you message Luke?'

I nod. 'That way, they can see we're serious about each other, they'll leave us alone and our careers will be saved,' I finish for him. 'We are geniuses.'

Matteo half smiles at this. 'Desperate times, desperate measures. And you're sure the Dollz and Ged and Liam won't mind being excluded?'

'Only if they find out. But honestly, it's a night-mare trying to get them to stick to the schedule as it is, without rounding them all up for 3 p.m. And don't forget we'd then need to include them all in the wed-ding celebration at Caesars Palace, which might be a hassle,' I say, justifying my actions. 'This way is sim-ple, just me and you and back here for our wedding night.' A shoot of lust rips through me at the thought of Matteo seeing me in my wedding underwear. Just the thought of how he'll strip it off me. What he'll do. How he'll do it. I swallow down the butterflies rising up from my stomach as our eyes meet. 'Then to-morrow we're on the Grand Canyon Safari all day for our honeymoon.'

This is the happiest I've ever been in my entire life.

'Honeymoon?' Matteo looks worried. 'You do re-member that this is all pretend, don't you?'

'Of course.' I force a laugh as I adjust my sheet. 'Of course.'

* * *

At breakfast, the whole group is sitting at the usual booth picking at a selection of pancakes piled high, drizzled with maple syrup and a generous side of crispy bacon. 'At least we'll be outside where it's warm,' Liberty is saying to Ged and Liam. 'What's the plan?'

'I asked Connie to book us the Happy Half Hour Cabin with the full drinks package for Kev's BIG birthday,' trots out Tash, smoothing down her skintight gold metallic skimpy dress.

I take a second to absorb what I am seeing. *What the hell?* Tash has come dressed to kill. She is wearing red sky-high gladiator sandals, and her hair is perfect. Whereas we are all in full regulation Daytrip Barbie and Ken wigs, oversized sunglasses, pink check bucket hats with a photo of Ged and Liam on the front, tight white T-shirts with a photo of Ged and Liam on the front, hot pink short shorts and white knee socks. As per the effing schedule.

The Dollz are eyeing Tash up and down with interest and Ged is giving me *Well? Say something* eyes.

I am flabbergasted. Is it too much to request that everyone sticks to the arrangements? My mind flicks ahead to this afternoon. *Apart from me, of course.*

'Erm, nice outfit, Tash. Very nice. But we don't have much time before our turn in the Happy Half Hour Cabin. Are you planning to get changed before we leave in...' I make a big show of checking my phone. '...thirty seconds? It's booked for twelve. The limo should be outside waiting to take us there.'

Tash bursts out laughing. 'You and that schedule. This is about Kev's BIG birthday. It's *not* about the stag do. So, if anyone should change, it's you lot.'

'No,' I say carefully. 'If you check the itinerary, I booked SlotZilla for day one. Day two, roller disco. Day three, the High Roller and day four, Grand Canyon Safari. Day five, optional shopping day, or Omega Mart, before we do the birthday gig for Eddie at Talent Star. And day six, fly home.'

'But it was my idea to book the Happy Half Hour Cabin,' she says stubbornly.

Sister Kevin is standing behind her dressed smartly in chinos and a polo shirt. He looks very uncomfortable but at least his bust nose from the roller disco is healing nicely. 'And then we have something special planned that we are doing.'

'What's that?' asks Big Mand.

Sister Kevin's cheeks immediately redden. He fiddles with the neckline of his polo shirt and loosens the button. 'Erm, it's a birthday surprise.'

'Exactly how old are you?' Big Sue demands.

'Oh, for God's sake. We haven't got time for this!' Tash yells. 'To the limo. Let's go.'

Matteo raises his eyebrows at me. I bet he wishes he'd not bothered agreeing to come to this. But at least Tash and Sister Kevin won't be around to witness our wedding.

'And you can talk!' Tash bellows, pointing at Matteo, who's dressed in a casual dark denim shirt rolled up to his forearms, khaki combat shorts and sneakers. He looks magnificent but I suppose she has a point.

'I've invited Hank Junior,' says Liberty, standing with a hand on her hip. 'He also won't be in costume. Anyone got a problem with that?'

Dear Lord.

'No,' Ged and Liam say wearily in unison. 'Everyone else seems to be fine with hijacking our trip. But you do know you're on a pre-moon, *not* a stag do?'

* * *

Once the happy group have rained on Ged and Liam's parade, it's time to hurry to the waiting limo. Hank Junior joins us as we fly past the huge sphere artwork at reception. Liberty must have allowed him to wear his normal clothes today, and we are all impressed. Hank Junior scrubs up very nicely. He is all head-to-toe expensive designer clothes. The sharp lines and soft fabrics of luxury brands mould to his tanned and athletic body. The latest must-haves are on his feet. We pile in the limo.

'You sure as heck are funny, taking a limo,' Hank remarks. Talk turns politely to the High Roller and who has been on it before. Hank Junior gives us a list of what famous landmarks to look out for on our way round the world's tallest ever Ferris wheel.

'I might get motion sickness, and I have a fear of heights,' says Cherry.

How has this not come up already?

'Connie, did you bring sick bags or are they included in the ride?'

'I'm not great with heights either,' adds Big Mand.

What? This is news to me!

'We could wait on the ground for them?' suggests Big Sue. 'We could do some sight... seeing. While Libs looks after Cherry?'

The way she says sightseeing sounds weird. They are exchanging secretive glances. Oh. My. God. They are going to sneak off to buy engagement rings or get married or something. There's only room enough in the schedule for one couple to slope off behind everyone's backs and that's me and Matteo. Luckily, Tash is quick to pounce.

'No. We are celebrating Kev's BIG birthday and that's final. It won't be any fun if you lot don't come.'

The rest of us try not to take offence. All too soon, just three minutes later due to a slight hold-up in the traffic, and we arrive at the giant wheel, dotted with pods large enough to accommodate forty people each.

We clamber out, embarrassed. 'Connie, pet. How did you not know the hotel is practically next door to a giant wheel?' Cherry asks.

'We have had a lot going on,' I say, smiling through gritted teeth.

'And it's been excellent so far,' says Ged. 'Hasn't it, Liam? Franz has been the icing on the cake.'

As far as I can tell, they've hung out with Franz in their luxury suite more than they've been out and about.

'Brilliant. He's simply brilliant,' says Liam, craning his neck to peer up into the sky. 'Who knew there was all this going on in Vegas?'

Me. I knew. I have put a watertight schedule together.

As we walk to the entrance gate, I'm surprised to find the High Roller is so slow moving that it does not need to stop. People are being guided into the pods by staff and the doors locked. I show my tickets at the booth, and we are herded into a big queue. Tensions are gathering steam. Cherry is rubbing her belly and claiming to already feel motion sickness even though we are on solid ground. Maybe it is morning sickness and not the skip-full of sugar she has consumed. Before she has a chance to go to the toilets, the staff yell for the Cooper Party to come forward. 'Happy Half Hour Cooper party this way, please.'

Cripes. I hope Cherry can hold it for thirty minutes.

'This is Manny. He will be your bartender while on board. Drinks are free. Tips are welcome.'

The Dollz burst into laughter. 'Manny!' shrieks Tash, pointing at his badge.

'Manny!' howls Liberty. 'You couldn't make it up.'

Big Sue and Big Mand are creased up. They are also pointing to his badge. Manny holds up his badge. 'It is my name. Manny. Manny Fagnet. Why is this funny?'

'Ah, shite. I've wet myself,' yelps Cherry, choking on her laughter. She really isn't having a good day.

'We'll explain when we get in there,' says Tash, catching her breath. 'Come on, Manny *Fagnet*.' And off she goes, howling with laughter. At least the energy levels and raucous vibes have returned. Ged and Liam have also cracked up, which is nice to see. For a second, I thought this trip was going to be a disaster.

Poor Manny. He has no idea why we are laughing until Liberty whispers something in his ear. Manny gazes around the group before he shouts, 'I love it! I love it because it is funny. But it is funny because I also love fanny!'

Silence. Manny has taken things too far. Also, we are confused. Does he mean American for bum, or does he mean the English version?

'Who wants a drink?' he says, trying to recover the vibe, and luckily everyone is now in the mood to drink even though it is only noon.

Matteo sidles up to me. 'See? What did I say about you all being batshit crazy?'

He's not wrong.

As the drinks and colourful cocktails are speedily served by Manny, who has managed to get himself back in the good books by serving sparklers, giant straws and umbrellas with the drinks, Matteo sidles up to me.

'Nervous?' he murmurs into my hair.

I chew my lip. 'A bit. What if they don't turn up?' I say very quietly.

'If they don't, we can always ring them mid-vows and hurry them along.' He chuckles, wrapping his arms around me as we gaze out at the spectacular view.

I feel a little pang that Matteo is not taking it as seriously as me.

'OMG!' yells Liberty. 'The Eiffel Tower!'

Hank Junior corrects her. 'No. That is the STRAT Tower. It has the world's tallest rotating restaurant. I will take you there tonight for our... celebration.'

Liberty squeals with excitement and kisses him full on the mouth in response. They then exchange what I'm going to start calling a 'secretive' vibe.

Celebration? Not these two as well!

Matteo spots it too. 'Do you think they're... up to something?'

I dig him in the ribs. 'And look at Big Sue and Big Mand.' I nod discreetly to where they are standing whispering to one another and pointing downwards. Matteo and I glimpse out the window. We are directly over the Little Wedding Chapel. In fact, there are many wedding chapels. One on nearly every street corner. There are brides and grooms aplenty scurrying below us.

Tash points out the Bellagio fountain. 'That's where we're thinking of...' She stops mid-sentence.

'Thinking of what?' I ask, dreading the answer. *Getting hitched? Conceiving a baby?*

'Thinking of doing a live for Tash's followers,' supplies Sister Kevin smoothly. 'She wants me to be the sort of interviewer. Even though I've never done it before.'

Speaking of which. I whip out my phone. I keep forgetting the documentary I'm filming for Ged and Liam. I point the phone in their direction, but they are wearing disappointed expressions. 'But we wanted to do a live from there for TikTok.'

This squabble proves popular. Everyone wants to do a 'live' from the Bellagio.

Hank Junior breaks from Liberty, who has much to say on the topic, to approach Matteo and me. 'Hi,' he says. 'Can you delete any footage with me on, please?'

'Yes, sure. Sorry,' I say, instantly thumbing through photos to delete any with him on. 'I always forget to check with people.'

Hank Junior waits until I have completed the action. 'No problem. I just don't like my image out there, is all.' He swiftly changes topic. 'Liberty told me about the jerk who keeps following you round.'

Oh.

'Uh, yeah. He's just...' *How to explain?*

'Well, just to let you know. I'll take care of it.' Hank winks at me.

'Thank you, but what...?'

'You're welcome.'

'No. I meant, sorry, did you say, "take care of it"?'

He taps his nose.

What is happening here?

'Could you explain what you mean by that, please?' I can barely get the words out. Hank is smiling at me like your everyday, very rich playboy about town.

Hank laughs, shaking his head. 'You Brits.'

'But when you say "take care of it", what do you mean?'

Hank rolls his eyes as though I'm in on some sort of joke and wanders back over to Liberty. I turn to Matteo, who has gone deathly pale.

Oh, shit.

16

If it wasn't for Cherry throwing up all over the floor, I would have followed Hank Junior to find out exactly what he meant by 'taking care' of Luke.

'We know nothing about him!' I hiss to Matteo.

The barman is inspecting the mess with a horrified expression, but he has conjured a mop out of thin air and is scrutinising the sea of vomit sliding around the floor. Unfortunately, Cherry has positioned the contents of her stomach, a vibrant yellow liquid, between the group and the bar. He is trapped on one side and everyone else is trapped on the other. Tash is livid.

'Better out than in, as they say,' says Cherry, wiping at her mouth with a weary expression. The air is filled with a pungent, sickly-sweet smell. 'Morning sickness. I have morning sickness because I am pregnant.' Her tone is becoming increasingly angry. 'That's what happens when a man impregnates a woman without telling her.'

Cherry's words hang in the air, causing an abrupt halt to all the shrieking.

'What?' says Cherry, accusingly.

'You were... unconscious at the time?' Big Sue appears to swallow a lump in her throat. This is all getting very dark, very quickly.

'No,' Cherry says, impatiently.

A collective sigh of relief reverberates around the pod.

'Sometimes I can't feel it going in,' she explains, bluntly. 'It's a bit thin, that's all. Plus, I was unloading the dishwasher at the time. My mind was on other things. And he's going thin on top, did I mention that? He never warned me that might happen. I'm so bloody furious with him!'

She's not exactly painting the most romantic picture of wedded bliss.

None of us know where to look. Cherry has started to go nuclear on the world's tallest ride, and we are right at the top with half the journey still to go, and a pool of sick is taking up three quarters of the space. Oh, and the windows don't open.

* * *

Finally, we arrive back on solid ground. Matteo and I barely had time to discuss the Hank Junior situation because it felt as though we were being listened to the whole of the way down. Everyone was pretty much silent. Stunned at the bizarre predicament we have once again found ourselves in.

'Well, that was eventful,' murmurs Matteo. He has regained the power of speech. 'I'll have a word with Hank. Find out what he means exactly.'

I feel nervous as I watch him walk over to Hank Junior, who has his arm around Liberty's waist. She is looking adoringly up at him. He smiles when Matteo approaches. He puts a hand on Matteo's shoulder. They both laugh in a forced kind of way, and Matteo makes his way back to me with a fake smile almost splitting his face in two.

Before he can explain, we are yet again distracted. 'That was the most miserable fifteen minutes of my life,' wails Liam, gagging as he sprints from the pod.

Manny, who was far from professional in the way he kept screaming each time the vomit slid closer to him with each movement of the pod, has radioed for the cleaning team who are there to greet us with scowls. The ride doesn't stop, they remind us. They have less than two minutes to clean it up otherwise they have to go right round, trapped inside.

'Sorry, guys.' *Ah.* Poor Cherry. It's not her fault her thinning-haired husband put his sperm inside her while she was trying to tidy the kitchen.

I instruct everyone to walk back to the hotel, seeing as it is a lovely sunny day and approximately only a seven-minute walk. Because of the Cherry incident, everyone suddenly needs some fresh air and alone time. Liberty and Hank take the opportunity to slope off in the opposite direction. Likewise Big Mand and Big Sue.

Ged screws his eyes at Sister Kevin. 'Happy birthday, by the way. How old did you say—'

Tash grabs Sister Kevin by the arm. 'Connie, pet. Can you look after Cherry? Thanks, love.' And within seconds they are speeding away from us.

Oh, crap.

'Sure,' I say.

'We're going to pop into the Bellagio to do some filming,' says Liam. 'See you later, Connie, babes. And thanks for organising. Mwah-mwah.' He and Ged can't wait to get away.

'How many times?' Cherry says to me. 'I don't need a friggin' babysitter.' She marches off, furious with her husband and the world.

Everyone has disappeared. The coast is clear. 'Well, that was much easier than I thought,' I say.

Matteo fixes me a look that makes my toes curl. 'Time to get married?'

* * *

We make the conscious decision not to ruin the day by speculating over Hank Junior's remarks. In fact, we laugh it off as nerves.

'A lot has happened in the past few days. We're tired.'

'Of course, we are going to interpret things in unusual ways,' I agree readily.

'Maybe Hank is jet-lagged and behaving differently? Where did he say he flew in from?'

'Who knows? Maybe it is the Vegas culture and that's how they all talk?' I reason.

'Maybe it is the fake murderer's moustache Liberty has been making him wear that has given us a false impression of him?'

By the time we arrive at The Venetian, we have more or less convinced ourselves that Hank Junior is simply here in Vegas, without friends, for a quick relaxing break from his charity business that he runs to save animals and old people from neglect. And that if anything was *off* about him then Liberty would surely let us know. After all, she has a degree in mood management. She is practically a trained psychiatrist.

We hurry to our room to get ready, scampering along the maze-like corridors. Matteo holds the door open for me. I hesitate a fraction and try to quash the nerves before I go in. We're really doing this. We're going to pretend to get married. I'm going to transform myself from downtown Barbie to uptown bride.

Matteo studies me, smoothing back a lock of the wig hair from my forehead with tenderness. 'You okay?'

I summon a bright smile for him.

'You're like no other woman I've ever known.' He trails the backs of his fingers down my face and kisses me in a slow, languid way, as though we have all the time in the world. The weight of his hands on my waist ignites a fire deep within my belly as my body responds to him in its customary way. I loop my arms around his neck and press myself against him. The door closes with a click and Matteo holds my gaze. 'I will never stop wanting you.'

His words melt against my neck as his hands

loosen the straps and buckles of my outfit. I slide my hands beneath his shirt to feel his smooth, hot skin. He shivers at my touch.

'Constance,' he murmurs against my lips. The way he says my name sends delicious tingles up my spine. My fingers slip down to inside his waistband. He takes a sharp inhale, holding his breath as I undo the zip of his shorts. Our breathing quickens as he hardens and pulls me to him. We find a patch of wall to kiss against. He knots both my hands in his, holding them above my head as our kiss deepens.

We make our way across the room in a tangle of hands in hair, under clothes and between legs. 'I will never stop wanting to kiss you,' I whisper into his ear as he leaves a burning trail of hot kisses down my throat and along my collarbone, his fingers working their way inside my knickers. It causes an unholy throbbing of desire to pulsate throughout my entire body. I can barely breathe.

'Then don't stop.' Matteo pushes his fingers inside me, expertly sliding them back and forth. His thumb rubbing gentle circles on my sweet spot causes me to moan loudly.

A knock on the door snaps us out of the moment.

'Ignore it,' he groans, one of his hands tugging down my top to release a nipple for him to close his lips over, the other softly bringing me to orgasm. The knocking persists as I shudder against his hand. We lock eyes. I am properly panting. He's checking to see if I'm satisfied. I totally am.

* * *

When he eventually opens the door, two orgasms each later, we find a stunning bouquet of flowers on the floor outside. Matteo has the foresight to check that they are our wedding flowers and not another bouquet from Hank Junior to Liberty. As he hands them to me, it's as though we're having a conversation without words. It's time to get married.

'You shower first, then I'll go in,' he offers, checking the time on his phone. 'I'm guessing you'll need more time than me to get ready.'

So accurate. So thoughtful.

Once I disappear into the shower, my breathing returns to normal. It isn't until the warm water sprays against my shoulders and spine that I realise how overjoyed I am. I study my reflection. I'm so far from the mouse I used to be. It's as though Matteo lights a spark in me every time we get together. I become more. More alive. More adventurous. Just more.

When I emerge from the bathroom in a hotel

robe, I see Matteo is on the phone. He is pacing up and down.

'No, Birdie. I told you I'm busy this afternoon. Look, you meet the client, and maybe we can get together tomorrow to discuss it. Uh-huh. No. Then let him wait.'

He switches off his phone with an impatient growl, but breaks into a half-smile when he sees me. He throws the phone on the bed.

'I'm so done,' he says.

'You still have time for a shower,' I say. 'It'll relax you. Such a shame I broke that jar of soothing pond algae.'

A chuckle escapes his lips. He throws me a grateful smile. 'You're good for me,' he says, closing the bathroom door behind him.

His words dance around my brain, instantly catapulting me into action. Face. Hair. Body cream. Perfume. Outfit.

I have completed my 'no make-up' make-up and most of my hair when I hear Matteo turning off the shower. I take out all the garment bags from the wardrobe and lay them on the bed. The wardrobe door has a full-length mirror on the inside. I spend a few moments staring back at my reflection. My mother's eyes peer back at me. Would she do something as wild and reckless as this? I unclip my locket necklace, open it to reveal her photo and take in her young, vibrant expression. She was brave and bold and knew exactly what she wanted to do with her life. She loved singing with a passion and she loved me and my father with the same fierce intensity, as though we were the only two human beings on the planet. I see her staring back at me through wide green eyes.

I remove my hair curlers and let the freshly dried brown curls tumble down my back. I look just like her. I have her thick, shiny hair and her tall, slender frame. I have her cheekbones and long lashes. She is with me always.

'I'm happy, Mam,' I say into the mirror. 'I'm really, really happy.' I wipe a single tear from my cheek. She'd be proud of me. I know she would.

A movement catches my eye. It's Matteo. He's standing with an expression of compassion on his face. He gets me. He gets that I'm on a journey.

I return his smile, and he takes that as permission to come and hold me. He looks insanely hot in his wedding suit. Unbelievably handsome with his hair slightly damp, his face cleanly shaved and smelling of lemon balm. Fragrant aftershave blooms from his body as he holds me tight in his strong arms. He rests his chin on the top of my head and makes eye contact with me through the mirror. I feel an energy flow between us as a feeling of calm sweeps through me. We feel right. I sag against him, and we stay like that until I'm ready to be released.

'Is it okay for me to go?' he asks. 'I need to speak to the officiator in person. Something about the vows. I thought that you'd prefer the time to finish getting ready instead of coming with me?'

'Yes, please,' I say, quite relieved. It's bad luck for the groom to see the bride before the wedding, whatever the circumstances. 'Why don't I meet you at the gondola?'

'If you're sure,' he says. 'I can stay and help?'

'I'm fine. I'll be down in thirty minutes.'

I watch him go, the tuxedo hugging his tall frame in all the right places. His shirt is taut across his muscular stomach, his jacket close-fitting like it was tailormade. The trousers, slim-fit, flow loosely over his solid thighs and athletic legs. He turns at the door to give me one last smile, causing sparks to erupt like fireworks in my heart, before it closes.

I am so ready for this.

17

Twenty minutes later, I inspect myself in the mirror. That assistant knew exactly what she was doing. Everything from the insanely sexy underwear, hold-up stockings and complimentary sparkling body mist she shoved in the bag, to the exquisite sleeveless wedding gown that is flowing with my body with every slight movement I make. It wasn't an expensive gown, but it sure feels like one.

I admire the delicate layers of off-white chiffon falling gently to the floor. I trace the soft, simple lace of the V-neck plunging just below the breastbone because of the clever built-in straps. I reach behind my neck to fasten the tiny buttons. The dress is almost backless because the lace is cut out from the shoulder blades in a soft diamond shape to just above the waist. It makes my waist tiny. It's simple. It's classic. It's perfect for this wedding on an Italian gondola, floating on a canal in the middle of this crazy city.

My hair is teased into sleek waves, my lips are voluptuous and stained ruby red and my smoky eyes are huge, enhanced with black flicks of liner and fake lashes showing them off. My locket sits nicely on my chest, and sparkly earrings and a sweet diamanté headband complete the look. I slip my feet into some kitten heels that I brought with me and spritz myself with perfume. Anyone would think I was really getting married.

I feel a pang of wistfulness as my head is temporarily clouded by my heart.

I text Matteo to let him know I'm on my way, pick up my beaded purse and close the door behind me. It feels like a dream as I hitch up the skirts of my wedding dress to the ankle and walk along the carpeted corridors as people zigzag out of my way, no one batting an eyelid at the matrimonial attire. By the time I reach the floor with the canal and gondolas on, I have passed four brides already. I am not even out of place; there are so many people coming and going here.

I make my way to the gondola station, nervous excitement providing a spring in each step, as the charm of Venice, with its breathtaking architecture and stone-clad shopfronts, surrounds me. The ceiling is an almost cloudless blue sky, as though it is a bright sunny day in bustling St Mark's Square.

Matteo is waiting for me. He is standing deep in conversation with Elvis Presley who is wearing bell-bottom white trousers lined with colourful rhine-stones up the sides. He has a matching blazer, dark oversized sunglasses, thick black sideburns and hair slicked back into a perfect pompadour. He's certainly committed.

A giggle escapes my lips. I can't believe I'm doing this. It's insane. It's thrilling. It's exactly what my soul is crying out to do. I'm finally living an adventurous, messy, unpredictable life. And it's everything I dreamed it would be, and so much more.

The icing on the cake is the way Matteo's eyes light up when he catches sight of me walking towards him. He almost drops the clipboard that he's holding. Even Elvis is grinning broadly.

'Why, you've caught yourself a mighty fine filly, if I say so myself, ah-har-ha,' Elvis drawls in a thick Southern accent. He obviously never comes out of character. 'Are you two sweethearts excited? This is a mighty fine special day.'

I nod politely but I just can't take my eyes from Matteo. It seems as though he has a thousand things he wants to say but is lost for words. He reaches for my hand, and that dreamy smile is all I need. 'You look... stunning.'

'Back at you,' I say, leaning in close. I can practically feel the sparkles bursting from my eyes.

Elvis takes the clipboard from Matteo and hands it to me. 'Just tick the box and sign on the dotted line and we'll get your wedding vows underway.'

I can barely hold the pen for nerves, never mind read what I'm signing.

'You two lovebirds make a handsome couple, that's for sure,' Elvis is saying as he holds my bouquet for me. 'You seem perfect together. Have you been together long?'

Ah. Awkward.

'No. Not long,' says Matteo.

'You sure give the impression that you have a happy life together.' He takes the clipboard from me, hands back the flowers and leads us to a spectacular gondola, all white with elaborate gold swirls and edging. The seats are a deep plum colour. There's a gondolier wearing a striped T-shirt, a boater hat, red neckerchief and a matching cummerbund.

Matteo takes my hand and helps me climb down onto it, he follows, and lastly Elvis climbs in and sits opposite. We take our seats and Matteo shuffles closer to me as gentle romantic music begins to play. The gondolier croons along as he pushes us away from the jetty and onto the canal.

'I can't believe we're doing this.' Matteo's face is lit up. 'It's insane,' he whispers. He holds both my hands in his as we press even closer together.

'It's just another bonkers story to tell the grand-kids,' I quip.

Elvis winks at us. 'Ready?'

We both nod nervously. It feels so real.

'Now, not only is this little lady adorable, she's happy,' he says to Matteo. 'And it's your job to keep her that way for the rest of your days. Are you up to it, young fella?'

'Yes. I am.'

'Well, alright! Today is all about a promise. A promise to cherish one another, no matter what comes your way, with a love that's tender and true. A promise to stay honest and faithful when times get hard and confusing, 'cause they certainly will. And a promise to remember that any place is paradise, as long as you're together.' Elvis raises one of his thick black eyebrows and curls his lip as he gives us a piercing look. 'Today is about celebrating the special bond you two share. If you keep loving each other the way you've been loving each other, that bond is bound to last forever. Now, son, face your bride and... I see you're doing it already. That's a good sign.'

He peruses the clipboard where we have written our names.

'Are you, Xavier Matteo George...' Elvis tilts his head and checks with Matteo before continuing.

I totally forgot Matteo has the longest name in recorded history.

'...Marie-Carmen Torrado Grande...' Elvis pauses for breath. '...ready to take Constance Emily Cooper as your wife?'

'I am,' says Matteo, smiling.

'Then repeat after me. I promise to never step on your blue suede shoes. Or treat you like a fool. I promise to love you tender, and never return to sender. Like the sweet song of a choir. You light my morning sky with burning love. I'm just a hunk, a hunk of burning love for you.'

Matteo can barely stop chuckling as he obediently repeats every phrase while trying to gaze earnestly into my eyes.

Elvis is clearly enjoying himself too. When it's my turn, I can barely keep a straight face.

'I promise to never leave you in Heartbreak Hotel. Or have a suspicious mind,' I say. 'I promise to love you tender, and love you sweet, and never let you go. You have made my life complete, and I promise to always love you so.' Our eyes meet and for a brief second, I wish with all my heart this was real.

'You've chosen to exchange wedding rings, which symbolise the promise of lasting marriage and your devotion to each other.'

Matteo hands Elvis the boxes with our rings in.

'Like a fountain of love, flowing endlessly, these rings and the love they represent will nourish you, in this life and the next. But remember,' he says, dramatically and loudly, 'the ring is only a symbol. It shows the world that you belong to someone, just as they belong to your heart. But as you wear them, it's your care, devotion, and concern for one another that are the true signs of your love.'

Matteo slips the ring on my finger, not taking his eyes from mine for a second. I blink slowly. The emotion is welling up inside me.

I gulp down the temptation to cry happy tears as I slip the golden wedding band slowly onto his strong and capable finger. The matching platinum band against the raised gold looks simple and elegant.

'Lord have mercy, look at this beautiful love!' yells Elvis to our gondolier, causing us to start giggling again. 'Constance and Matteo, by the power vested in me by the State of Nevada and American Marriage Ministries, I now pronounce you husband and wife. You may now kiss your bride!'

Matteo leans towards me, a huge smile on his face. He has thoroughly enjoyed this experience. It has been so much fun. Everything I'd want in a real wedding. He kisses me lightly on the lips, leaving me tingling all over. 'You look so happy. I wish we could stay in this moment forever,' he murmurs into my ear.

I cup his face, a bloom of pride swelling in my heart. 'Me too.'

Elvis stands up and spreads his arms wide as 'Viva Las Vegas' bellows from the gondola speaker. 'Ladies and gentlemen,' he yells to all the passers-by, 'give it up for Mr and Mrs Torrado Grande!'

People walking along the sides of the canal, bustling from shop to shop or scurrying towards the casino, stop to stare, cheer and clap. It's then that I remember we need to be floating under the bridge at dead on 3 p.m. I have no idea where my phone is to check the time and, as I cast my eyes about, I re-member Las Vegas is the city with no clocks.

Matteo gets my drift instantly. 'No need,' he says, pointing at the bridge. The colour has drained from his face. I twist round to see what's going on.

Birdie is not the only one standing with her mouth agape. Ged and Liam are beside her, jaws hanging open, eyes wide with shock, hurt and disbe-lief. The Dollz are beside them, their faces a mix of incredulity and confusion. Tash is slapping her own cheeks as though we are part of an elaborate halluci-nation. Big Sue and Big Mand keep gawping at me then at each other. Liberty has both eyebrows as near to her hairline as they can get and her mouth a per-fect O. Cherry is grinning as she chews slowly on a length of sugary rope, a knowing smile splattered across her face. She gives us a sly thumbs up.

Only Sister Kevin is clapping along to 'Viva Las Vegas' until Tash whacks him with her handbag.

Oh. My. God.

Things could not have gone any worse.

Loud singing penetrates the haze of confusion.

Oh, wait. Things can get worse. Much worse.

My ears filter out the cacophony of noise and yells from the bridge to make certain.

No. It can't be.

A series of pitch-perfect notes and operatic singing booms out across the water. It sounds like Luke. He's singing 'Mi Amore Mi Amore'.

I swivel around to see where it is coming from. At that moment, a spectacularly showy super-gondola floats beside us. Luke is belting out the song dressed as a singing gondolier, complete with boater hat, cummerbund, unflattering striped T-shirt clinging to him and legs wide apart clad in flared black trousers flapping in the breeze while he thrusts the oar dramatically into the water. A familiar-looking bride and groom sit opposite gazing affectionately at him.

But when the super-gondola floats serenely past us, Luke does a double take, causing him to lose a beat in his singing. He squints hard at me, his eyes raking over my wedding dress. His whole face drops as realisation dawns. His gaze flicks to Matteo, before he abruptly stops singing.

'Connie?' he bellows as they float past. He twists round, bringing the huge oar out of the water to try to halt the gondola's progress as the music continues playing without him.

Then to everyone's horror, the oar bashes into the orange Donald Trump who is marrying the couple, and we see two rings fly up into the air and land in the water. The bride screams. The groom yells, and all the while Luke is trying to continue singing as though none of it was his fault. The bride leaps to her feet and bashes her bouquet of flowers against Luke's chest before pushing him in the water.

Tash is filming it all for her Instagram and has clearly recognised the famous bride.

'You bastard! Find my wedding rings!' she screeches. 'And you can forget all about the million-dollar fee while you're at it! I'll sue you into the shitting ground for this.'

We float along, staring up at our friends, aghast. It's hard to know where to look. Luke is splashing about in the water trying to make for the side while lots of people are shouting at him, and the bride is squawking about her dream wedding being ruined.

We glide under the bridge, momentarily out of everyone's sight, and take a moment to stare at one another.

'This was so not the plan,' I say. 'Ged and Liam are going to be furious. And Luke, he *was* actually here for work after all! Oh my God.' My hand flies to my mouth.

I can hear him splashing about as a fast-forwarded reel of all our interactions with him plays out in my head. All I can recall is him repeatedly trying to convince us that he was in town for work and nothing else. Panic churns in my stomach.

Matteo puts his hand to his forehead. 'Give me a moment to think of something.'

To give Elvis his credit, this is not his first rodeo. 'You wanted to seal your love privately. I get it. You're a hunk of burning love. And she's a cute patootie. But I'm not sure your guests seem so understanding.' He indicates to the gondolier to park up as quickly as possible. He jumps up onto the seat and almost hops out of the boat. He flicks through his paperwork as we clamber out after him.

Matteo holds out his hand to help me out of the gondola. 'I'll tell them this was all my idea.' His hand is strong and capable. His kind, dark eyes are swimming with reassurance. His smile is comforting and safe.

I feel an overwhelming rush of love for him. He's keeping a level head amidst all the madness as usual.

Then Luke, still swimming to the side of the canal, hauls himself out, exhausted. He looks flabbergasted. Which is understandable. I'm sure I would too if I'd just lost a million dollars and my singing partner had refused to believe me on the multiple occasions I'd tried to tell her I was here for work. As the water drips off him, he gives me a filthy look.

I watch him stomping away without looking back. This wedding has clearly done what we needed it to do.

'Forget him. That's karmic payback for the way he went on in York.' Matteo's face grows serious as he tugs me to him. 'Do not feel guilty.'

I can hear the thundering of feet over the bridge. I don't have to turn around to know that it's everyone charging towards us for answers.

18

Matteo puts a protective arm around me, squeezing my shoulder as the footsteps grow louder.

'We'll have to tell them it's all fake.' I flap my hands about, my bouquet slapping against my dress.

'How can we deny we're married in front of Birdie?' Matteo reasons smoothly. 'If we admit it's all fake, it'll defeat the purpose.'

'What will we do?' A light film of sweat forms on my brow as I take in huge gulps of air.

Matteo takes my hand gently. 'Breathe. It'll be okay, I promise. Just play along and we'll come clean with them later.'

'I can't!' I wail. 'I can't hurt my friends' feelings like this.'

Elvis, looking frantic and desperate to get out of here, starts to tear a strip of paper from his clipboard. 'Well, have a nice life together.'

The Elvis music is still bellowing out. It all seems so surreal. Such happy, celebratory music against this sea of angry, perplexed faces and yelling from the group as they push through the crowd to get to us.

'Erm, what are you all doing here?' I yell over to them.

'What are *we* doing here? What are *you* doing here?' booms Big Mand, eyeing my wedding dress and flowers as they get closer.

'It's not what you think,' I say to Ged and Liam as they reach me. *Oh, God.* They have tears in their eyes.

'It looks a lot like you were getting married to me,' Ged sniffs. He picks up my hand and spots the lovely, smooth, thick golden wedding band on my finger, reflecting the light.

'No. No, we're not,' I explain, trying to hush him. 'I mean, we are. But we're not. This is all a huge misunderstanding.'

Elvis curls his lip, hooks his thumbs into his trouser waist and strikes the pose. 'If I had a dollar for every time I heard that, lemme tell y'all.' He lets out a deep, rumbling chuckle before bellowing, 'Viva Las

Vegas, ah-har-ha.' He holds out the slip of paper. 'Here you go, son.'

'Thanks. Is that the receipt?' Matteo says dazedly, taking it from him just as everyone gathers closely around us.

Elvis laughs. 'No, son. Why, that's your wedding certificate.' His voice really does carry considering the music and the disgruntled chatter from my friends and the screaming bride in the other gondola.

'Our what now?' Matteo says, snapping into business mode. His eyes scan the document. He instinctively tries to give it back to him.

Elvis sticks both his hands up. 'You'll need to show that if anyone asks if you're legally wed.' He rolls his eyes. 'Lordy, you young folks and your internet. It's like you don't know what to do with a piece of paper. Don't worry, we'll email a copy to you.'

'But we opted for the...' I hiss from the side of my mouth, trying to keep my voice from carrying over to Birdie, who is hovering at the back of the group. 'For the *pretend* renewal of the vows option. The *non-legal* version.'

Elvis flicks through his clipboard.

'Nope. You young 'uns ticked this box.' Elvis shows me and Matteo the box that we ticked. 'And you signed right here.'

Fuck me.

'Yeah,' chimes Cherry, poking her head between us to speedily read the page. 'You're married alright. That's an official document and those signatures give this overweight Elvis lookalike the authority to marry you.'

'Viva Las Vegas and congratulations on your matrimonial life together,' says Elvis, scurrying away. 'I have another happy couple to officiate in five minutes.'

He leaves us standing there. Facing everyone. I turn to Matteo. He looks stunned.

Elvis has left the building.

'You're married!' shrieks Liam. 'You got married without us! You are our *best woman*. The person we trust most in the whole world. The *only* person we asked. We wanted you to play the biggest part in *our* wedding because you are our *family*. Apparently, you don't feel the same.' He bursts into tears.

Then Ged gives me a desolate look, and he also bursts into tears.

Then I burst into tears.

Then Matteo yells, 'What the fuck is happening here?'

Then Cherry tells him off.

Then Birdie screams that she'll never work with Matteo ever again.

'And you can fuck off as well, pet,' Cherry tells her in between biting off chunks of her sugar rope. 'Go on, you miserable cow. Sling yer hook.'

Birdie is fuming and releases a tirade of what we all presume are French expletives at Matteo, before she whips her coral-coloured hair violently over her shoulder and stamps away on her skinny legs.

Matteo immediately stiffens beside me. This scenario is escalating unnecessarily.

Liberty, Tash and Sister Kevin are the only ones to find it hilariously funny.

'I love weddings,' says Sister Kevin, grinning down at Tash.

'Congratulations, Big Guy,' says Big Sue, patting me woefully on the back.

'Yeah, Big Guy,' says Liberty, trying her best not to howl with laughter. 'Congratulations. I hope you'll both be very happy.' She attempts to give me a hug but I'm too upset to respond. Instead, she leans in. 'Don't worry. I'm just joking. We'll fix this, Connie, babes. We'll take care of it. I promise.'

'Take care of it.' Cherry inhales sharply. 'Guys. I've just remembered something.' She turns to Liberty. 'You sound just like Hank Junior.'

Oh, God.

My head snaps up. 'Where is Hank Junior?' I ask suddenly.

Liberty shrugs. 'He's gone to take care of something, he said.'

'He's gone to *take care* of something?' I dart a look at Matteo.

'Uh-huh,' Liberty says. 'Why?'

Cherry presses her fingers to her temples. 'I overheard him on the phone last night in the club. Said he was making a hit for someone. And that he was taking care of it. Hang on. Where did I get this?' Cherry says, distracted by the rope she's been chewing the whole time. 'What even is it?'

'Where did he say he was going?' Matteo asks Liberty, a look of incredulity washing over him.

'He didn't say,' Liberty says.

'Fucking hell. I can't believe this is happening!' Matteo drags his hands slowly down his face. It seems as though we've found his tipping point. To be fair, it is way higher than mine.

How could I get so swept up in everything that I forgot that Liberty put an accidental hit out on Luke?

I grab Liberty's arms. 'Tell Hank Junior that the Luke situation has already been *taken care* of.'

'What do you mean?' she says, confused.

'Hank,' I say. 'He told me and Matteo not to worry about Luke because he would *take care of it*, you know, as in...' I jiggle my head.

Big Sue and Big Mand are suddenly very interested in this swift change of topic. 'What's the ten four?' she asks me, her face serious.

I gulp. 'How do I explain this?'

'Quietly,' says Big Sue. 'We're in the middle of Las Vegas's busiest hotel with cameras and microphones hidden all over the place. Capeesh?'

Is there really any need for this level of paranoia?

'There aren't any in our room, we've checked,' says Tash, winking at Sister Kevin.

'Look, Connie. What the hell are you going on about?' says Liberty, shrugging out of my grip.

'I think you accidentally put a hit out on Luke,' I say to her.

'No, I didn't. I just told Hank about Luke, and he asked me if I wanted him to... take care of... the situation...' She trails off. Her hand flies to her mouth. 'Oh, shit.'

At the mention of Hank Junior, Cherry suddenly springs back into the game. 'Yes. Libs. Hank Junior literally said he made hits for a living and laughed about it. I thought he meant records. What does he really do? Did he say?'

Liberty shrugs, shaking her head.

'Cherry, do they still hang people here? Even if they're British?' Big Mand asks.

'You've all just confessed to being accessories to murder,' says Cherry, her eyes darting up and around. She has gone very pale. 'They fry people in the electric chair here. I'm going to be sick... again.'

Liberty puts a hand to her chest. 'And I think I'm going to...' Her eyelids clang shut. Like a toppling tree, she falls backwards towards the canal. Big Sue, renowned for her agility and speed, dives to catch her and lays her gently on the ground.

'Right. Get her flat on her back with her legs in the air,' booms Big Mand. 'High in the air. That's it.'

'So, just put her in her favourite position then?' says Sister Kevin, winking at Big Mand, even though this is very clearly not a winking-type scenario and is wildly inappropriate.

Tash elbows him sharply in the ribs. Poor Sister Kevin. He's always just out of sync. On any other day we'd have laughed this off, and perhaps mentioned that Liberty often brags that reverse cowgirl is her favourite position, on account of her having two round apples for bum cheeks. But not today.

'Never a dull moment, is there?' trills Tash. She looks borderline deranged. 'Come. Come along,' she squeaks to Sister Kevin, as though he's a chihuahua. 'Come. Come with me. Come. Let's leave them to this madness. I don't believe one word of it.'

Sister Kevin, who could be undercover police for all we know about him, holds up a hand. 'Everyone stay right where you are.'

Thank the Lord. Maybe he is the police. He's the right shape. He can confirm our bungling innocence to Interpol.

He draws himself up to his full height. He is a veritable man-mountain, oozing calm and confidence. He looks us all in the eye with absolute assurance.

Such a relief.

'I saw this sort of thing happen in a film once. Maybe *Die Hard*, or was it one of the Bournes? But the most important thing to do is *not* panic.'

His words roll over us like tumbleweed, sucking the hope from our very souls.

Feckin useless. Unbelievably shitting, effing, bollocksing useless.

Tears prickle my eyes, blurring my vision. It's not his fault he's a buffoon. 'Thank you,' I whisper, all the strength draining from my voice.

Matteo stands rigid, staring at him, opening and closing his eyes slowly and repetitively as though he is hoping to blink himself awake from this nightmare.

'I think you'd better take him with you, Tash,' barks Big Sue, taking charge. 'We need to workshop this mess.'

Big Sue towers over Liberty, while Tash yanks Sister Kevin away from the scene.

Cherry rummages through Liberty's bag and pulls out her phone. There follows an awkward few minutes, while the phone refuses to recognise Liberty's unconscious face, even though Big Sue and Big Mand are holding open her eyelids while Cherry hovers over her.

'What are we doing?' Liam frets.

'Hank Junior's phone number,' says Big Sue in answer. 'Could save us a lot of trouble. She can tell him the target has already been neutralised. He is to stand down. He needs to cease and desist.'

Of course. So simple. A wave of gratitude for quick-thinking Big Sue envelops me.

'We're in,' says Cherry, flicking quickly through Liberty's contacts, while Big Mand gently slaps her face.

'No. No. No,' mumbles Cherry. 'Christ, who's Phat-Dawg? Her contacts read like a who's who of Pornhub. There's no Hank Junior. And no recent calls made or received. He mustn't have given her his number. And no spicy pics of the two of them either. Typical hitman behaviour.'

'No wonder he didn't want to be in any of the photos,' I say, remembering the High Roller.

Liberty lets out a quiet groan and winces as she comes to, then immediately snatches her phone back. 'We didn't need to ring each other because we've barely been out of each other's sight since we met.' She rubs her head. 'And PhatDawg is my plumber, you cheeky bitch.'

'Libs, hun, where do you think Hank Junior might be?' Big Sue asks Liberty.

'He could be anywhere,' she croaks, trying to sit up. 'My ankle. I think I've twisted it.'

We let this information percolate. It is not good.

Liam is still very tearful as I walk over to him. 'I'm so sorry, Liam.' I hang my head in shame. 'It was only supposed to be a fake marriage. Something to throw Luke and Birdie off our scent.'

'She's right,' says Matteo, behind me. 'We never meant for anyone else to see us. You all seemed so busy with other things, we didn't want to hijack your special week. We just wanted to spend a bit of time getting to know each other... alone.' He sighs heavily. 'It doesn't matter now because, apparently, we're *legally* married. We've got the rest of our lives to get to know each other.' He waves the certificate around, his voice rising with each word. 'And we're also caught up in a potential murder, so what does any of it matter anyway, in the grand scheme of things?'

'So, you're saying our being married doesn't matter?' My voice comes out shrill. My eyes have overfilled again. A solitary tear spills down my cheek.

'I didn't say that,' Matteo says, annoyed.

'You did,' says Cherry. 'We all heard you.'

Suddenly there's an atmosphere between us.

'Look, the wedding is the least of our worries,' says Matteo through tight lips. 'Can we... just sort out Hank Junior first? Then we'll all sit down and talk about what to do next. But Liam, Ged, none of this was Connie's idea. It was all mine. Don't be angry with her. This ridiculous mess is all my fault. I pushed her into it.'

'Well, technically, it was my idea,' corrects Cherry.

'You didn't push me into it,' I say sharply. 'I wanted to marry you. And I thought you wanted to marry me.'

Matteo gives me an exasperated look.

'None of this is helping,' booms Big Mand as she heaves a barely mobile Liberty up and over her shoulder. 'Come on. Why don't you two give each other some space? We can point fingers later.'

'Fine, yes,' Matteo agrees, a little too readily for my liking. He is no longer holding my hand or gazing at me in a star-struck fashion.

Why does he need space? From me? We've only been married two minutes.

'And that's the forty-five minutes up,' says a man with a video camera. He smiles at Matteo. He is wearing a *'Weddings at The Venetian'* polo shirt and an amused expression. 'You can have as many stills from this footage as you like as part of the wedding package,' he explains cheerily. 'As well as footage from the onboard gondola video camera, of course. We'll email you the links, and you do it all on the website.'

We stand, stunned, as he bends to snap shut his equipment and pack it away at lightning speed. He scuttles off through the crowd with his tripod over his shoulder, as though this bizarre scene is very much his normal day-to-day experience of Vegas weddings.

'Fuck me.' Matteo rakes a hand through his hair, the other holding our wedding certificate. 'This day just keeps on giving.' He sounds exhausted with it all, and I can't blame him, but his words cut right through me.

Deep breaths.

Deep breaths.

19

'Mandeep, I'll help you carry Libs to her room,' Big Sue commands. 'Cherry, you can stay with her. This is no situation for a pregnant lady. Matteo and Connie, you'd better warn Luke what's happening, and see about getting that video evidence back. Did anyone see the photographer's name badge? Ged and Liam, we'll use your room as headquarters.'

'Roger that,' says Big Mand dutifully.

'Roger that,' says Ged. At least all this talk of being jailed for murder has snapped him out of his sulk with me. 'Although we need to make sure Franz isn't there.'

'You have a naked butler in your room even when you're not there?' asks Big Sue.

'He likes to write poetry between shifts. He's a job-bing actor-slash-model. He's very sensitive. I'd hate to subject him to this horror show.'

'I'll give Luke a call,' I say, realising for the first time that I'm still holding my bouquet. 'If I can re-member where I put my phone.'

'It's in the room,' says Matteo. 'You gave it to me before we got...' He leaves the sentence hanging. He obviously can't bring himself to say the M word.

'Right.' My hands are shaking, and my head feels heavy. I can't tell what he's thinking, only that he has a disappointed air about him. Is that for me or this situ-ation? I can feel everyone watching our stilted interac-tion. 'I'll head there now and ring him from our room,' I say quickly. I need to get out of here before it stifles me. I can't bear to see that look in Matteo's eyes a moment longer. 'I need to change anyway.'

'No time,' barks Big Sue. 'Sorry, Connie, pet. Time is of the essence here. Luke's life could depend on your finding him before Hank Junior does.'

I gulp.

Ged and Liam form plans for a search party with Big Sue and Big Mand. I listen in a sort of daze as they agree to split up and do a sweep of the casino, the re-ception and bars between them.

'I'll meet you in Ged and Liam's room,' I say. I can

hear the break in my voice. I need to keep it together. I take a deep breath in and force a smile. 'I'll What-sApp you how I get on.'

'No.' Cherry puts a hand up. 'WhatsApp is compromised. It's like giving a running report straight to the police. You might as well sling yourself in jail now and throw away the key.'

Cherry is being very dramatic, and it is not helping.

'Okay. What do you suggest?' I say sharply. 'Telepathy?'

She raises an eyebrow.

'Right. Sorry. I'm a bit... all over.' I've made a right tit of myself. I just can't believe I'm into my first hour of married life and this is what's happening. I should be having my garter twanged and a champagne toast, not trying to find a bloody killer and prevent a murder. I can't even make eye contact with any of them. Deep down, this whole Luke mess is all my fault.

'Wait,' says Matteo, striding over to me. 'I'm coming with you.'

'No. It's fine. I'll manage.'

He reaches out to gently take my arm. 'Look, I know this is all' – he blows out his cheeks – 'completely insane, but at least let me come with you, in case Hank Junior shows up for Luke.'

That's a good point, but his words about needing some space echo in my mind.

'Thought you needed space?'

'Do *you* need space?' he asks.

'I'm not the one who's furious about being married.'

'Who said anything about being furious?'

'Your face did.'

'My face told you I was furious? My *face* had a conversation with you without me knowing about it?'

He's being facetious and this is absolutely not the time. My nerves are in shreds as it is.

'Well maybe I *do* need some space, if you're going to be like that about it.'

'Like what?' Matteo shrugs his shoulders.

We're having a marital spat. *An actual marital spat.* Less than ten minutes in.

'Surely you can get it annulled if you both hate the idea so much, babes,' says Cherry. 'Didn't Britney Spears do something similar with a few of her husbands?'

'Is that what you want?' I ask Matteo, my voice paper-thin.

'Is that what *you* want?' Matteo says, glaring at me.

'For God's sake. We'll all go up to the room together and sort the MO out from there,' barks Big

Sue, heaving Liberty up from the ground. 'Mandeep, could you grab her legs, please?'

'Here, let me help,' Matteo says, taking Liberty from them and flipping her easily over his shoulder before marching towards the lifts.

As we walk solemnly along, I notice Matteo is keeping his distance, deep in thought.

We all scamper after him, tourists parting like a biblical sea to let us through.

Once we're in the lift, we have the delight of the mirrored wall casting a giant well-lit reflection. Big Mand and Big Sue are still in their Barbie outfits and wigs. I've only just noticed that Cherry is wearing silk pyjamas with cherries printed all over them. Matteo has Liberty slung over his shoulder like a passed-out drunk, her arms and hair hanging down. Ged and Liam are in a state of panic, clutching at each other. And there's me. My beautiful make-up running down my upset face. My hair dishevelled while my wedding dress remains pristine and gorgeous in stark contrast. I catch sight of my locket hanging round my neck. What would my mother make of all of this? Good job she's inside the locket and can't see my eyes full of tears and my lip wobbling. What a wedding party.

The lift stops several times, and each time people

hesitate when they get an eyeful of us and say they'll wait for the next one.

My gaze is drawn to my husband. *My husband.* Matteo has not taken his eyes off his shoes, the panel of buttons, the ceiling, since we got in the lift. It's as though he is searching for a way to fix this mess. Honestly, I don't know whether to laugh or cry.

'Nice dress, Connie,' says Cherry, quietly. 'Really pretty.'

'Yeah, babes,' says Big Mand. 'You look lovely.'

'You make a gorgeous bride, babe,' adds Big Sue. 'Don't worry. We'll get all of this sorted, Big Guy.'

Matteo blinks slowly. His face softens as he tilts his head, waiting to see how I'll react.

Big Guy. I'm going to be saddled with that unflattering moniker forever.

I don't know what it is, but it causes me to snort. I remain staring at the group through the mirror. We look a right clip. Big Sue catches my eye, causing me to smile, then I snort again.

Big Mand starts laughing. 'You couldn't make this shit up, could you?'

'At least we got to see you get married,' says Ged, calmly. 'Even if it wasn't the full Disney princess wedding we were after.' He squeezes Liam's hand and raises a smile.

I feel an instant sense of relief.

'No. No. This is exactly how I pictured my dream wedding,' I say to the mirror. 'My husband carrying another woman over his shoulder. My friends in tears, my work colleague having lost a million dollars and no doubt blaming me, and a possible prison sentence hanging over us. All we need now is for the lift to break down, or for Hank Junior to be standing outside when the doors open.'

Matteo's mouth curves slightly as he looks me dead in the eye. 'Well, you wanted a bonkers story to tell the grandkids.'

I take a beat to stare back at him.

He's letting me know we can get past this. In our very short time together, I have tested his boundaries on multiple occasions and each time he has come through for me.

I reach out to squeeze his hand. Besides, he's too handsome to stay mad at. 'Best strap in then,' I say, exhaling loudly. 'Because I doubt we'll have a shortage of those to tell.'

'And in her defence, she...' says Ged, looking at me through the mirror. I wait for him to say something encouraging to Matteo. Something to give him hope that a life with me won't be one long, fruitless string of fraught and embarrassing situations. His smile slips. 'No, sorry. I took off there without a place to land.'

Matteo rolls his eyes and, within seconds, we're all howling with crazed laughter. And then it comes to me.

The mother of all ideas.

'I've got it.' It seems easier to keep talking to the group through the mirror. 'The murder hasn't happened yet. If we keep Luke close to us, then Hank Junior can't get to him.'

'But that means spending more time with him.' Matteo doesn't sound thrilled. 'Isn't that the opposite of what we wanted to happen?'

'Only until Hank Junior can be found and this misunderstanding cleared up,' I argue. 'We keep Luke alive and no crime will be committed. And no crime means we don't go to jail.'

'Makes sense,' says Big Sue.

'Yeah. It does,' agrees Cherry.

'Roger that,' confirms Big Mand.

'Thank God,' gushes Liam. 'I'd rather have a married best friend than one on death row.'

'Let's finish this mission, make sure everyone is safe, and then we can get our pre-moon back on track,' Ged says forcefully, rolling up his frilly sleeves. 'Now, who's for a medicinal cocktail? I make a great

Skanky Lady with a twist.'

Liam is gazing adoringly at Ged as he bosses us all about.

Big Sue is beaming at them like a proud parent.

'And can someone track down Sister Kevin? It's killing me not knowing how old he is,' says Big Mand as the lift pings, and we all shuffle out towards Cherry and Liberty's room.

* * *

Once Liberty is laid on the bed, I go in search of ice for her ankle while Matteo runs to our room to get my phone, leaving the group to bicker about who should 'babysit' Luke.

I wander back through.

'He's not staying with us,' says Ged, eyeing Liam. 'We've got Franz to consider.'

'And he can't stay with us,' says Big Mand. 'Because...'

'Because you're both lesbians now?' says Cherry.

'Because we only have one bed,' says Big Sue. 'And because we don't like him.'

'Well, he's not staying here. He fancies me too much,' claims Liberty.

'Well, he can't stay with us,' I say. 'We're newlyweds.' My face flames at the thought of our first night of wedded bliss.

There's a knock at the door, causing us to jump a mile.

'I'll get it,' I say when everyone but me runs to hide in the bathroom, leaving Liberty furious and exposed on the bed. 'It'll be Matteo.'

I gingerly open the door. It's Tash and Sister Kevin. They pile in just as Matteo arrives with my phone. I take it shyly from him.

Gah! I wish we could get a few minutes alone. Away from this insanity.

'Just in time,' I say to Tash. 'We need you both to keep an eye on Luke for us.'

Tash's eyes flash. 'No. Not possible.'

'But you literally said you thought the hitman stuff was nonsense.' Cherry puts her hands on her bony hips.

'I have an idea,' says Sister Kevin.

Oh no. I squash down a wave of despair, inwardly groaning as I make eye contact with Matteo. His lips are twitching.

'We do drop-off points.' He strides over to the bureau at the side of the room and picks up a large printed sheet of the hotel and casino layout. 'We take turns throughout the night. We do two hours each and then swap. That way we keep him on the move and outfox the killer.'

'Blinking hell, Sister Kev. That's not actually a bad idea,' says Big Mand.

Tash inspects the map, handing it to me with a quizzical look. 'How are we even supposed to find our own suites on this?' she sighs.

I take it and quickly study it. The map is simply a whole jumble of lines, directions and advertisements. The Venetian is a very complex hotel with many floors and thousands of rooms.

Sister Kevin whips it from my hand. 'Allow me.' Within seconds he has located the spot we're in and pointed us in the direction we need to go for each of our rooms. 'I haven't been navigating enemy terrain for this many years without learning how to read a map,' he says, beaming at Tash.

Thank God. He's military. No wonder he was so tight-lipped about it all. He'll be off duty or some such. I breathe a sigh of relief.

Big Sue gives him a look of admiration. 'Now all we need is eyes on the target.'

'Roger that,' confirms Sister Kevin with a quick salute.

I'm just about to ask which regiment he's with when Tash answers for him.

She hangs off his beefy arm. 'He's a professional gamer,' she boasts. We take a beat. Is there such a role? 'In his spare time. Tuesday nights, mostly.'

Once again, my heart sinks. 'I'll ring Luke.'

We listen to Luke's phone go straight to voicemail.

'He's either blocked your number, is refusing to pick up or he's dead already,' says Big Mand.

I race over to the phone on the cabinet beside Liberty and ring reception.

'They might ring his room for us,' I explain. I replace the handset when, after five minutes, the number rings out.

'We're wasting time,' warns Big Sue. 'We need to split up. Connie and Matteo, you go down to reception to find Luke. Ged and Liam, you come with us to find Hank Junior.'

I see my best friends turn pale yellow and feel a stab of guilt in my stomach.

Matteo walks over to them. 'It'll be okay, guys. We'll find Luke and make sure everything is sorted out. If you see Hank, do not approach him. Ring me, and I'll come to where you are.' They are looking at him in awe. 'Do you understand? None of you approach him. It's too dangerous.'

My heart is swelling to five times its size.

* * *

Matteo and I hurry down to reception to beg, beg, beg the staff to help me.

'Wait in line, ma'am,' I'm told.

Gah!

The clock is ticking. I'm scanning the passing hordes frantically, while the never-ending queue of guests checking in seems to get longer, not shorter. I have rung Luke's number fourteen times. Still no answer.

By the time we get to the front, I'm a gibbering wreck. 'Can you tell me which room Luke, erm, Luke...' *Oh, God. What's his surname?*

The receptionist raises an eyebrow. 'I have a long line of people to check in, ma'am.'

'Try Count Nikolai of the House of Glucksburg!'

She taps the keyboard, shaking her head as though I've asked her to type in Beyoncé Giselle Knowles-Carter.

'Try Nick, Nic. Nicholas. Nicky! For Christ's sake, he's a famous opera singer! He's always on TikTok showing off!' I end up yelling at her.

She gives me a pitiful shrug.

It is clear that Luke has checked in under a pseudonym.

'Perhaps if you tell me what the urgency is?' she asks, taking in my wedding dress.

'He's disappeared! Now will you help me find him?'

She smiles serenely. 'Yes, ma'am. Lord knows people never "disappear" in this town, especially husbands. Especially *new* ones. When they've accidentally married the wrong bride.' She gives me a pointed look. 'I'll call the police for you now.'

Such unnecessary sarcasm.

'No police! No need. I'll find him myself.'

FFS.

20

'I have an idea,' says Matteo. 'This way. Follow me.'

When we arrive at the media suite, the penny drops. 'A video?'

Matteo nods. 'It's not ideal but what options have we got?'

They are only too happy to take my poor credit card from me, swipe it through their machine and settle me in front of a green screen. 'You look great,' Zonia, the camera operator, says, giving me a thumbs up.

I literally look like the bride of Dracula if she'd been recently dug up, thrown down a wind tunnel and run over by a truck several times.

'Okay. Let's do it.' My nerves are starting to get the better of me.

They count me in as the camera starts rolling.

'This is an urgent appeal for my, erm, singing partner, Luke. If you are listening, please come immediately to the...' We were in such a rush we didn't get a plan together first! 'Erm, please meet me at the love sign right now, or as soon as you can get there. Please hurry. There's something I urgently need to tell you. And it's not great. You really need to come meet me. Please. And I'm sorry you lost your million dollars, but it really wasn't my fault. And I have something even more valuable for you.'

Zonia is gaping at me in disbelief as they shout, 'Cut!' from behind the camera. 'Are you sure that's the message?'

'I'm sure.' *I mean, what's more valuable than your own life?*

In the ten minutes it takes Matteo and me to race to the love sign, over half a billion people have gathered with phones aloft to hear what the 'not great' news is that I have to tell Luke.

'It's proposal girl!' I hear them chanting. 'She's come ready to marry him!'

Feckedy feck feck feck.

'I'm not sure this was such a good idea,' says Matteo, sounding worried. He can say that again.

I really know how to make a bad situation worse.

'Too late now,' I say, craning my neck over the crowds to see if Luke has turned up.

I sweep my gaze from one side of the love sign to the other and just as I'm about to change my mind I hear, 'CONNIE! I'm here! But I don't want to talk to you!'

OMG.

Luke is such a show-off. He's using his powerful stage voice. Who needs a PA system when you've got him? And why is he emerging from the giant O of the sign? Hanging on to it with one arm and dramatically reaching out with the other. I'm sure you're not allowed to climb on it. It very clearly states that the letters are an art installation. Anyway, he's there. He's waving and yelling because he has a massive crowd of people filming him. Yes, he's nothing short of an attention-seeking missile, and yes, he's got that air of pompous entitlement, and yes, he's got a big fat tongue, but at least he's alive. The crowd parts to let us through. A zillion things are running through my mind, but when I reach him all I can manage is an exasperated smile.

'Can we have a word?' I say.

'Sorry? What was that?' he shouts, pointing to a nearby tripod on the ground. 'Can you speak up? I'm live-streaming.'

'CAN I HAVE A WORD?' I try again. I really don't want to draw any more attention to us.

He too seems a little deflated. 'That depends. Are you here to apologise for ruining my wedding? My life?'

'It wasn't your wedding. It was "a" wedding and you were only singing at it.'

He leaps down. And when he gets up from his superhero landing, he shakes his hair, sweeps his gaze across the crowd and flashes his white teeth while they film him.

It's all I can do to refrain from walking away and letting Hank Junior do his worst.

'Is this about the million dollars? Did you find the rings?' He looks as though he's trying to convince himself. 'Have you changed your mind about marrying me?'

'No, nothing like that,' I say. There's a disappointed groan from the crowd around us.

Luke looks startled. 'But you said you had something more—'

'Look. Can we go to my room and talk?'

'HO, HO!' Luke laughs maniacally, like a pantomime villain, into his camera. 'The fair maiden wants me to goeth to her chambers!'

This reunion has not gone how he expected, and now he's acting like a children's entertainer. I simply don't have time for it.

I swivel round and march away. 'Fine!' I yell. 'Deal with the hitman on your own then!'

* * *

'What do you mean someone might be coming to kill me?' Luke is saying on a loop. His voice has become a high-pitched shriek. 'I thought you were coming to tell me that you'd changed your mind. That... that... that you want me, not him.'

Infuriating.

'Why would I change my mind? I've told you so many times that we are work colleagues and nothing more.'

It's like he doesn't want to acknowledge that Matteo the Magnificent is now my legal husband. We all heard Elvis, clear as day. We are legally wed.

We are back at Ged and Liam's room for the rendezvous. I decided against my own chambers for obvious reasons. I am hungry. I am tired. I am unbelievably disappointed with how my wedding day has gone so far, and I just want Luke to accept what is happening.

'Then why would you make a video trying to win me back?' he says, almost losing it. He is sitting on the sofa and Ged, Liam, Franz and I are all standing around him. 'And why is this guy naked?'

Matteo has stepped outside to take some calls. Tash and Sister Kevin have disappeared to do some emergency tidying up for when they have to take their turn 'babysitting'. Liberty is resting her leg, and Cherry is guarding her. Big Mand and Big Sue are making their way back, having abandoned the search for Hank Junior.

I remain calm. 'I clearly stated that I had some not so great news,' I repeat through clenched teeth. 'If you'd answered your phone, then none of this would even be happening right now.'

'I beg to differ!' he shrieks. 'I often put it on silent to calm my mind. All the pinging gets on my nerves. It's WhatsApp. It's never-ending.'

'We're getting sidetracked,' I say. 'The main issue is that we need to keep you hidden until we sort out the, erm, issue.'

'Issue? ISSUE? You are saying that somewhere inside this hotel is a hitman with a contract out on me, and it's just an issue!' His eyes have gone all froggy. 'What is being done so far? Have you called the police? Interpol? The CIA? The FBI?'

'The YMCA?' Ged offers. 'The RSVP?' He and Liam have done nothing but sit quietly and stare at Luke while his meltdown unfolds, but they are growing weary.

'I said someone in this hotel might be trying to *take care* of you,' I say resignedly. 'We don't know for sure what that means exactly, but until we are, we thought it best to keep you safe.' *What's not to understand? We have been having this same conversation on repeat for an hour.*

'None of us are qualified to deal with this sort of situation but, honestly, we're all doing well not to freak out,' Ged says, trying to calm him. 'Mind, to be fair, we're not the ones with a killer on the loose. Or the ones who just lost a million dollars. Who pays an opera singer a million dollars to sing at their wedding? Was it Gaga? Was it Kim? Not J-Lo again? That veil covering her face didn't budge an inch, even when she was whacking her flowers over your head. Was it fixed to the dress?'

How is that helping?

'And the police?' frets Luke. 'I'm calling the police right now. Where's my phone?'

I had the good sense to remove it earlier when he

threatened to ring Princess Anne, King Harald of Norway, and CNN. Given Luke is a royal, and an international celebrity, presumably he's feared for his safety before now, but we need a bit of time to establish whether this is a real bona fide threat first, so that we don't get into trouble with the authorities or cause a diplomatic incident – or worse, annoy Nancy by being late for our next performance. 'Have you done this before?' I ask him.

'Done what before?' Luke flaps his hands about. 'Feared a crazy assassin is after me? Got mixed up with the wrong crowd of lunatics?' He raises his eyebrows as he sweeps his gaze to each of us. 'Unfortunately, that's something we royals always have vaguely in the back of our minds.'

'Listen. On the basis that the last place the killer will probably look for the stalker is Connie's room, I suggest that Luke stays with Connie and Matteo tonight for the first drop-off,' says Liam.

'Yes, makes sense,' agrees Ged.

'No, it doesn't,' I argue. They just want rid of him.

'Excuse me,' says Luke, his voice breaking. 'Can we circle back to the use of the words killer and stalker? What is going on here? Do you mean you know who it is?' Luke is taking in terrified gulps of air. 'Can't you explain that I'm here for work, not for stalking purposes? And FYI, I've never stalked anyone in my life.'

'Not killer. He meant the person who is going to *take care* of you, and by stalker, well, erm, that's just a loose term we gave you when you kept following me from country to country!' I'm losing my temper at it all now. 'If you'd only just listened to me in the first place, in York, we wouldn't even be in this mess, would we?'

Luke surprises us all by collapsing like a pack of cards and slips with a thud onto the floor.

'He even falls like a posh person,' remarks Ged.

'Yes, that was a real swoon, wasn't it?' adds Liam.

The door flings open. Matteo, Big Sue and Big Mand burst through the door arguing among themselves about who isn't babysitting the first shift. They stop immediately when they see Ged, Liam and me gathered around Luke's crumpled body.

'Fucking hell. We're too goddamn late! They've killed him!' yells Big Sue.

'Why haven't you hidden the body?' demands Big Mand. 'Why is it just lying there? Why are you all just gawping at it? No body, no crime. Doesn't anyone listen to podcasts?'

We all let her words hang in the air for a beat.

'Honestly, is any of this even real?' I ask the universe. 'Can someone please pinch me? Can someone shake me awake, because I've obviously been roofied and slipped into a coma?'

Matteo speeds across the room. 'Are you okay?' he asks, taking me in his arms.

'Yes, I'm fine,' I say, pointing to Luke. 'But it's been a lot for him to take in. He just fainted, that's all.'

And none of us could be bothered to catch him.

'Thank fuck,' says Big Sue. 'I wasn't looking forward to chopping that huge body up in the bath. What is he? Six three? Six four?'

'Okay,' I say. 'Let's rein it in. This is not a Hollywood blockbuster. This is a pre-moon-slash-work-trip-slash' – I half smile at Matteo – 'romantic minibreak. Everyone needs to get a grip.' I take a deep breath in. 'Big Sue, what's the ten twenty?'

'No, no, no, Big Guy,' says Big Sue with an exasperated groan. 'How many times? It's what's your twenty for where you are, or what's the ten four for what's happening. Capeesh?'

'Perhaps we could speak English while we sort out what's what?' suggests Matteo firmly. He has such an authoritative manner that we all nod obediently. 'Any news on Hank Junior?'

We shake our heads.

'We've decided you and Connie should keep Luke in your room and guard him first,' Liam informs him.

'Good idea,' agrees Big Mand.

'No. Absolutely not,' Matteo says firmly.

'But it's the last place the killer will look,' says Liam. 'And he's far too high-maintenance to stay here.'

'I think we might have to go to the police,' says Matteo.

'But what if they think we're the guilty ones for agreeing to have him "taken care of"?' Big Mand asks.

'But we didn't,' I say.

'I know, but how can we prove it? Don't the hotel have us all on video admitting exactly that?'

Matteo exhales loudly. 'Okay. Just for one night.'

'Who were you on the phone to just now?' I ask. Literally everyone is listening in.

Matteo looks me dead in the eye. 'Birdie.'

I swallow down a jealous urge. 'Oh.'

'About work.'

'Oh.'

'About her threatening to pull the plug on the deal. If she walks, the singer walks. If the singer walks, the deal with the record company falls through. It's that simple.'

'Ah. And is she okay with you now?'

'No.'

'Oh.'

I'm discovering I'm not what you call a natural conversationalist under pressure.

Just then, his phone pings. He reads the message. 'It's her. She wants to meet me.'

* * *

'Matteo just needs to sort things with Birdie,' Ged says soothingly as we walk a groggy Luke back to my room. 'She's threatened to quit in the heat of the moment. When she calms down, she'll be okay. You know what the French are like.'

All ooh-la-la and sex appeal?

We plonk Luke on the chaise longue. None of this has properly sunk in. Liam fixes him a double brandy from the minibar but ends up drinking it himself.

How could such a beautiful day end so badly?

I recap the events of today in my mind. The search party came up with nothing. It's as though Hank Junior has disappeared. He doesn't want to be found. Matteo looked so disappointed to leave but he didn't exactly put up a fight against Birdie. He never even gave me a chance to ask him to stay. He just pivoted and walked out. Walked out to where? Her room? My body shivers at the thought of him in her room. She'll do anything to get the two of them together. This might be just the catalyst she's been after. I don't trust her one bit.

How, on my wedding night, did I manage to end up sharing a room with Luke while Matteo is in a room with Birdie? How?

It pinches at my heart. I reach for my phone. No message from him.

* * *

'I wonder what time Matteo will come back.' Liam yawns, a few hours into them helping me babysit Luke. They are clearly getting bored, and all the miniatures have been drunk. 'It's just the butler... He might... need us.'

Ged is snoring, slumped face down: half on, half off the sofa. Liam shakes him awake.

'Just go,' I say, waving them towards the door. 'We'll be okay.'

Luke has not moved a muscle since we arrived. He is staring glumly into space.

'Are you sure?' checks Ged. 'We can wait.'

'I'll be fine. He'll be back any minute.' I'm not in the slightest bit sure what time he'll be back, but I really don't want to spoil Ged and Luke's pre-moon any more than is necessary. 'I'll phone Big Sue if anything happens.'

'What do you think might happen?' Luke shrieks, suddenly wide awake.

'Nothing,' I say. 'Nothing will happen.' *Please God.*

'Okay. Well, we'll leave you to it. If you're sure.' Liam is discreetly nodding towards Luke, who is slumped on the chaise longue. His face is haunted and thoroughly miserable.

'I'll be fine,' I assure them as they leave.

'I'm having a shower,' says Luke, getting up and walking over to the bathroom. 'I might as well stay in there. It'll be easier for housekeeping to mop up the blood.'

I roll my eyes. 'Whatever.'

* * *

Luke takes an age in the bathroom, so I seize the opportunity to get out of my wedding dress. It takes a few minutes to undo the tiny delicate buttons and shuffle out of it. I hang it back on its hanger. I admire the gorgeous underwear the bridal assistant advised me to get. Aside from the haggard face and messy hair, it looks stunning. I stare at my reflection. What a shame. What a waste of a wedding night. We had Caesars Palace booked and everything! I really hope I get another opportunity to show this off to Matteo. And, as if I manifested him to return to the room right this instant to see me in all my glory, the familiar beeping sound of the room key at the door indicates Matteo's arrival. I assume a sexy pose with which to greet him.

At the same time, the bathroom door opens. I instinctively scream out to Luke, 'No, don't open the door!'

But as I spin back round to see Matteo standing there, I notice a look of hurt darken his eyes.

'Too late,' he says as he watches Luke emerge from the bathroom in a towel and not much else. Matteo sees me in my underwear, shifts his gaze back to Luke, who has suddenly decided to stir things by smiling for the first time today as he looks me up and down appreciatively.

A thunderous expression crawls across Matteo's face.

'I meant for Luke not to open the door,' I explain. 'And it's not as bad as it looks.'

'It never is,' Matteo says.

'There's nothing going on,' I say quickly, grabbing my robe to cover up.

'I know. I believe you.'

'And what took you so long?'

Matteo's face colours as he crosses the room to-wards me.

'I see,' I say, feeling a pang of jealousy.

He shakes his head. 'No. Whatever you're think-ing, it's not that.'

'So, what happened?'

'After my meeting, I went to reception to see if they had another room available.'

'Oh. I see.'

He lifts my chin so that he can see my eyes. 'For us. Another room for us. I didn't want to share our wedding night with... that prick.' He nods towards Luke.

Oh.

He exhales loudly. 'But I had to wait so long in the queue that by the time I got to the front there were no rooms available anyway.'

Oh.

Matteo turns to Luke. 'Get dressed. It's someone else's turn to babysit you.'

21

I wake to the WhatsApp group buzzing with messages. We are due to go on the Grand Canyon Safari today and the group is split. It is seven o'clock in the morning. I slide my eyes over to Matteo, who is sleeping soundly next to me, and turn the volume down on my phone. I take a moment to admire the back of his silky hair, his toned shoulders, the tanned skin of his arms disappearing beneath the pillows.

LIBERTY

Forget it. I'm not going.

CHERRY

I'm popping downstairs for breakfast. Does anyone want a jam sugar donut?

BIG SUE

The Grand Canyon is one of the seven wonders of the world. Why wouldn't you go?

BIG MAND

It's eight, isn't it?

LIBERTY

Everyone knows the Grand Canyon is where they hide all the bodies.

TASH

What bodies?

LIBERTY

Bodies in general.

BIG SUE

Be specific, because it's a four-hour drive there and a four-hour drive back. Does Hank Junior have that kind of time to spare? He did say he was only in town for a few days.

BIG MAND

I'm not sure Hank would dispose of the body. Isn't that the sort of thing you ask the minions to do?

ME

Can you all stop clogging up the group chat.

CHERRY

Is it a Barbie and Ken day?

ME

Yes. We are doing the group montage and video.

TASH

How do you get pizza out of a wig?

BIG SUE

Back to the bodies.

BIG MAND

It's only one body and it's Luke.

BIG SUE

He's royalty. This could spark a diplomatic incident. A code red.

TASH

Shit. What do we do about Luke?

CHERRY

He'll have to come with us.

BIG SUE

Roger that.

Oh, God. They're right. So, that's that sorted. Matteo will not be impressed when he reads all this chat. Luke was not very gracious last night when Matteo offered to frogmarch him round to Tash and Sister Kevin's room, so I ended up going just to keep the peace. But when we got to their room, they were out. Then we tried the next babysitters on the list, Big Sue and Big Mand, and they were also out. The only person who picked up their phone was Liberty, who sounded so upset over Hank Junior that Matteo and I didn't have the heart to make her suffer Luke for the rest of the night, so we ended up bringing him back to our suite where he crashed out on the sofa. By that time it was 4 a.m., and we were all shattered, and our wedding night was ruined.

So much for the babysitting schedule.

* * *

'So, this is fun,' says Liam in a terrified voice as we all gather in the Hello Helicopter hut for a safety briefing delivered by our helicopter pilots.

'We'll be taking off at zero nine hundred hours,' one of the pilots says. 'In answer to your... many questions, make sure your wigs and Stetsons are secure. There's nothing we can do if things fly off. No, there are no parachutes on board. No, there is no free bar service. And no, I've never crashed a helicopter before.'

Everyone sags with relief.

'Just a light aircraft. But to be fair to the old girl, we did all survive. Well, nearly all of us.' The pilot gazes off into the middle distance, deep in thought. It's then I notice he only has one arm.

Gah!

Matteo and I exchange a worried glance. Things have been strained because of Luke and the lack of sleep and the lack of respect shown by the Dollz for not sticking to the agreed babysitting plan and, of course, the ruined wedding night. Thankfully, the pilots split the group in half and Luke is put in with Ged, Liam, Big Mand and Big Sue. Cherry has had to duck out because she's afraid of flying while preggers. She says she's already starting to show. She will stay in The Venetian and eat freshly baked cookies. Matteo climbs in after me and Liberty, who is wiped out, while Tash and Sister Kevin sit up front.

'This is like a dream come true,' he says. 'I never thought I'd get to do this.' He beams at Tash. 'You're truly amazing.'

'I know,' she says, giving him a bashful flick of her lashes as she pats his leg.

Before we know it, we are lifting off the ground. The noise of the rotors is deafening. We can only hear the sound of the pilot in our ears as he gives us a running commentary on what we are about to see below. He has had to tell Tash and Sister Kevin several times, before take-off, to stop mauling each other's faces off. He is finding it very distracting, and it is causing some concern for the rest of us. We would prefer the pilot to keep his eyes on the skies and not on Sister Kevin's hand sliding up and down Tash's thigh.

We focus on the view and our jaws drop as the helicopter flies over Las Vegas. We see all of the iconic features and grand hotels haphazardly clumped together in a blaze of spectacular colour. The city is huge but when we reach the outer rim and see the vast desert, we realise how dwarfed it is in comparison, and how isolated. We see the main highway heading out of the city, busy with cars. It is breathtaking. I've never seen anything like this in my life. Matteo and I are huddled as close as you can get. We all keep making eye contact and pointing at stuff, trying to relay how amazing the sight is, but the underlying insanity of yesterday's events is weighing heavily on us and we all look shattered. I'm trying to keep a smile on my face for everyone's sake and it is making my cheeks ache.

When we land, I realise that the real journey is only just beginning. This is my first day as Matteo's wife. He is my husband. Is this the beginning of something or the end?

Big Mand and Big Sue have wandered hand in hand over to the edge of the canyon further down from us with Tash and Sister Kevin. While Ged and Liam are busy doing selfies, Matteo pulls me to the edge away from the group.

'Are you okay?' he asks me.

'Not really, no,' I say truthfully. 'I'm gutted that between Birdie and Luke, we didn't get to... you know.' I feel the heat rise to my cheeks. Matteo cups my face.

'I'm working on it.' He's just about to kiss me when we are interrupted by the pilot yelling for us to gather round.

He introduces us to our tour guide for the day, Bran. The day is very structured, and it is crucial we stick to the plan.

Good luck with that.

'We'll start with the Sky Walk, on the Southern Rim.'

A small snigger escapes from Liberty. She recovered from her huge fainting session and sprained ankle debacle and when she realised that she'd missed her date with Hank and that she'd have no way of contacting him, she fell into a deep sleep until this morning. She has woken looking fresh and fabulous.

'Rimming isn't for everyone,' Bran warns.

Tash giggles. 'Speak for yourself.'

'Ma'am. If you don't mind, the Rim is quite a dangerous albeit spectacular place, and you don't want to ruin the experience for yourself or others.'

'Amen,' barks Sister Kevin, and none of us can hold the guffaws in any longer.

We are going to be *that* group.

Bran rolls his eyes, the humour passing him by, or maybe he has heard the jokes a million times before. 'If anyone has a fear of rimming, DO NOT be sick over the edge. DO NOT try to go back the way you came. Simply continue in the same direction until you are back on solid ground.'

'Does anyone here have a fear of RIMMING?' barks Big Sue in a jokey fashion. 'A fear of RIMMING, anyone?' She winks at Ged and Liam.

They pretend to be aghast.

I'm so relieved things are back to normal with them.

The guide does not, repeat, does *not*, appreciate the British sense of humour. Even Luke is trying to relax into it. I've noticed he is regarding everyone suspiciously and sticking to Liberty like glue as though she is a mobster's moll and will defend his life when her shady boyfriend shows up to shoot him.

A while later, we are staring into a giant abyss. The view is spectacular. The atmosphere is otherworldly. It's a truly spiritual, moving experience. Matteo is standing next to me almost in a trance as he soaks in the majestic wonder of the rocks, the sculptured formations. The impossible size of it all. This is one of those moments that I'll never ever forget. It's almost sensory overload; my brain can barely comprehend everything that is going on. And here I am, sharing it with my husband. I really need to stop calling him that in my mind. He will probably want an annulment. The thought of being married to him for real fills me with joy, though. Which is ridiculous, I know. But the heart wants what the heart wants, as they say. I take a sneaky peek at him. His near-perfect profile, impossibly handsome and lost in thought. His slim, athletic body and strong, toned arms as he leans casually on the rail of the wooden and steel bridge.

'Rimming isn't half as bad as I imagined,' I whisper to him, causing him to snort out loud. His eyes are sparkling with laughter as colour rushes to his cheeks. 'Is it everything you hoped it would be?' I say, giving him a wide-eyed look of innocence.

'Stop,' he says, barely keeping it together. After a beat, he replies, 'You don't seem the rimming type.'

Now it's my turn to blush. Heat rises up my neck. 'What type do you think I am?' Electricity crackles between us. What a conversation to be having, dangling four thousand feet over a sheer drop into the Grand Canyon on less than three hours' sleep.

Matteo's eyes grow dark as he steps towards me. I feel the heat emanate from him as our bodies make contact, causing my heart to beat slightly faster. His hair, caught in the breeze, is falling across his forehead. I have a sudden urge to run my fingers through it, grab hold of it and pull him towards my lips. 'The marrying type,' he says. There's no hint of mockery in his voice whatsoever.

I feel weak at the knees. My legs are going to go.

'Move it along, lovebirds,' bellows Bran. 'We need to be at the Mule Station in twenty minutes.'

I have a million questions to ask. They are all the same version of *what happens now?*

Matteo smiles at me. It lights up his whole face. He has a quiet confidence about him, an intelligent, curious expression ever-present in his eyes. He thinks this whole marriage, this whole trip, is bonkers because he's sane and normal and lovely. I must try to reflect that in my own behaviour.

Luke catches up to me while we are being paired up with our horses for the next part of the safari. We are trekking across the forest area to the east of the canyon. A minibus ferried us to a huge hunting-lodge-style wooden motel-slash-café-slash-gift-shop-slash-excursion pit stop.

'I'm sorry,' he says with a pained expression. 'I'm sorry I came here. I realise now it was a mistake.' He scrubs a hand over his face with a sigh. 'A big fucking mistake.'

'What do you mean?'

'I knew you were coming to Las Vegas and I took the job on purpose.' Luke stares down at the ground. 'That was so wrong of me.'

'We all make mistakes,' I say bluntly. I don't want

Matteo to see us talking. Not when he's so pissed off with Luke. 'Forgive yourself and move on.'

'Help me make it right,' he says, his voice losing its usual power, his eyes pleading. 'I'll do anything. I don't want to die. You have to call the hit off.'

'Sssshhh,' I say quickly. 'And I did not put a hit out on you. Jesus. It was an accident. Not even mine. It was... It doesn't matter whose fault it was. We'll sort it. Just try and stay out of my way.' We both happen to notice Matteo throwing a hard look Luke's way.

'I get it. I'll book myself on to the first flight out of here,' he says in earnest. 'I promise. I'll never pursue this again. I got carried away by my feelings for you, but I can see that you and him...' He indicates Matteo. 'Well, you're married to someone else so that's that. But I hope this hasn't put you off working with me again.'

He stands, hands in shorts, peering at the ground.

'To be honest, it has. We absolutely can't work together. I'm going to resign from the Sinfonia when I get back. I'm sure I'll get a chance to sing with another orchestra. Our last tour wasn't such a disaster. They might still give me a good reference.'

Crestfallen, he puffs out a long breath. 'I'm sorry. If anyone should resign, it's me. I've been a spoiled, over-privileged brat all my life. It's time I grew up and took responsibility for it.' He puts a hand to his breastbone. 'Please forgive me.'

A quick dip of his head and he's gone. I see him move to the front of the queue. He leans towards Liberty and the two remain deep in conversation. She throws me a half-smile when he's finished and gives me a thumbs up. Our troubles are nearly over.

A movement at my side causes me to turn. Matteo is astride a horse, feet in stirrups, muscular thighs gripping the flanks, strong hands holding the reins, a moody gleam in his eyes. *Jesus wept.* Could he be any sexier?

'Ready?'

Under his watchful gaze, I make a haphazard mess of trying to mount my steed. I'm burning with embarrassment when he slides easily from his horse and walks it over to help me. He ties it to the wooden rail and saunters towards me.

'May I?'

'You may.'

We've been here before. Matteo holds me steady while I grab hold of the saddle and hook my ridiculous sandal in the stirrup. He is standing very close behind me, his hands gripping my waist. I'm going to positively evaporate if his hands go any lower or higher.

'What was all that about?' he says in a low voice. 'Was he bothering you?'

I shake my head. 'The opposite.'

Matteo gives me a quizzical look.

'He's going to get on the first flight out of here tonight. He's going to resign from the Sinfonia.'

I swish my ponytail from my neck, exposing it to him. I bite my lower lip enticingly and blink slowly at him. It's as though a spark has been ignited.

'Please don't,' he says in a low groan that only I can hear. His eyes skim my body. I'm wearing tiny Barbie hot pants and a bra top. With one fluid move, he hoists me up onto my steed.

I watch him mount his own and pull it round to my side.

'Okay then. One down, one to go,' I say, smiling at him. 'We might just get a night to ourselves after all.'

'I can't wait,' he says, smiling at me. 'I'll try to make another reservation for Caesars Palace.'

His phone buzzes.

My chest tightens as he pulls it out of his pocket.

He throws his head up to the sky with a sigh. 'Birdie suddenly has another job offer. She's leaving tonight.'

'But that's great, isn't it?'

'It means we need to bring the completion date

forward for the record we're working on. She wants me to go back to LA with her to finish it.'

'She wants you to leave tonight?' My whole stomach drops. 'That's so out of order.'

'Either I leave with her or she pulls the plug on the whole deal.'

22

Not that I'm thinking with my loins, but we'll not get to consummate our marriage, and that annulment is looking easier and easier to obtain. Nor is that the most critical issue of the day. Obviously, Matteo pursuing his lifelong dream to produce a global smash hit for one of the world's most successful pop stars is very important. While the threat of Luke being murdered by accident and us all going to jail for it is still an issue very much hovering on the periphery of my mind. But still, I can't help feeling gutted that my gorgeous wedding dress and beautifully crafted underwear have gone completely to waste.

'You're going?' I say. I can't believe it. 'You're just

going to do what she tells you, the moment she snaps her fingers?'

This outburst coming from a chronic wimp.

I see his face harden. 'I hardly have a choice.' He reaches down to pat his horse, the atmosphere between us suddenly tense. 'I have people depending on me.' He applies pressure to the horse with his legs and canters away from me.

I throw my head back and groan with frustration. I remain at the back of the horse trail. I should be admiring the gorgeous view but instead my eyes are glued to the back of Matteo. What does this mean for us as a couple if Matteo always jumps to it when Birdie snaps her fingers? If this deal is a success, will other artists expect him and Birdie to be the dream team they hire, always as a pair? If so, will we never be free of Birdie?

'Admiring the gorgeous view, are you, pet?' Tash cackles. She is riding her horse with knee-high socks on. Her high heels are hanging from the saddle.

'Something like that,' I say.

'I feel like this has been such a spiritual journey,' says Tash, not picking up on my flat, depressed tone. 'It's made me totally rethink my decision to have baby Vegas outside of wedlock. Seeing how happy you and

Matteo are together. It's made me hanker after a huge fairy-tale wedding instead. A proper one. Not like your quickie accidental one. No offence, like.' She stares off into space. 'I want a big fuck-off Jennifer Lopez meets *Bridgerton* meets the Kardashians wedding with sweeping staircases and golden thrones aplenty.' She flutters her eyes at Sister Kevin.

He's so big, they've given him a very short but wide load-bearing mule. His feet are only inches above the ground. He's yelling 'Yeehaw!' and waving his pink Stetson like a cowboy.

'When you know you know,' she says, cantering off to catch up with him.

It's lovely to see Big Sue and Big Mand behaving like love-struck teens when they think no one is looking. They've barely spoken to any of us. A softness has consumed them. Even the way they walk and hold themselves seems different. They only have eyes for each other, their foreheads always touching. You'd think they'd only just met. I observe them riding side by side, gazing at one another, silly grins on their faces, laughing at private jokes and taking *every* opportunity to touch the other's arm or face or leg.

I see Matteo up ahead, avoiding me. We have only a few days left of our minibreak and, so far, it has been nothing short of a romantic shambles. Ged rides alongside him. I wish I could hear what they are talking about. Matteo is smiling at Ged and thanking him for something. Then Ged's face is looking horrified. Then Matteo looks awkward. Then Ged does a fifty-point turn on his horse and almost gallops towards me.

'He's leaving you?' he yells at me as he overshoots by a few yards and, as I twist in my seat, I can see him pulling on the reins to get the horse to stop and turn around. He pulls up alongside me all flustered. 'I welcome him to the family. Which was very big of me considering the trick marriage throwing shade on my own nuptials. But anyway, I welcome him to our little family, I invite him for drinks, just you, him and us to celebrate your nuptials, and he tells me he has to leave. For work! On your honeymoon! It's not on, babe. It's not on. I'm seething.'

Ged sets off a chain reaction. Seconds later, everyone is fuming.

'Hey, Libs, Matteo is abandoning Connie on her honeymoon!' bellows Tash down the line.

'What? That's outrageous!' Liberty shouts back. Her voice echoes around the canyon perimeter.

'Totally out of fucking order, pet. Isn't it, Sue?' barks Big Mand.

'Abso-fucking-lutely. Who jilts their bride the day after they get married?' Big Sue is livid.

'He's deserting her in her hour of need, Mandeep,' Ged says. 'Did those Elvis lyrics mean nothing?' His voice is a high-pitched squeal that releases birds from the trees around us.

'It isn't our honeymoon,' I try to argue. Gawd, this is excruciating. 'He has to work. Just like we do.'

Matteo is trying his best to twist round on his horse to defend himself, but it is nigh-on impossible to control these beasts. 'I'm not abandoning her! I'm securing a hugely important business deal. For our future together and—'

'That doesn't matter,' Tash cuts him off. 'Connie. Today is the first day of your honeymoon, and Matteo is leaving you. End of. Who does that?'

Matteo has fallen foul of the entire group. They haven't given him a chance to explain.

'He's worse than Luke!' bellows Liberty. She is incensed. 'Men. You're all fucking useless!'

Luke has the good grace to avert his gaze.

The trip back through the ancient forest, overlooking thousands of years' worth of volcanic erosion and natural wonder, is atmospheric and spiritual and emotive for all the wrong reasons. Matteo seems desperate to press on ahead, but Bran, the guide, who has the obvious hump, says we must all stick together and stop bickering so loudly because we are ruining the glorious experience for other groups of hikers and travellers.

The day has ended in another disaster. Typical.

When we reach the helipad to go back to Vegas via the Hoover Dam, the girls forcefully insist we are put in one helicopter and all the men in the other, so that we don't get contaminated with masculine toxicity. It's like a bad dream as I gaze forlornly out of the window at miles upon miles upon miles of mindblowing mountainous rock.

* * *

When we finally arrive back at the hotel, Liberty is restless. Because she missed her dinner date, she has no idea how to contact Hank Junior to sort out the mess.

'Fuck it. I'm going on a gambling rampage,' she says, looking like an angry Barbie doll. 'I'll ring Cherry and find out where she is.'

'Well, me and Kev will join you. I'm in the mood to let off some steam,' says Tash, her arm around his neck.

'We'll come,' says Big Mand. 'I could do with a loosener. Sue?'

'Christ, yes. Feels like all we've done since we got here is work and take care of people.'

She's not entirely wrong.

'We'll probably chill for a few at the private cabana,' adds Liam, taking Ged's hand lovingly. 'It's been such a tiring day. And we don't like to leave Franz on his own for too long. He's written us a poem and he's looking forward to giving us a couples massage. We'll try to meet you in the casino before dinner.'

'Okay, then,' says Luke awkwardly. 'I guess this is goodbye. I'd best go before someone... you know... tries to kill me.'

I try to hide my surprise. It is clear that everyone thought he'd left already.

'Good luck,' says Liberty, at least trying to sound genuine. 'I'm sure everything will be fine. Now I think about it, I'm 100 per cent sure Hank Junior was joking.'

We all take a beat.

'Probably,' she says. 'I was just trying to make you feel better.'

Luke seems about to cry.

'Good luck,' I say, feeling a tiny bit sorry for him.

'Luke,' says Matteo, approaching the group. 'I've arranged for the concierge to have all of your belongings packed and waiting in the car for you. It'll take ten minutes. Just wait at reception with this.'

Matteo hands him a receipt. Luke tries to shake his hand, but Matteo isn't interested.

'I'm sorry for all of the upset,' Luke says to him. 'I truly am.'

We watch him scurry to the check-out desk, waving his piece of paper. He can't wait to get away.

'That was nice,' I say to Matteo.

'Don't speak to him!' bellows Tash. 'You need to make him suffer before you forgive him.'

Matteo's lips form a tight line. He seems at the end of his tether. Poor man.

Thankfully, Sister Kevin pulls Tash away. 'Catch you later, man.' The two men exchange raised brows.

Liberty, Big Sue and Big Mand follow them over to the lifts.

'And that's our cue to leave too,' says Ged. 'Coming, Connie?'

I blink a few times because my eyes are glassy. Is this goodbye?

Matteo holds my gaze. 'Can we at least talk before I go?'

'I think you've said enough,' says Liam, coming

over to put his arm around my shoulders. 'How dare you hurt our best friend? Our best woman. Our beautiful lost soul. How dare you crush her like this?'

That's a bit much, but Liam is very dramatic under stress.

'It's fine,' I say to him. 'It's fine. We need to sort things out. I'll see you guys later. I'll come up to the pool. I need to sort out the logistics for the birthday gig tomorrow. It's somewhere up on that floor.'

Hearing me sound normal and back to my efficient self helps me convince them that I'll be okay, when inside I have melted into a pool of mush. My pulse is racing, and not in a good way. I'm hot, sticky and desperate to get this conversation with Matteo over with. He has chosen work over me. It should be relatively short.

We make our way to the lifts along with crowds of new tourists with their suitcases and pull-along bags. A heaviness settles over us, laced with disappointment. This magical minibreak has taken a very wrong turn, and I have no idea how to fix it. I stand in a numb trance staring forward until we reach our floor. There's only Matteo and me getting out. We walk the corridors in silence, navigating each bend as though we know them well, until we reach our room. Matteo whips out his key and holds open the door for me.

'Wait,' he says, reaching out his hand to gently thumb away a tear from my cheek. My eyes have pooled with tears. Matteo can barely hold my gaze. I know this is tearing him up too.

'I'm fine. I'm fine.' I sniff, stopping in the doorway to face him. 'I think I'll go to the doctor's when I get back. There's something very overactive about my tear ducts.'

Matteo half smiles. He reaches up to smooth away strands of stray wig hair. 'I wish things could've been different.'

'Me too.'

We go inside and stand at the picture window. Floor-to-ceiling glass affords a stunning view over Las Vegas. The twinkling lights, the water fountains, the taxis and limos gridlocked on the Strip. The towering hotels, windows glistening in the bright sunshine. Everything about this place screams 'have a fabulous and unforgettable time'.

'I understand,' I tell him. 'I completely understand why you have to go. And why' – I drop my gaze to the floor – 'and why we have to annul this marriage.' I swallow a lump in my throat and will away the rest of the tears threatening to fall. I'm a grown-ass woman. I can deal with this head-on. 'We can't possibly stay married. That would be insane. I'll get on to it as soon as I've finalised the birthday bash for Eddie at Talent Star.'

'Wait. You're doing something for Eddie?'

'Yes,' I say. 'You've heard of him?'

'Who hasn't heard of him?' Matteo drums his fingers against his thigh while he stares back out of the window. 'That's a huge deal. Well done. He only books the best.'

My heart lifts at his words.

'Connie. About the wedding,' Matteo says, stepping closer. 'I meant what I said.'

I close my eyes and send a silent prayer out into the universe.

'Please don't play me like a fool,' I say. 'You can be honest with me. I don't need you to spare my feelings. Just because we promised to cherish one another, no matter what comes our way, with a love that's tender and true. A promise to stay honest and faithful when times get hard and confusing.'

Matteo is admiring of my excellent memory.

'I had to learn a lot of lines very quickly for the Sinfonia. It's greatly improved my memory for lyrics,' I explain.

'What else did we promise each other?'

'Well,' I say, biting my bottom lip. 'You promised to never leave me in Heartbreak Hotel. Or to have a suspicious mind. You also promised to love me tender, and love me sweet, and to never let me go.'

The words hang in the air. It's almost as though Elvis knew what was coming our way.

Matteo takes my hand. 'I'm not abandoning you. And I meant everything I said. Yesterday was one of the happiest moments of my life. Second only to being handcuffed on stage with you at that music festival and listening to that song you wrote.'

I clear my throat. 'The song that definitely wasn't about you?'

'Yes. The song you wrote that was called "Matteo, I Love Everything About You". The one that definitely wasn't about me.'

'Uh-huh.' That was excruciatingly embarrassing. It was a masterclass in oversharing.

Matteo lifts my chin, forcing me to lose myself in his dark swirls. He blinks slowly, his lashes sweeping his eyes clear. Seeing me upset is killing him. His emotions are written all over his face.

'I'm in love with you, Connie.' His words explode in my brain like fireworks, lighting up my entire body from within. 'I'm just a hunk, a hunk of burning love for you.'

A giggle escapes my lips. I arch towards him, my head tipping back, lips parted and plumped for action. Just as I'm about to tell him that I love him too, there's a thumping on the door.

'Ignore it,' he says.

'What if it's the killer?'

'Definitely ignore it then.'

The thumping grows more insistent. 'Matteo? *C'est moi, Birdie. J'ai besoin de te voir. C'est urgent.*'

23

Matteo opens the door to an anxious-looking Birdie. She spots me immediately and leans forward to whisper in his ear.

'What? How did that happen?' Matteo says loudly in a strained voice, stepping away from her. 'I don't understand. Can't they get around it somehow?'

Birdie shakes her head. Her usual cool exterior and nonchalant poise have deserted her.

'Have you tried talking to him?'

Again, she shakes her head. 'He's on the plane. He wants to see us as soon as he lands.'

'And the investors?'

'Furious.'

Matteo rakes his hand through his hair as he swivels back towards her. I see his lips pressed tightly together, his eyes dull. It must be bad, whatever she said. Matteo links his hands together, resting them on the crest of his head as he groans loudly. 'Fuuuuuuuuck.'

'I don't know what to do,' Birdie says, putting a hand to her throat. 'I thought they were okay with it.' She huffs. 'I should have stayed with them at the studio.'

Matteo moves his hands to his pockets. 'Yes, you should have. Instead of following me here on some wild goose chase. And trying to cause trouble between me and my wife.'

Nobody could have prepared me for the jolt of feeling that swooshes through me at the sound of Matteo calling me his wife. Birdie studies me for a second, and even from the far side of the room I can see her face go red. Matteo sounds really annoyed with her. Part of me is secretly very pleased and I'm loving how he is standing up to her. She's nothing but a bully, at the end of the day.

'What time does he land?' he asks forcefully.

Birdie checks her phone. 'One hour.'

Matteo walks towards me. Birdie hovers by the door because no one has invited her in.

'Does this mean you're not leaving today?' I whisper as he reaches me.

He shakes his head. 'Doesn't look like it.'

I half smile.

He half smiles back, his face hidden from Birdie.

Our eyes have a short conversation.

Mine are saying, *Yippee. I'll see you later and perhaps we can pick up where we left off. You saying you love me, and me saying it back because I didn't get the chance to before.*

His are saying, *I'll spend my entire life making up for all of this and I'll adore you for the rest of time.* Probably. Whatever is going through his head, it has brought a sparkle to his eyes.

'Good luck,' I say, reaching for his fingers, aware our every move is being monitored. 'See you later?'

He blinks slowly, a genuine smile spreading across his face, lighting it up. He raises my fingers to his lips and stares at the wedding ring he placed there, before dipping his head to place a light kiss on it. 'Don't take it off. We have a lot of unfinished business, Cenicienta.'

His words send a shiver of excitement up my spine as I watch him walk out the door with that annoyingly sexy but firmly rejected French floozy. A smile spreads across my face from ear to ear.

Matteo. Is. In. Love. With. Me.

* * *

The moment they have gone, I race over to the bureau. It is adjacent to the picture window, overlooking the city. My heart is bursting, my pulse is racing, and song lyrics are zipping around my brain like electric sparks. I need to get them out before my head explodes. Matteo and I have been given a glorious second chance to get this right and, this time, I'm determined not to let anything, or anyone, get in the way.

I rip off my wig, kick off my ridiculous skyscraper sandals and tiny Barbie outfit and sling on a hotel silky dressing gown so that I might give in to this overwhelming desire to express my thoughts and feelings.

What seems like seconds later, I am opening a notepad full of scribbles and lyrics. I'm banging out a beat with the pencil, but I need more. I need a piano. Think. Think. That's it! The Cocktail Hour. Jumping up, I race over to the wardrobe to grab some clothes. I pull on some joggers and immediately spot one of Matteo's sweaters. Slipping it over my head, I breathe in the manly scent of bergamot and woody spice. Perfect. I hurriedly lace up my sneakers, grab the notepaper and room key and head out into the corridor.

I'm passing by Liberty and Cherry's room when Cherry bursts out of the door cackling with laughter, stumbling into the corridor. She is dressed to kill. Her flaming-red hair is silky and salon fresh. It contrasts perfectly with her green silk baggy trousers and bra top.

'Cherry, wait for me, man,' Liberty is yelling from the room.

'No time! I've missed five fucking days' worth and I'm going to friggin' well make up for it. Ooh, look. Connie's here!' Cherry launches herself at me in a cloud of tequila fumes.

Liberty pokes her head round the door. 'You better come in.'

Gah! I'm in the throes of being a musical genius!

'I'd love to but Matteo... He just said he loves me!'

'Okay. That's lovely. Let's celebrate,' says Liberty.

Cherry grabs my arm. 'No, she's coming with me. We'll celebrate downstairs.'

'No,' says Liberty, grabbing my other arm. 'We're all going to go back in the room until we discuss this like adults. What did you say when he said he loves you?'

There's so much tugging and pulling that none of us notice the door sliding quietly shut.

'Don't worry.' Liberty holds out her hand, palm up. 'Cherry, where's your key?'

'What key?'

'The room key.'

'I don't need one. I'm going out all night to gamble and drink irresponsibly.'

'But why?' I intervene. 'You shouldn't be drinking in your' – my eyes flick to her belly. It still looks swollen. Like she's swallowed a netball – 'in your delicate condition.'

'I'm not preggers!' she yells. 'I got my period! Total bloodbath. Absolutely everywhere. Never been so relieved in all my life. It must have been the stress of thinking I was preggers making it late. I'm just so effing gutted that I've missed out on all that free booze. And look at the size of this.' She points to her belly. 'It's all sugar but it'll melt with the booze.'

'Congratulations,' I say. 'Why don't you two sort out your room key at reception while I go sort things for tomorrow's show at Eddie from Talent Star's birthday bash?'

'Fuck that. I've missed out on nearly everything. I'm gonna be binge-drinking and doing all the things.

Doubt I'll have time for that freebie show. Eddie can shove it.'

Liberty visibly swallows. 'She'll be fine after she's had a messy one tonight. No worries.'

'And you're coming with me.' Cherry stabs Liberty in the chest with a pointy talon. 'To cheer you up. She's devastated Hank Junior hasn't tried to find her,' she tells me.

'And that he could be a hitman?' I add.

'No. Just that he's done a runner. Like all the rest. It's so sad, pet. Let's find a new cowboy for you. One with a real trash-tache.'

Liberty looks genuinely forlorn. 'I really liked him.'

'Sorry,' I say, rubbing her arm. 'I'll meet you guys later. I just have to do this... erm, thing.'

I'm not two steps from the lift when they ping open and Big Mand and Big Sue clamber out, weighed down with bags. Big white paper bags with gold rope handles that I recognise. They immediately try to hide them.

'Shopping. For costumes,' says Big Mand too quickly.

'Oh, yeah?' I really want to pry but I'm in a rush myself so I'm going to have to let it go. 'Can't wait to see them,' I say, jumping in the lift just as the doors are closing.

Big Sue yells at me. 'We can't make the birthday bash tomorrow, sorry!'

And the doors close.

WTF!

Ping. The doors open and Tash and Sister Kevin are waiting in the foyer. 'There she is! I've been messaging you all afternoon,' she says.

'Sorry. My phone's been off. And by the way, Matteo says he loves me. What's up with you two?'

Tash, hanging from Sister Kevin's arm, beams at me. 'We're going to see Celine Dion at the Bellagio. She's doing a one-off performance tomorrow night and Kev won us tickets at the craps table,' she squeals. 'He had to lose eight hundred dollars first but then he hit the jackpot with these tickets!'

'Wait. Tomorrow evening? But we're working tomorrow, at the birthday bash as a favour for Nancy, remember? And then it's the last night of Ged and Liam's premoon.' She'll never squeeze in the Celine Dion concert.

Tash's face falls. 'It's okay. It's fine.'

Phew. Tash is the lead vocalist. She's far too professional to drop the Dollz in it like that. Thank God.

'You can do the birthday bash without me. No one

will notice I'm missing. And Matteo loves you? That's so cute, babes.'

Gah!

* * *

It doesn't take me long to locate the Cocktail Hour bar or the grand piano that sits in the darkened corner. I'm not even going to ask anybody if I can play it because there's no one around. The bar doesn't open for another hour. I sit down and take a deep breath in. I take a deep sniff of his scent on the sweater and let images of Matteo swirl around inside my head until I feel the endorphins flooding my brain and my insides vibrating with excitement. Keeping my eyes closed, I put my fingers on the piano keys and start to play. Goosebumps cover my arms at the sound of my voice, the raw emotion mixed with the heady rush of adrenaline. As my voice grows, so does my confidence in these lyrics. Every now and then, I stop to adjust the key or scribble a new line down or change the tempo slightly before picking up where I left off.

This has to be the easiest song I've ever written. I feel light-headed with euphoria. Once I've cracked it, I check the time. I have ten minutes left to record.

'Sorry, ma'am. You can't be in here,' says a waiter. 'Staff only.'

'But I am staff. Kind of. I'm the entertainment. The singer from England,' I say pleadingly. 'I just need ten minutes to finish rehearsing.'

He tilts his head and studies me. 'Proposal woman?'

'Yes.' I sigh.

'Knock yourself out,' he says, grinning. 'By the way, we were all rooting for the other fella. The hot Latino one, not the posh show-off one.'

'Me too.' I giggle.

'Mind if I stay and listen?' he asks. 'While I set up the tables?'

Yikes. An audience so soon? 'Well, I only just wrote it. I was just sort of practising really.' My nerves have just plummeted through the floor, down through the layers of rock to the earth's core. Such is the sensitive nature of a creative's confidence.

'I promise, you won't even realise I'm here,' he says, wiping down the tables.

I swallow a lump in my throat. I guess he is doing me a favour instead of throwing me out. I will simply keep my eyes closed and pretend he's not here. 'Yep. Sure. No problem.'

'What's it called?'

'"Matteo the Magnificent, Volume One".'

I shrug.

I prop my phone up on the piano, press record and spread my fingers across the keys, ready to go. My wedding ring twinkles in the solitary light swinging above the piano. I take a beat to admire it. The smoothness of the shape. The contrast of the platinum band against the raised gold running round the middle. A warmth spreads through my body as I cast my mind back to Matteo sliding it on my finger, his eyes not leaving mine. I hear Elvis's words echo round my brain as though he is standing in front of me. 'The ring is only a symbol. It shows the world that you belong to someone, just as they belong to your heart. But as you wear them, it's your care, devotion, and concern for one another that are the true signs of your love.'

I play the opening chords and hear the shy sound of my voice lifting the words, teasing them out, releasing them into the world. I forget all about the waiter listening. Just like with the Sinfonia, I'm at my best when I completely let go and exist only in the moment. Flashes of me on stage push me to reach for those higher notes, stretching them, controlling them with precision.

By the time the second verse and chorus come

around, I am belting out this tune for all it's worth. It seems to take on a new life, a new fire. My eyes are clamped shut and all I can hear is my own breath as my fingers crash down on to the piano keys. I am no longer in full control. All of the tension of the past few days rushes from my body. All of the gruelling practice I put in for the opera tour is paying off big time. All the sexy and sass taught to me by the Dollz has given me an edge. A perfect melting pot of my singing experience to date.

I AM ON FIRE.

When I finish the song on the haunting melody that I began with, I am breathless. I hear the waiter slow clapping. He is joined by a few more people clapping. *Gah!* My eyes spring open.

The waiter is beaming. Next to him, Matteo is standing watching me. He gives me a long, burning look before he strides across the room and pulls me into a passionate kiss. 'Connie,' he says in a hoarse voice when we break free. 'That was... magnificent.'

I immediately blush. He's already guessed half the song title.

'You wrote that?'

I nod.

'Just now?'

'Uh-huh.'

'Wow.'

I blush even deeper. 'What are you doing here?'

'We were on our way to the recording studio when I heard you singing.' Matteo points to a security team at the bar entrance and Birdie staring at me with a stunned expression on her face. My chest is pounding as I'm rooted to the piano stool. 'You have a really powerful voice. It carries. Like a really long way.'

'Blame the Sinfonia,' I say. 'Was it too powerful?' I'm desperate for more praise.

'No. Not at all. It was perfect. What's it called?'

Busted.

My face is a raging furnace.

Matteo laughs. 'I see.' He rubs his face. 'Oh, man. I will never tire of this.'

A screaming mob of women start harassing the security team to get to whoever they are protecting. Birdie makes a frustrated gargling sound.

'Sorry I can't stay. Send me the video. Who knew my kisses fizz like champagne?' He leans over to place a light kiss on my lips. 'You're right. They do.'

Glittery tingles race through my veins.

'By the way,' he says over his shoulder as he follows Birdie back out of the bar, 'the sweater looks great on you.'

24

The next morning brings a whole new challenge. Matteo kept texting me all night but failed to make it back, which was very disappointing. Whoever he and Birdie are working with is sure working them hard. Must be a right perfectionist. I have heard nothing from the Dollz since they all dropped out of today's gig. Nothing from Luke so fingers crossed he must have made it on to the plane. I race down to the breakfast meet point. Ged and Liam seem very smug. There's something fresh and wholesome about them. They look like they have been in a spa for the last three years.

'OMG,' I say, flabbergasted. 'You're not yellow. It finally faded.'

Liam smiles at me. 'Thanks to Matteo.' Liam launches into this whole story of how Matteo organised a beauty therapist to come and paint them purple last night. Apparently, it has neutralised the yellow tone and turned them back to their normal colour. 'Then we had the whole works.'

'The full VIP Detox, Deflate and Diminish package,' Ged gushes. 'I've never felt so energised.'

'I thought you'd cast Matteo out of the family into the dark abyss?' I remind them. 'On account of him having to save his company from ruin to secure the jobs of his poor staff whose livelihoods were hanging in the balance?'

'We were only defending your honour,' says Liam sheepishly. 'But when we stopped to think about it, Matteo was really stuck between a rock and a hard place, wasn't he?'

I nod.

'He's very thoughtful. I'll give him that,' says Ged. 'When I asked about Luke, he told me he'd taken care of everything to see him safely on the plane, so unless Hank Junior has contacts in the UK, he'll survive this ordeal.'

'He told you that? When?'

Ged makes a big deal of searching his memory. So much must have happened since yesterday evening.

'Yesterday. Right after we got back. He came to see us. He was gutted we were so upset with him.'

'He was very manly about it all. Wanted to assure us his intentions were honourable and that the legal side of the wedding was a genuine administrative error.'

'Did he give any indication as to what he thought might happen? Annulment-wise?' I ask, trying to sound casual.

Liam shakes his head. 'No, love. But can you imagine waking up to that face every morning?' he says, a dreamy glimmer in his eye.

Ged coughs loudly. 'Meanwhile, back on planet Earth, Connie, you can't seriously want to stay married to a man you've only just met. You've barely been on a date with him, never mind agreeing to spend the rest of your lives together. How could you possibly know he's the one for you? I mean, just look at the way Luke turned your head in the beginning. Are you sure you want to commit to Matteo? What do you really know about him? What toothpaste does he use, for Christ's sake? What's his go-to Netflix binge-watch?'

He's right. Ged always manages to get right to the nub of things. But all I have to go on is my gut feeling. 'I love him. And he loves me. He just told me.'

Ged and Liam beam at me for a few moments before swooping me into a big hug. 'Well, that's good
enough for us,' says Liam. 'Now, what's on the pre-
moon agenda today?'

I step out of the hug to swipe my phone. 'This
morning is supposed to be a visit to the weird and
whimsical, immersive, psychedelic art exhibit at
Omega Mart, followed by Eddie from Talent Star's
birthday bash. It's up at the pool, where you have
your private cabana. At least you'll get a great view of
all the entertainment.'

'Apparently, he has a famous DJ flying in,' says
Ged, ever one to keep his ear to the ground. 'Our
concierge told me yesterday.'

Just then my phone pings. I hope it's Matteo and
not the Dollz confirming they are dropping out of today's activities.

Shite.

'Why have you gone pale?' asks Liam. 'Oh, God. Is
it an update on the killer?'

'Worse. It's Nancy. She's reminding me that we
need to give a top-notch performance for Eddie, because she owes him big time and has promised him
the works.' I gulp.

'What's the problem?'

'I'm missing a few Dollz, is the problem,' I say, explaining the situation. 'And so, I might need you guys as backup if they don't show this afternoon.'

Ged and Liam are usually very keen to join me on stage.

'Of course we'll help out. Even though it's our premoon and we didn't come here to work.' Liam sounds disappointingly on the cusp of not wanting to do it.

'So, we have Big Mand and Big Sue sneaking around like loved-up teens.' Ged is ticking off a mental list. 'Cherry has gone nuclear because she's no longer pregnant. Liberty is designated carer. And Tash and Sister Kevin are doing what exactly?'

Oh, God.

'They've won some tickets.'

'What sort of tickets?'

'Just tickets.'

'To do what?'

Gah!

'To see Celine Dion.'

'CELINE BLOODY DION?' yells Ged.

'WHERE?' says Liam.

'She's doing a one-off at the Bellagio.'

They remain motionless for a few seconds. Liam develops a tic in his eye while Ged grinds his teeth very loudly.

'I'm sure the pool party will be so much better,' I

say. 'And you guys love being on stage. All that attention.'

They remain unconvinced.

'I promise we'll have a blast.'

I should not be making promises I can't keep. What is wrong with me?

'Who will be at this pool party of Eddie's? Isn't he, like, ninety or something? How old is Nancy? She's had more than a few laps round the sun.'

'No idea. Thirty-nine?' She's got to be sixty at least. I am making an already bad situation much worse. 'But I do know that it will be the event to go to.'

Ged huffs, turning to Liam. 'Look, she's pulling her earlobe.'

I immediately stop, sandwiching both my hands in my lap, my eyes wide, feigning innocence.

'Too late, sister. Cancel the Omega Mart. We're going to try and get tickets for Celine. What table did they win them at? Liam, darling, put on your finery. We're going gambling.'

This birthday bash is going to be a disaster if there's just me to entertain Eddie. The Dollz bring all the energy and fun. Sparks fly when they are on stage together. Crowds clap and cheer. They get out of their seats to join in the twerking. They get ridiculously hot and sweaty trying to copy their moves, especially slapping pretend sexual partners on their behinds as they take them doggy style. Crowds have been known to sing along from start to finish, such is the playful atmosphere the Dollz create the moment they strut onto stage. They are mesmerising.

I can already hear Nancy shouting down the phone at me that if Eddie had wanted a melancholy singing statue for his birthday, he would have ordered one.

* * *

I check my phone again to see if Matteo has messaged. Nothing yet. A feeling of emptiness unfurls in my stomach. I have to fight the urge to send him a thousand silly texts thanking him for being so kind to my friends. I just want to know what he's doing. Where he is. What he's saying. I want us to be hanging out together.

Instead, I message the group chat and demand a meeting at the love sign. I tell them there has been a change of plan. We are no longer going to the Omega Mart this morning, but we need to discuss Eddie from Talent Star's birthday bash instead. His party starts at 2 p.m. We are expected on stage at 4 p.m. I tell them Nancy has been in touch. She is expecting *all* of us to be on top form for it and to do something special as a surprise. What does that even mean? I'm hoping for a rapid response. A plethora of suggestions to come flooding in.

They do not.

Where to start? I slip my phone back in my pocket and head to the casino. Surely Cherry with her flaming-red hair and cloud of dissatisfaction at the world will be easy to spot, but I'm met with a burst of colour in every direction. The blinking neon lights, the loud trilling, bleeping and blooping of slot machines merge into one gigantic seascape of blazing psychedelic colour and noise. The casino is vast and there are so many people walking around. Someone taps me lightly on the shoulder.

'Hi there.'

For a moment I can't respond. I stare dumbstruck into a pair of piercing grey eyes.

'You look like you've seen a ghost.'

I nod rapidly.

'It's Hank. Hank Junior. Remember?' he says dryly.

I continue nodding. An icy fear roots me to the spot as I feel beads of sweat break out on my lip.

'Hi,' I squeak. My heart is hammering against my chest. 'We've been... erm, looking for you.'

He tilts his head, far from overjoyed. 'Funny. Because I've been looking all over for you.'

I gulp. 'You have?'

He screws his eyes. 'You seem nervous, ma'am.'

I shake my head, biting my lips together.

'You still on for the job?' He slides his gaze around as though recording activity and movement in the near vicinity. His jaw is set as he rubs his stubble.

'What job would that be?' *The one where you kill my innocent unrequited lover?*

Hank Junior gives me a hard look before a rumble of laughter escapes from his mouth. I notice it doesn't reach his eyes. 'What job? Very funny.' He takes a few steps away from me. 'And tell that friend of yours, I don't appreciate being stood up. I'm not the sort of man to play games. I'm a person of my word. Even if she ain't.'

He sounds very cross.

I'd hate for him to 'take care' of her too. 'She fainted,' I explain. 'Liberty fainted. She wanted to meet you but we had to take her back to the room. That's why she stood you up.'

His face softens for a split second before resuming a scowl. 'She fainted?'

'Uh-huh.'

He shakes his head. 'Sounds unlikely. She doesn't strike me as the fainting type.'

'It was unusual circumstances.'

He eyes me warily. 'Really?'

'Yup, siree. They sure as heck were.' *Oh, God, where is this coming from? He'll think I'm taking the piss.* 'We want to cancel the job,' I blurt.

He stops in his tracks. Now he looks downright thunderous.

'Excuse me?'

It's then I notice he has two burly security guards hovering around. I notice the earpieces first, the dark suits and the way their eyes are continually darting around the room.

'We want to... we need to cancel the "job",' I say slowly. 'The erm, "package" has already been taken care of.' I do air quotes.

Hank does not respond. He is not a happy chappy.

I swallow a lump in my throat. 'Please? Can we cancel the job?'

Hank Junior is fuming. 'We had a deal. The payment has been made.'

'Did we? Has it?' My voice is so high-pitched I'm surprised I haven't attracted every dog from miles around.

'Yes, ma'am.'

'So, we can't cancel?' I think I'm going to cry. Does this mean they'll track Luke to England? Hank Junior is so intimidating and yet all he is doing is standing a few feet away, talking. He has such a powerful aura. He has a real hardness to him that wasn't there before. Maybe Liberty has had a lucky escape.

He shakes his head. He's standing, legs wide apart, arms folded. A solid mass of man. With a bored sigh, he says loudly, 'A deal's a deal. I'll be seeing y'all later.' It sounds more like a threat.

No, no, no, this isn't happening!

Holding my breath, I watch him walk confidently away. My legs are wobbling, barely able to hold me up. I reach for the nearest table to rest on and sag into an empty booth.

Fuck.

25

I'm hyperventilating, hunched up in the booth. What do I do? I haven't had a proper full-on panic attack for years, but I recognise the signs immediately. My skin feels cold and sweaty. I wipe at my brow, gasping to control my breath. I grab the sides of the table and squeeze my eyes shut, trying to control the inner turmoil.

'You okay, Big Guy?'

My eyes snap open. It's Big Sue.

'Thank God!' I cry, putting a hand to my chest to help get the words out. 'It's him. He's back. He found me.'

Quick as lightning, Big Sue slides in beside me. 'Who's back? Luke?'

I shake my head. 'Hank Junior.'

Her face drops. 'What did he say? Did you tell him to cancel the job?'

'Yes, but he said it's too late.' I panic. 'What does that even mean?'

'Tell me everything that happened.'

'I think he's angry that Liberty stood him up. He said something like payment had already been made therefore there was no backing out of the deal.' The words are tumbling out of my dry mouth. 'And he looked really mean. And he had two bodyguards. And he was standing with his legs too far apart and...'

'Stick to the relevant details, babe. Did he mention' – she lowers her voice – 'Luke?'

I rack my brains. What did I say? What did he say? Where's Cherry and her memory when you need her? 'He just said it was too late to cancel.'

'Does that mean too late because he's already "taken care" of him?'

Fucking hell. Poor Luke.

'Have you tried ringing him?'

I shake my head. 'Ged said that Matteo told him he made sure Luke got away safely. He should be in the air by now. Oh God. What if there's a killer on the plane? We'll not know if he ever made it until he lands. And even then...' I trail off, clenching and un-

clenching my fists at my sides to stop my mind spi-
ralling with terror.

Big Sue's thumbs are whizzing over her phone.
'I'm messaging the group. We need an emergency
meeting. Now.'

'It's no use. Everyone is off doing other things. I'm
on my own for the birthday bash. It's going to be a
disaster. Nancy is going to kill us. Ged and Liam won't
step in because of Celine *must-see* Dion.'

'Breathe, hun,' she says softly, taking off her
Barbie ponytail and rooting around in her bag. She
pulls out a small hairbrush. 'Can you quickly brush
the tats out of that for me please?'

This is absolutely not the time for caring how we
look.

'Please. While I get the troops together. And try
not to blame Celine. She's had a tough few years,
babe. Namaste and all that.'

'Okay,' I say, taking the wig and hairbrush from
her. I stare numbly at my phone, lying on the table in
front of me, while I gently stroke tats out of her wig.
The rhythmic action is oddly soothing, and the shine
on the white-blonde synthetic material is very satisfying. Big Sue has messaged that the eagle has landed.
Code red. Usual rendezvous point. How is anyone
supposed to know what the heck she means? They'll

never reply anyway. Too busy living their best lives while I sit here frozen with panic, brushing a wig.

Ping. Big Mand is on her way.

Ping. Liberty is on her way.

Ping. Cherry is on her way.

I see dots travelling across the top of the chat. Tash is typing. Tash has stopped typing. Tash is typing again.

'Not sure she'll leave day-drinking in the run-up to a Celine Dion concert for this,' I say.

Big Sue smirks, thumbing out a message at high speed. 'She will.'

Ping. Tash is on her way.

What a sisterhood. A lump forms in my throat. And I'm part of it. I'm a stone's throw away from getting a hashtag blessed tattoo.

'Come on, let's go,' orders Big Sue, sliding out of the booth. 'That panic attack of yours subsided yet?'

Gosh. It has.

'I'll take that back, thanks.' Big Sue tips her head down and secures the wig neatly into place.

I half smile, handing over the brush. She's so incredibly effective. She's one of those people who gets the job done. Minimum fuss. If the world goes to shit, then Big Sue is who you'd want in charge. I check my phone to see what she wrote in the group chat:

Sisters before misters.

I blink slowly as we take a moment.

'Sisters are like stars. We shine brightest when we love and support each other,' Big Sue says, her voice soft as an angel, before she quickly clears her throat and recovers herself. 'Capeesh?'

'I absolutely capeesh. I capeesh totally.' Emotions are getting the better of me. 'I capeesh so much.'

'You're just spoiling it now, Big Guy.'

I stifle a giggle as she flits her head, indicating for me to follow. 'Where's the rendezvous point?' I ask. 'The love sign?' Because I think I love Big Sue.

'Too obvious,' she says as we scurry through the casino and into the shopping mall. We pass by all the boutiques, the shops selling oversized sweets, cookies, milkshakes. We pass the designer clothes shop that Hank Junior took us to in order to gallantly get Liberty out of her wet things. We come to an abrupt halt. 'We're here.'

My eyes dart about. 'Here? The bridge?'

'How do you think we all caught you sneaking off to get married?' She points to the gondolas floating underneath, the gondoliers singing to their passengers, their voices carrying over the water to the crowds gathering to watch. 'Don't you read all the messages? Or were you too busy getting married?' She nods down to the water. There are several white and gold wedding gondolas floating nearby. The scene gives me a wistful pang of longing. 'How does it feel?' she says. Big Sue's face has taken on a slight glow of embarrassment.

'To be married?'

She nods.

'To be honest, I have no idea. We haven't yet had the chance to...'

'You haven't consummated the marriage?' she says, sounding shocked.

'Well... there have been a series of pressing issues to contend with since... you know. And he has got a lifelong dream hanging in the balance. Which Birdie is threatening to ruin. It's been a lot.'

'Sorry,' she says, her hand landing heavily on my shoulder. 'Sorry you didn't get your special day.'

I stare down at the glistening water. 'It wasn't supposed to be real anyway.'

'But your feelings are real, aren't they?'

'They are.'

'Have you told him?'

'Not yet.'

'Don't worry, Big Guy. We'll get this "situation"

sorted and then we'll put things right with you and mister lover lover.'

I put my hands in prayer, smiling. 'Please don't. I promise you; I can handle it.'

The Dollz have a horrendous track record when it comes to interfering with my love life.

Thumping footsteps on the bridge alert us to the arrival of Big Mand. She reaches us and immediately bends double, catching her breath.

'Where have you been?' I ask.

Her head jerks up, her eyes connecting with Big Sue's. 'Nowhere,' they say in unison.

I suppress a tiny smirk. 'Okaaaay.' I won't pry, but they are being very, very cute.

Next to arrive is Liberty. She is holding Cherry upright. Cherry's chin has flopped down onto her chest. 'It's okay, she's just a bit tipsy. Nothing a strong coffee won't fix.' Liberty props Cherry against the bridge railing and we watch her slide slowly down to the floor. Legs akimbo, head slumped on her shoulder, red hair splayed across her face. Not what I'd call battle ready.

'We're here!' yells Tash. Sister Kevin is clamped to her. My heart sinks. I hope she's not pissed as well.

'Where have you been?' I ask as they approach.

Every single casino serving free booze from here to the Mo-jave Desert?

'Nowhere,' they say in unison. They are out of breath and clearly agitated. Sister Kevin's cheeks colour.

My eyes dart to Big Sue, who immediately inspects her nails. What are they all hiding? I make a mental note to quiz them later. After all, I did spot them all hiding from each other in the wedding department at Macy's. But at the moment, all my brain can think about is Hank Junior and what to do about him.

I'm pinning my hopes on Tash having a sensible pharmaceutical solution to the Cherry situation. Maybe we can hook her up to one of these vitamin drips that seem to be everywhere. Tash drops down to check on Cherry. 'Nothing a good strong coffee won't fix,' she says, echoing Liberty, as she straightens back up. She seems sober as a judge to me, if not overly confident in the powers of caffeine.

'I know just the place,' says Ged from behind me. He and Liam hold up takeaway coffees, their pupils the size of dinner plates. 'Turbo Charge Cannonball Coffee. It's amazing.'

'We've been awake for nearly thirty-six hours,' says Liam, twitching. One of his eyes is independently straying to the left. 'I'm incredibly focused right now. And we're so full of energy. I might never sleep again.'

'Perfect,' says Liberty, stooping to grab one of Cherry's arms. I bend down to help.

'We need a plan,' I say. Even now that the Dollz are all here, this birthday performance is going to suck big time. Nobody will have their head in the game because of Hank Junior looming over us. I really hope Eddie is some kind of geriatric who won't notice.

'Agreed,' says Liberty, sounding too quiet. She makes eye contact with me as we hunch down over Cherry's limp body. I notice the dark circles beneath her eyes and her pale complexion. 'I'm sorry I caused all of this, Connie. I really am.'

'It's not your fault,' I'm quick to say. 'How were you supposed to know Hank Junior was a mobster?'

She shrugs. 'I still feel guilty. And...' She turns her wet, dull eyes to the gondolas peeking through the balustrade. 'I really liked him, you know?' A lone tear trickles down her cheek. 'I'm always the bloody bridesmaid. Never the bride.' She wipes the tear away with the back of her index finger.

I reach out to stroke her shoulder. 'For what it's worth, I think Hank Junior genuinely likes you. He seemed angry about your no-show but then really concerned when I told him you'd fainted and that's why you didn't turn up.'

'Did he?' she says, a shade brighter. 'Such a shame.'

I smile sympathetically at her. 'Shame he's a hitman?'

'Shame he didn't give me his number. Can you remember which direction he went in?'

What? How desperate is this woman?

Liberty huffs out a small laugh. 'Fuck's sake, Connie. Your face! As if! My standards are low but not that low.'

Cherry takes that moment to zing back to life. 'Jackpot! Put everything on red. Or black.'

We heave her back to standing and head off in search of this uber-powerful coffee. 'Let's all get some,' says Big Sue. 'It'll turbocharge our tactical briefing.'

* * *

Twenty minutes later, we are staring bug-eyed at one another. With pupils the size of manhole covers, we attempt to put a plan together. My heart is pumping like a jackhammer at twice its normal speed.

'Why is Tash twitching?' barks Big Mand, making it sound like all one word.

'Never mind her, what about Hank Junior?' Liberty asks.

'Never mind Hank Junior, what about our Birthday Bash performance?' I ask. 'We should really go and get ready for it.'

Blank expressions.

'It's on the schedule,' I remind them, waving my phone. 'The gig we are doing at the pool party, remember? The reason we are sitting here tactically meeting about it?'

All of a sudden, the floor, the neon lights flashing above the bar, acrylic nails and the diamanté stuck to them become objects of extreme interest.

'The one we are contractually obliged to do as a favour for Nancy.'

Blank stares. Nobody can be bothered.

'It should be fun,' I say, trying to sound convincing. 'And it'll be much safer if we stick together and...'

'And hide in plain sight,' Big Mand finishes. 'Good thinking, Big Guy.'

'If it's a pool party, should we go in swimming costumes?' asks Big Sue.

'Yes. Makes sense,' agrees Cherry.

'And did we bring swimming costumes?' asks Big Sue.

'No,' says Cherry.

My poor credit card. It will have organised its own funeral, obituary and wake by now.

I cross my fingers, praying no one can be bothered to go and buy any. 'What will we wear instead?' asks Big Sue. Her extra-long legs must be hollow because she seems least affected by the caffeine.

'I will make bikinis out of these,' Cherry says, pointing to the round cardboard beer mats. She holds two up to her breasts with an air of incredulity, as though wondering why she has never before thought to do this.

I flick through the schedule on my phone and pretend she did not just say that. 'There is a stage poolside, on the fourth floor, and we're on at 4 p.m. We need to be suited and booted. It's glorious sunshine so whatever we wear needs to be cool.'

'We'll do the pink Stetsons with our pink sequined bra tops. Grab whatever short skirt you have or hot pants or sarong in a bright colour and we'll do the Barbie white sandals. We'll keep the wigs on. End of.' Tash purses her lips. 'Agreed?'

We all nod obediently.

'And if he's not happy, one of us can do him a lap dance afterwards,' she says.

Absolutely not happening.

'As for Hank Junior,' says Big Sue. 'We'll just have to wait until after the show to do a recon. Connie, you ring Luke as soon as he lands, okay? Make sure he's alive.'

'And if he isn't?'

Gah! I immediately regret asking this. After some eye contact, we leave the question hanging in the air. Where it can stay. Forever.

We agree to meet in my room once we are all ready, to have a quick run-through before the pool party begins.

My phone pings. It is from Nancy. She has heard that we are too busy messing about, gambling, sight-seeing, getting married, etc, and that is *not* what she is paying us to do. I read the rest of the text aloud. 'Eddie from Talent Star is very well connected, do not cross him under any circumstances.'

'Right, Libs. Looks like we'll be needing to do our Hot Garbage routine on him,' Tash says forcefully. 'You take the lead. Let's give this old fucker a flaming heart attack.'

26

I race back to my room, turning the last corner to find Matteo is at the door. His face lights up as I walk casually towards him down the long, never-ending corridor.

It's funny how the simple act of walking has become the most awkward action possible now that I'm married to a gorgeous hunk who *loves* me. I'm overwhelmed with excitement. I instantly speed up, thinking better of it once my elbows start pointing outwards like a Nordic speed walker.

Now it's as though I've forgotten what a normal speed is. I've gone too far the other way; it feels awfully like I'm walking in slow motion. And my hands? I wipe some non-existent hair from my brow. Now where do I put them? I suddenly get the idea to wave at him with one of them just for something to do, while I'm laughing at what a coincidence it is that we've arrived at the same time.

Obviously, I'm too far away to explain what I'm laughing at. So, for some reason, I just keep waving and laughing. Much longer than is acceptable. I am also walking too close to the wall because I'm trying to focus on his handsome face, and not the picture I've just knocked off the wall with a loud thump.

He stands watching me with an amused expression while I display signs of acute dyspraxia, trying to discreetly put the picture back up and rehang it. Let me tell you, hanging pictures is not easy. And the weight of these things can be very deceiving. I am fucking exhausted by the time I reach him.

He is literally biting his lips together.

'Hello,' I say in a breathy, low voice. I'm too tired and stressed to even begin explaining what that spectacle just was.

He opens the door for me. His eyes are glassy, and his cheeks are pink. I may need to give him a moment to compose himself. He really is trying very hard to be gentlemanly and not to laugh. He clears his throat. 'You okay?' he asks.

'Oh, God. I forgot to tell you. Hank Junior showed

up while I was looking for the others in the casino. He's really mad at us for wanting to cancel. He basically said it was all too late and that the deal had been done. Please tell me you're sure Luke got safely on to the plane.'

He puts his arm around me. 'He did. The driver sent a confirmation email of the airport drop-off. Try not to worry. Las Vegas is a crazy town. It may all be bravado on Hank's part. But I'm here for you. I won't let him do anything to harm you or the others.' He dips down to kiss me. His lips are soft and warm. His touch is like a rejuvenating elixir as a wave of calm envelops me. When we draw apart, he is smiling.

'How did things go? Did you manage to sort things with Birdie?' I ask, instantly soothed.

'Kind of. But that's not why I came back. I have something I hope you'll like.' He sounds very excited. He leads me over to the floor-to-ceiling window. The sight of the city bathed in sunlight and sprawled out before us is stunning, simply breathtaking. 'Stay here. Don't move. Keep looking out of the window.'

Matteo is doing something in the room. There's a zipping, some clicking sounds; he's plugging something in. It's all very, very mysterious.

'Okay, turn around.'

'What's this?' I ask, pointing to a picture of me on the large TV screen in the room.

'It's you at the piano in the Cocktail Hour bar,' he says, and presses play.

I gulp loudly. It's the video he asked me to What-sApp him. How cringe. But as soon as I hear it, I realise he's tinkered with it. He's added amazing acoustics, some bass, subtle layers of sound. It's extremely clever. It's absolutely amazing. He's taken my song and made it a million times better. I am wide-eyed and speechless.

He gives me a shy smile.

We are silent as we watch the close-up of me on screen, eyes closed, lost in my own world, belting out the track. Singing about how excited I feel, how lucky to have found my special someone just at the right time and how, if only he knew, that inside I'm a blazing furnace, burning for his touch.

It's only when it ends that I realise I've been holding my breath.

'What do you think?' he asks quietly.

'It's incredible,' I whisper. 'I can't believe that's me. Thank you so much.'

'That's only part of my surprise,' he says. 'What time are you performing today?'

'At 4 p.m. Up at the poolside. Everyone is coming

here to rehearse beforehand. Sorry. I should have asked you first. I thought you'd be with...' My voice cracks. I can barely get the words out. I really don't want him to spend any more time with Birdie. We've only been married a day, and he's spent more time with her than me.

Luckily for him, all of this whining is very much internal.

'That's okay. I need to get back to the recording studio. I'll see you at 4 p.m.' His eyes rake over my face. 'Hey. I'm almost done. Birdie is behaving herself. The client is happy. Just two more hours and it's a wrap. I promise. By the time you've finished your gig, you and I will be officially on our...'

A wave of jubilation flows through my veins. 'Honeymoon,' I blurt, just as I hear him say, 'First date'.

He pulls a yikes face when he sees the look on mine. 'Honeymoon it is.'

'No, it's fine. I meant first date too,' I say, fake laughing to disguise my embarrassment.

'Honeymoon.' He places a hand on his heart, smiling. 'I insist.'

I swallow hard. He must think I'm insane. He has married a lunatic.

'Besides, I think we have sort of missed the boat

with the whole first date and let's get to know each other properly phase.' He takes my fingertips in his. 'All I know is that since the moment we met, it has been like stepping on to an out-of-control roller-coaster. And even though I have no idea what's coming... I have no desire to get off.'

A warmth radiates throughout my entire body as I realise what he's saying. He pulls me towards him just as there's a loud thumping at the door.

I jump a mile.

Matteo marches to the door. My heart is in my mouth as he checks the peephole and swings the door open. 'Come in, ladies. My wife has been expecting you. Make yourselves at home,' he says as they all troop in. 'Minibar is that way. There's champagne in the ice bucket. Toilet for throwing up is that way. I'll see you all later.'

They all stop dead in their tracks.

'You're staying married?' Cherry asks.

'As in legally hitched?' Big Mand says.

'You're twanging the marital garter?' says Tash. *Makes no sense.* 'Flashing the wedding knickers?' *Makes less sense.* 'Fondling the wedding giblets?' *Borderline unnecessary.* But Sister Kevin is finding her hilarious.

'Are you sure, both of you?' Liberty asks.

Matteo pauses in the doorway to make eye contact with me. My face flames. I give him a shy nod. Raw emotion flickers across his face, detectable only by me. 'Yes, we are,' he says and closes the door.

Cherry swirls round. 'Fuck me, Connie. Imagine ringing those wedding bells every night for the rest of your life. Lucky cow.'

* * *

Somehow, we all manage to stay focused as we run through the rehearsal for the birthday party. Practising the Hot Garbage finale has cost me a bedside lamp, Sister Kevin's glass of beer (kicked clean out of his hand) and a curtain rail. Liberty had mistakenly assumed it would hold her full weight as she grabbed hold of the curtain while coming out of a complex upside-down splits routine. Finally, after two solid hours, we stop for a quick break while we all scroll through our phones. I have no messages from Matteo, but I do have one from Ged and Liam posted to our private group chat. They are asking if I am absolutely certain that staying married to Matteo is what I want. I send them a video note back because I'm too excited to think straight, never mind text.

'I know it sounds crazy,' I say, quivering with the

effort of trying to control a face-splitting grin, 'but I just feel like my best self whenever I'm with him. For the first time in my life, I feel brave and reckless and... like I just want to skip everywhere because I'm so bursting with joy. And it's so scary but at the same time...' A brief glance behind me indicates I have a rapt audience as the Dollz eavesdrop, keen to understand why I've suddenly become so talkative and expressive. '...but at the same time, deep down, it's hard to describe but I just know it's meant to be. Because I feel a sort of calm. Like my mother sent him to me. To help me. He's like a dazzling light guiding me out of the dark place I've been in for so long.'

I press send and turn round to see why there is such a silence. The Dollz are standing staring at me. Big Mand, famously unemotional and detached because of her job of yanking babies from the often-torn vaginas of overanxious mothers, has tears streaming down her face. Cherry is also sniffing and wiping her wet cheeks. Liberty is sniffing hers up, dabbing her eyes as she tries not to smudge her mascara. Even Sister Kev has a slack jaw as he gives Tash a pensive look.

There's a loud knock at the door, making us all jump.

'It's Hank!' shrieks Tash. 'He's come to get rid of all the witnesses.'

Cherry, snapping to attention, is cool as a cucumber now she's back to her sane self. 'We haven't witnessed anything, pet.'

'Kev!' Tash yells. 'You go.'

Sister Kevin looks pleased to be of some use and strides to the door. He yanks it open, chest first, ready for some confrontation. 'Connie. It's the dry-clean service. I guess it's your wedding dress.' He carries a big plastic suit bag over his arm and lays it out on the bed. We take a moment to ooh and ahh over the dress, visible through the clear plastic.

'It's so pretty,' says Cherry. 'But I'd have gone for a more off-white if I were you.'

'Hmmm,' says Liberty, running her hand lightly over it. 'And maybe something a bit more fun? In silk? With a cowgirl theme?'

'No,' says Tash. 'It definitely should have been more princessy. More showstopper. More underskirts. The more the better. Don't you think so, Kev, hun?'

Sister Kev visibly swallows, like a giant mouse caught in a trap. 'I like it. It's elegant and understated.'

'Connie, babe,' she says, swiftly ignoring what he just said. 'If you'd bothered to include us in your top secret plans, we could have helped style you up.'

'And she'd never have been able to reach a decision in time,' says Big Sue diplomatically. 'So, it's just as well they sloped off in secret. I totally get it.'

Big Mand's cheeks flush. 'I mean, it's not like we have to tell each other every single blinking thing, do we?'

Before we can debate this startling revelation, there's another thump on the door.

'Christ, we'll never get ready in time at this rate,' moans Liberty. 'Part of me wishes it was Hank so that we can just get this over with.'

Our nerves are in shreds.

Sister Kevin charges back over to the door. 'It's a message,' he says, thanking the concierge and slipping him some dollars. 'In a posh envelope.' He carries it over to us. He hands it to me.

'Why me?' I'm quick to say. 'Give it to Big Sue.'

'It has your name on it.'

I take it gingerly and turn it around in my fingers. It's a small red envelope.

'That is so sinister,' says Cherry. 'You better open it. It might be a death threat.'

Not helping.

I slide my finger under the seal and take out a thick piece of beautifully crafted white card with embossed writing. 'It's an invitation.'

'To where?' says Cherry, looking over my shoulder. '"Your attendance is requested at The Little White Wedding Chapel at midnight."'

'It says, "Come for the free booze, stay for the wedding",' I say. 'Whose wedding?'

'Maybe it's a mistake? Or someone Matteo knows?'

'Would anyone mind if I just went downstairs for a little gamble?' Sister Kevin looks shattered. This week has been very full-on. I imagine Tash has been very high-maintenance and the cracks are beginning to show.

'If you must,' she says sharply. 'See you at the gig?'

'Of course. Sure.' He doesn't sound sure. 'I'll be there.'

We wait for Tash to run into his arms for a lengthy snog, but she stands rigid, unmoving. They exchange a frosty goodbye before he leaves.

'Whoa,' says Big Sue. 'What's going on there?'

'Nothing,' Tash says. 'We're just... tired.'

'Yup,' agrees Cherry. 'You can say that again. I'm frigging exhausted. Feels like we've been here forever.'

'Well, after today's gig for Eddie from Talent Star, we have only one day left before we fly home,' I say, staring down at my wedding ring, wondering what my dad will make of it all.

'So much has happened,' says Big Mand. 'It's ridiculous to think you're going back a married woman, Connie, babes. Five minutes ago, he was your Mr Window Seat on the plane to Benidorm and now, you're building a whole new life together.'

We let those words sink in.

I. AM. A. MARRIED. WOMAN.

Omigodomigodomigod.

'It's funny to think of how your life can change so dramatically all because of a chance meeting,' says Liberty with a faraway look in her eye.

I wonder if she's thinking of Hank.

27

An hour later, and the whole staying-married incident has put me on a high, excitement-wise. It's insane. It's ridiculous. It's the most alive I've ever felt, and I am bursting with joy. I want to yell and scream and dance around. I instantly text messaged Matteo to make sure he is sure about what he said. I reread his instant reply.

If you are sure. I am sure.

OmigodOmigodOmigod.
This is happening. This is really happening. My heart is skipping into a sweet shop and bouncing around on fluffy marshmallows.

'Connie!' yells Tash. 'Which floor? I need to press a button.'

'For frig's sake,' huffs Liberty. 'Get your head in the game, pet. I've just asked you five times which floor. You can drool and moon all you want after we get this gig out of the way. And don't forget. Hank Junior is still loose somewhere in this hotel.'

Liberty brings us all back down to earth with a bump.

Big Sue's eyes dart to the security camera in the lift that we are currently squashed into. 'For fuck's sake, Libs, we may as well hand ourselves in now.'

It's as though she has tempted fate because, just as the lift doors open on the fourth floor, Hank Junior is waiting to greet us as we step out. His eyes shoot straight to Liberty. 'May I have a word?' he asks politely. He is dressed casually. No Stetson, no fake moustache and no toothpick. He is actually really attractive in a quirky sort of way. It's such a shame he's a wrong 'un.

A forlorn expression crawls across her face. Her eyes glisten as the sunlight pours into the lift. It is over 30 degrees; the sun is high in the sky and there is a pool party in full swing on the other side of the patio.

We all stand in front of her, hands on hips. We respond collectively with a hard, 'No.'

Hank Junior stands his ground. He holds his hands up. 'Just one minute.'

'We're due on stage in five minutes,' I say.

'I know,' he says, looking perplexed. 'Why do you think I'm here?'

'It's okay, Big Guy. Leave it to me,' Big Sue says, stepping forward. Her tall frame is clad in a miniscule sequined bra top and hot pants. Her white-blonde Barbie ponytail is swinging. She's as far from terrifying as the rest of us. 'You heard the lady. Back off.'

Hank Junior shakes his head as though he's losing patience.

'Why don't we all discuss the, erm, issue, afterwards?' I say to placate him.

'I'd like to discuss the *issue* now, thank you very much, ma'am,' Hank Junior says with an expression of incredulity.

'But what if we don't want to discuss the friggin' issue?' barks Cherry. Her eyes are flashing angrily, her flaming-red hair is swishing and her hands are clamped to her bony hips.

Hank Junior almost jumps at the ferocity in her voice. He immediately holds up his hands again. 'Okay. Okay.'

'What's going on?' Matteo is striding up to us with a face like thunder. He squares right up to Hank Junior. 'Leave these women alone. They've told you it was all a misunderstanding. Why can't you just accept it and move on? We're all sorry for the inconvenience, but for your own good, just drop it.'

Hank Junior is livid. His face is puce. Liberty steps between them. Hank Junior immediately drops his shoulders. Liberty looks up at him with huge, sad puppy eyes. Hank Junior seems to melt instantly.

'I'm sorry,' she says simply.

He can't take his eyes off her.

'I thought we had something special. But you weren't being honest with me,' she says quietly, her voice breaking.

Hank Junior hangs his head. 'Is that why you stood me up?'

Liberty nods. 'Why didn't you tell me who you really are?'

He shrugs. 'Would you still have been interested in me, or just what I could do for you?'

Liberty lets out a puff of air while the rest of us hold our breath, watching the scene unfold in silence. I notice Matteo has his fists clamped to his sides, ready to pounce if anything goes wrong.

'Hank, I never wanted to hire a hitman. I told you

about Luke because... well, I just didn't want you thinking that I was interested in him. That's all. I didn't mean for you to "take care" of him.' Liberty does air quotes. 'I just wanted to spend time with you.'

This is it. This is the bit where it could all go horribly wrong for us. If Hank refuses to back down, we are all in serious trouble. I feel Matteo slip a hand into mine. My eyes flit to his. We're a team. He's got our backs. It would be a lovely poignant moment if we weren't so dreading Hank's next move.

Hank is staring at Liberty. Myriad emotions battling it out before, surprisingly, a broad smile almost splits his face in two. 'Oh, man,' he says, amused. 'Hitman? What are you talking about?'

'You're a hitman,' she says, her lip wobbling. 'Cherry overheard you talking about making hits and being very thorough, and you called yourself *the* hitman of Hollywood.'

'No, I ain't.' He chuckles. His eyes are sparkling. 'Well, I am. I do make hits but not those kind of hits.'

'So, you haven't...' Liberty mouths the rest. '...*killed Luke?*'

He looks horrified. 'No! Why would I do that? I barely know the guy.'

'But you said you'd "take care of him".'

'Yeah. As in bribe him to move to a hotel on the other side of town. Far away from you.'

'But then why wouldn't you let us cancel the *job*, so to speak?'

'Because I had no clue that you thought you'd hired me to do a hit on someone,' he says, adjusting his hat and stuffing a hand in one of his jeans pockets. 'Besides, he'd checked out of his room by the time my assistant got round to it, so I figured problem sorted.'

'Well, what are we talking about?' she asks. 'Why were you so angry with us?'

Yes. Wouldn't we all like to know? I'm not the only one in the group leaning forward. Matteo grips my hand even tighter.

'You, disappearing on me for our date after we'd...' His gaze travels the length of the group. We're encroaching on their space. 'After we'd said all that stuff to each other. And then suddenly wanting to cancel this gig for my' – his cheeks are burning red – 'for my BIG birthday.'

What?

Hank's chin dips down. 'Jeez! I admit it. I was looking forward to you girls playing at my party, and I got real upset that you wanted to cancel. And I had no idea why.' He gives Liberty an earnest look. 'I like you, Liberty. I really, really like you.'

My hand flies to my mouth. *Oh, my effing word.* We got this whole thing all wrong.

'You're Eddie from Talent Star?' I gasp. 'This is *your* birthday party?'

He nods.

'And you go by another name because...'

'To safeguard my privacy and to keep fame-hungry wannabes at bay. Yes, ma'am,' he finishes for me. 'It's hard to know who you can trust these days.'

Isn't it just?

I think the penny is about to drop by the way Liberty is looking adoringly at him. 'I never made our date because I fainted when I found out you were a hitman, and by the time I came round, it was too late.'

'So,' Hank Junior-slash-Eddie says, 'you're still into me?'

Liberty's cheeks redden.

'Even though I'm just a boring billionaire talent promoter... and not a hitman?' He chuckles.

Liberty squeals and leaps into his arms. I think he has his answer.

'Excuse me,' asks Big Mand, interrupting their embrace. 'How big is this BIG birthday exactly?' She gives Tash a pointed look. It's like she's thrown a lit match into a box of fireworks. It releases all the built-up tension as we crack up, howling with laughter.

'I'm forty,' he says, holding Liberty close. 'That too old for y'all?'

Liberty shakes her head. 'You might be older, but it doesn't mean you're old.' She reaches up on her tiptoes to plant a kiss on his lips. 'I'll just have to make sure I always keep you feeling young.'

'On that note. Haven't you ladies got a show to do?' he says.

'Come on, girls. Let's show these fellas just how entertaining we can be.' Liberty swivels on her high heels, bum cheeks wobbling like jellies beneath her ridiculously short hot pants. She blows him a kiss over her shoulder, a silly grin spreading across his face.

As we walk away, I glance back to see him and Matteo shaking hands and patting shoulders. Two striking alpha males. Two sizzling hot specimens of—

'CONNIE!' yells Ged from his private cabana. 'Over here!'

We walk over to see Ged and Liam in a state of exhilaration. 'You'll never guess what!' Liam yells as we all gather round.

'You're the best *best* woman in the whole world!' gushes Ged, clamping his hands together over his heart. 'Thank you so much. It's been a dream come true. We couldn't have wished for a better end to the pre-moon.'

I have no idea what they are talking about.

'I know we asked you to ask Matteo to pull strings but...' Liam stops to catch his breath. 'This is something else.'

The pair of them are gibbering wrecks. 'What do you mean?'

Before either of them can answer, their faces drop and I find myself staring right into a pair of electric-blue eyes. 'Hi. I hear congratulations are in order. You and Matteo. He also tells me you ladies are the hottest show in town.'

We all blush at the praise. The Dollz are rooted to the spot. He makes eye contact with them all.

'I'm looking forward to seeing you perform.'

We have no words. We stare unblinking at our pop idol. It's definitely not Barry Styles this time.

'We're all totally, like, obsessed with you,' says Liberty. 'But we'll have to catch you later. Lasses, let's get on stage.'

Liberty is very keen to begin showing off for Eddie. Her enthusiasm is infectious and because we are all high on adrenaline from meeting a pop icon and avoiding jail, our confidence is through the roof.

'For the Dollz,' says Big Mand, stretching her

hand out. We form a circle, each putting a hand over hers. She gives me a knowing smile. 'Once a Doll, always a Doll.'

My heart swells a thousand times too big for my chest. This moment of powerful friendship is overwhelming. Tears prick at my eyes.

'For fuck's sake, Connie.' Cherry huffs with laughter. 'This isn't Benidorm all over again, love, is it?'

'It is actually,' I say, wiping a stray tear away. 'You were there for me then, and we're all here for each other now. To friendship.'

'To friendship,' we all chant as we stride onto the stage to give the show of a lifetime.

28

As we stand looking out at the audience, the atmosphere is electric. The DJ has whipped everyone up into a frenzy with his banging tunes. Jets of cold-water vapour are bursting from the DJ booth to cool down the bikini-clad revellers, and from the stage roof, streams of ticker tape and coloured smoke bellow out at regular intervals.

Hundreds of people are dancing by the pool, lounging on inflatables, being squirted with foam jets, relaxing on the private cabanas under straw-roofed parasols and, generally, just having an amazing time. I've never seen anything like it. Palm trees dot the sur-rounding area with huge swathes of bunting and balloons strung between. There's a giant bird of paradise in the air with a brightly painted trapeze artist dangling from it, doing an amazing acrobatic routine. Giant screens show partygoers splashing around in real time.

Every now and again, Eddie flashes up on screen, clinking glasses with people. Mostly women. Young, hot, gorgeous model-types. I chuckle to myself. If anything will trigger Liberty, it will be that. Those girls won't stand a chance against her. Then the screens show us on stage, lined up and ready to go. We take a final look at one another, a silent message of *Good luck, let's sock it to them.* This party ambiance is highly infectious, and we can't wait to be a part of it. The DJ introduces us to a roaring cheer.

We stride to the front and take our positions. I'm first to lead, a cappella. I lift the microphone to my lips and belt out the opening line. There's a brief moment of silence where everyone in the place turns their attention to the stage, before the DJ blasts out our opening track. The whole place jumps at the same moment, hands reaching for the sky, hair flying, cocktails in the air as we take over.

Matteo, Eddie and Sister Kevin are standing to the side of the stage. They have a perfect view. Matteo and Eddie have been in deep discussion between numbers. As talent promoters and producers in the music industry, they must have much in common. Every now and then, Liberty runs up to Eddie during a number to give him a kiss. He seems delighted with the attention. I, myself, am behaving professionally and am not allowing my libido to run away with me. Even Tash has resisted the urge to dry-hump Sister Kevin. I have, however, noticed them exchanging tender looks and knowing smiles, so hopefully they are over whatever spat they were having. Once we are off stage and over at Ged and Liam's cabana, all is revealed.

'Soooooo, me and Kev have a bit of an announcement to make,' says Tash. She takes his hand and swings it back and forth like you do when you're four years old. She has a goofy grin on her face.

'So do we!' blurts Big Mand, taking one of Big Sue's hands in both of hers. Big Sue baulks at this shock announcement and immediately goes the colour of the Skanky Lady cocktail she is holding.

'Hold your horses there, lasses. Me and Eddie would like to say a few words first.' Liberty is beaming up at Eddie and he is beaming at her.

'Right after I make this toast,' Ged says. 'About our pre-moon.'

'It's like announcement Top Trumps,' Matteo

murmurs in my ear, causing me to giggle. Ever since
we ironed out all the misunderstandings, it has been
like a weight has lifted. 'I have to ask you something.'

'Sure, what is it?'

'How do you like surprises?'

I don't get the opportunity to answer him because
Ged raises his glass. 'Can I just say that this week has
been...' But he doesn't get the chance to finish because a loud squeak from the PA system almost
deafens us. The DJ stops playing.

'Party people, we have a special surprise for the
birthday boy. Where is he? Eddie, if you can, give us a
wave.'

Eddie swivels round and is caught on the big
screen. He frowns playfully. This must be a genuine
shock to him.

'And Connie Cooper, where are you? Could you
make your way to the stage, please?'

Oh, my God. What is happening? I cast my eyes
around the group in panic. Everyone looks confused
except Matteo. He has a... I'm not sure what expression that is, but the DJ has more to say.

'Come on. Don't be shy!' He laughs into the microphone. 'And while we get set up, here's a trip down
memory lane.' He plays some moving background
music as images of Eddie throughout the years ap-

pear on the screens. Eddie as a cute baby, Eddie as a scruffy-looking toddler, Eddie with a series of terrible haircuts, Eddie dressed in hand-me-downs with dirty cheeks and a raggedy bike held together with string. It is clear Eddie had a very humble upbringing. Liberty has a pained look in her eyes as she clings to Eddie's arm. Eddie laughs, clearly mortified, but is being gracious about it because his reactions are live on some of the giant LED screens.

Matteo nudges me and whispers, 'Go on. Go to the stage. There's a surprise waiting for you.'

I make my way through the crowd, over to the stage area and behind the curtain. I'm greeted by a team of security man-mountains. They immediately block my way.

'Oh,' I say, feeling intimidated. 'I was told to come to the stage by my... boyfriend. Well, actually, he's my husband now.' I start giggling out of nerves, and because it feels weird to call Matteo my husband out loud.

'Who is that, ma'am?' asks one of the guards in a tone that suggests he gets this all the time.

'Matteo. Matteo, erm, Tolleado, no, that's not it.' I pause, trying to remember what my husband's name is. 'Marie-Carmen is one of the names. Grande is definitely the last one.'

The guard shakes his head. 'Ma'am, seriously? You want me to believe that you don't know your husband's surname, but you married him anyway?'

When put like that...

I nod.

'Guys. She's with me. Let her through.'

I peer between the sets of beefy arms and nearly choke with shock.

'Hello again. Don't be freaked out. Matteo is producing my next album,' the mega-superstar says quietly, leaning towards me. 'Matteo played me your new song. I love it,' he says. 'I thought we could sing it as a surprise for Eddie. He manages my US tours. Your lyrics really speak to how grateful I am to the universe right now. I couldn't do any of this without the support of my loyal family and friends.'

I feel genuinely faint. One of the world's biggest pop stars is asking me to sing with him. To be spontaneous. I nod mutely.

Oh my.

'Now?' I squeak. 'As in right now, on stage... with you?'

He smiles that enigmatic smile, and I go to complete mush. 'Come on. The VT is just about finished.'

'So, erm, you're the one working with Birdie and Matteo?'

'Yeah. They're great.'

I nod. *One of them is.* 'I don't suppose you could give Matteo the day off tomorrow, could you?' I ask, receiving a wink in response.

'Congratulations. I heard all about your accidental Vegas wedding. We've all been there.' He laughs.

I make a 'yikes' face. 'You don't have to give Birdie the day off, though. I'm sure she would like to work tomorrow. All day long. Without any breaks if you can manage it, please.'

This is met with a snort of laughter. 'She's so fucking intense, right? I like you. We'll get on just fine. Come on. Let's knock 'em dead with your lovely song.' He hands me a scrap of paper with my song lyrics and which bits he is going to sing and which bits he'll harmonise over.

'Wow. Great. Let's do it.'

'Just one thing. What's it called?' he asks.

Matteo the Magnificent, Volume One.

'Well, erm, I haven't really...' Then it comes to me. '"Girls Gone Rogue". It's called "Girls Gone Rogue" because that's how this whole haphazard week has been. I took a risk. I stepped way, way, *way* out of my comfort zone to completely and utterly amaze myself. You know, when women lean on each other, lift each other up, we can achieve anything, do the impossible.'

He laughs understandingly. 'Welcome to my world, lady. Ready?' The next five minutes are like floating in clouds, looking down on myself from afar. It passes in a complete rush of adrenaline. One minute we are leading the crowd to sing happy birthday to Eddie, and the next we are dedicating my song's debut to him. Matteo has made a special backing tape and set it up ready. When? When did he have time to do all of this?

It sounds incredible. I have no problem singing it this time round. Every single note is fresh in my memory. I search for him in the crowd but there are too many people between the cabana and me. I close my eyes and picture him listening to his song.

Our duet goes down very well. Mostly due to my famous singing partner being one of the most popular artists on the planet. When we take a bow together, the crowd cheers and I can't help doing a special shout-out to Ged and Liam. The crowd roars. A special shout-out to my Dollz. The crowd roars again. And a special shout-out to Eddie for not being who we thought he was. The crowd roars again. They will clearly celebrate anything.

When I get back to the cabana, Matteo is there, waiting nervously. 'Was that too much? Should I have warned you?'

'Yes, and yes,' I say, laughing. 'But what a thrill! OMG. There is no way on earth I'd have done that if you'd warned me in advance. I'm about as spontaneous as a regular flat white with soy milk and no foam. Did you know he wants me to feature on his album?'

Gah! It's like a dream.

Matteo nods, visibly relaxing.

I stare at him. 'I can't believe you made this happen.'

He clears his throat, embarrassed. 'Your talent made this happen.'

How in the name of all that is sacred will I be able to match such a grand gesture?

'If you two can stop drooling over each other for two seconds, I have an announcement to make,' says Tash loudly.

'Wait. Hold on. I'm not listening to a word until you tell us exactly how old Sister Kevin is,' says Big Mand. It has become a fixation. One that we are all on board with. We gather around Sister Kevin.

He squirms. 'I'm...' he begins to say, when Tash bellows it out for him.

'For fuck's sake, he's thirty-four!'

Sister Kevin looks surprised.

Then Tash looks surprised back. 'Thirty-seven?'

He shakes his head.

'Not... not forty?' Tash says. I can't help but notice her hand resting on her belly. It reminds me of Cherry when Cherry thought she was... *Oh, my goodness.* Tash is observing Sister Kevin intently. I wonder if he is inadvertently ageing himself out of the baby-daddy market.

Or is it too late for that?

'What's wrong with forty?' says Liberty defensively. She gives Eddie an adoring stroke on the cheek.

'Just let him tell us,' says Big Mand, the frustration clearly getting to her.

Sister Kevin has a wide grin on his face. 'I'm twenty-four.'

Tash drains of colour. 'But you can't be. I'm almost thirty-two. You're still a baby.' Her voice fades on her lips. If I thought it was bad to marry someone without knowing their full name, then I think planning to have children with someone without knowing how old they are might be a close second.

'MILFs are all the trend these days. A huge age gap is nothing,' Cherry says, waving it off. 'Just look at Hugh Jackman. His wife is in her seventies now.'

'They're famously divorced,' says Big Mand.

Sister Kevin swoops Tash up into his big, beefy arms. 'Don't worry, old woman. I'm sure I can think of plenty of ways to keep you young.' He is laughing hard at his own joke. Tash's eyes grow wide as she glares at him.

Oh no.

'Tash? Tash?' Sister Kevin is asking as he deposits her back on the ground. 'Are you okay, babe?'

Tash has become unresponsive, like a mannequin version of herself, frozen in time.

But then, uncharacteristically, she bursts into tears, slaps Sister Kevin hard on the chest and runs away. Once again, he turns to us, baffled.

'What did I do this time? What did I say?' he pleads.

'Dude,' says Big Sue. 'Old woman?'

His face falls a hundred feet.

'She's very sensitive underneath that cold, brash exterior,' explains Cherry. 'You'd think butter wouldn't melt but it's the little things that get to her. Mind, she has been very emotional this whole trip. Her hormones are all over the...' Cherry trails off and frowns sharply at Sister Kevin. 'Go after her.'

He visibly swallows as her words sink in, and he darts off in the same direction.

'Poor boy,' says Big Sue. 'She'll go apeshit over that comment. I doubt there's any coming back from that.'

'Not unless she's...' Cherry says.

'No,' says Big Mand. 'She wouldn't have. Would she? Things weren't that serious between them, were they?'

Matteo gives me a knowing look. Now is not the time to admit we saw them in Macy's wedding department. Along with the rest of the group.

'I'm sure they'll be fine,' I say to lighten the mood. 'Big Sue. What was your news?'

'Nothing that can't wait,' she says, reddening slightly.

'Libs, weren't you and Eddie about to say something?' asks Big Mand.

'No. No, I don't think so,' she says, looking at Eddie. Liberty is also behaving oddly.

'Champagne, anyone?' says Eddie loudly. 'I'll have some sent over. Liberty, honey, there's someone I'd really like you to meet.' He pulls Liberty away and she is very keen to go.

'What is going on with you lot?' says Liam. 'I'm getting seriously weird vibes from the lot of you.'

'Forget that,' Ged says. 'Connie, babes. You just sang your own original song on stage in Las Vegas. My mind is officially blown.'

'I know,' I say. 'It's totally surreal.'

'So, what now? Does this mean you'll stay over

here?' he asks Matteo. 'Are you taking our Connie back to LA? What's the plan?' Ged loves a plan as much as me. We live our lives by lists, agendas and schedules. They're our security blanket.

Oh, God. I'm going to need a plan.

29

'Did you guys get an invitation?' says Liam, holding up a slip of card identical to the one that was delivered to my room. 'Who is it from?'

'No idea,' I say. 'Are you going?'

We are lounging on the cabana. Matteo is networking, the Dollz are dancing, Liberty and Eddie have been welded together since we came off stage. The birthday party is showing no signs of ever ending.

'What if it's Big Sue and Big Mand?' says Ged theatrically, his mouth gaping open. 'What if they're getting hitched while we're here? They might have planned a military-style wedding.'

Oh. That would make sense. They *were* looking at rings.

'When would they have had the time to buy wedding cargos? They've been full metal jacket since we got here.'

Images of how excited they were in the shop flood my mind. 'I'm not sure they'd wear wedding combat gear, guys.'

Ged raises an eyebrow.

'Tash and Kev have been behaving very oddly. What if it's them?' says Liam.

Oh. That would make a lot of sense too. 'She could be preggers, and he may have proposed.'

'Let's not leap to conclusions,' says Ged.

This is very much the pot calling the kettle black. Not so long ago we all thought Hank was a hitman.

'Or maybe it's Liberty. Look at the way they are glued together,' Liam speculates.

'Nah. Too soon,' Ged says. 'Although he is forty and a billionaire, he might do this sort of thing on a regular basis. This is Las Vegas.'

'Unless...' I peer at them. 'Unless it is you two, and you're trying to call my bluff?'

They feign innocence. 'Honey, if we were planning a secret wedding, you'd know about it.'

He's right. They couldn't keep a secret to save their lives. None of us will forget the time Liam admitted in a job interview that his guilty pleasure was eating jars of organic baby food while quilting. He didn't get the job. But we do have too many quilts.

'I guess we'll have to get all spruced up for it. It's quite romantic, don't you think? A midnight wedding on our last night here?'

'But surely if it was one of the Dollz getting married, they'd say?' I shake my head, wondering whether to reveal that I've seen nearly all of the Dollz in Macy's. It could be any of them. 'I'll probably give it a miss. I'm sure Matteo would rather spend the night alone with me. If that's okay with you guys?'

'NO!' squeaks Liam. 'We *must* go. We must. I couldn't bear to not find out. You need to be there to see who gets married, babe.'

'Who is getting married?' says a sharp voice.

Ged jerks upright, spilling his drink.

Gah!

Like a disgruntled ghost, Birdie is floating before us. She is wearing a barely-there bikini made of two fine strips of coloured tape criss-crossing her nipples and a loose chiffon kaftan. I'll be honest, it's awful. Very in your face.

I shield my eyes from the sun. It's time to face her head-on. I'm a married woman now. It's time to start acting like one. Butterflies flit around in my stomach at the thought of being Matteo's wife. 'What are you doing here? You're not welcome. You've done every-thing you possibly can to keep me and Matteo apart.'

She has the good grace to bend her face into a shape that looks vaguely guilty. 'You're right. Sorry,' she says with absolutely no remorse whatsoever in her voice.

'Making him work all through the night just so he can't consummate his nuptials,' blurts Liam. 'Who does that?'

What did I say about keeping secrets?

'I don't know what you're talking about. I haven't seen Matteo since yesterday evening,' Birdie says snippily. 'He's obviously been too busy producing your amateur track to do what he's being actually paid to do.'

'I beg to differ,' I say, defending Matteo. 'Your client has asked if that amateur track of mine can fea-ture on his new album.'

Birdie's jaw drops to the floor. 'But... how? Why didn't Matteo tell...?'

'Perhaps because you've been treating him disrespectfully since you got here.' I fold my arms and stand up straight. I'm an inch taller than her even though I'm in bare feet and she's in high mules. 'My husband is a very talented man. He has a successful business to run, and he is *married*. So why don't you back off, stop with the emotional blackmail, and behave professionally for once?' My heart is pounding in my chest. I've never stood up to a bully like this.

As my words sink in, Birdie lifts her chin and regards me through her long lashes. *'D'accord.'*

Oh, my word. While that felt incredibly satisfying, I hope I haven't just made everything worse.

I'm too busy watching her flounce off in a huff to notice Matteo standing nearby, listening to every word. I can't tell what he's thinking. He puts his hands together to slow clap me, his eyes crinkling at the sides as he walks over. 'Glad to know you have my back.'

If only he knew how I feel about him. In this moment I'd do anything for him.

I am flooded with joy, and all I want to do is be close to him, touch him, listen to every word he has to say.

He takes my hand. 'Mind if I steal my wife away for a few minutes?'

Gah! I will never tire of hearing that.

The music is pumping out around us. 'We never did get a first dance,' he says, leading me to a small clearing.

We never got to do a lot of things.

He twirls me out and back in again so that I'm pressed up against him. Sparks shoot down to my toes as our foreheads touch. With a wide smile, he dips me backwards. I'm still wearing my tiny sequined bra top and hot pants. He must be getting a right eyeful of underboob.

'So, how's married life?' I say as we sway in time to the music. Keeping hold of my hand, he moves behind me, flicks the hair from my neck to lightly nuzzle it, before swirling me out and back in again.

We do a two-step in time, one hand on his shoulder and my other clasping his. 'So far so good,' he says dryly.

I instinctively lift my leg for him to put a hand beneath my knee and lift it to his waist. He puts his forehead to mine, yanks me closer and runs an appreciative hand down the back of my thigh. We grind gently against one another, me with my hands clamped round his neck, him with his other hand firmly round my waist. I dip backwards once more, pushing my pelvis against him. His eyes flash as I curl back up, bringing my lips to his, brushing them lightly.

'I've missed you,' he says in a low groan, tracing my cheek with his lips, trailing downwards to nuzzle my neck again. It sends electricity coursing through my veins. I can feel his breath become ragged. He wants me. He wants his wife.

I close my eyes, my head rolling backwards to give him full access. He places gentle kisses on my throat, his hands now roaming my back, pulling me towards him so that every inch of our bodies are touching. He tangles his hands in my hair and pulls my head back up, his eyes trained on my lips as he dips his head to kiss me. His every desire is unleashed as he hungrily slides his lips against mine. I wind my hands tighter into his hair, eager to match his passion.

'Get a room, you two,' Cherry says, swaying over to us. We spring apart. 'Look.' She points through the crowd to a couple cavorting on a giant inflatable flamingo. It's Sister Kevin. He is getting down on one knee. He's stretching out his hand. Tash is taking it in hers and gazing at him with a blissful look on her face.

'I think we can guess who sent the invitation then,' Cherry says.

'You got one, too?'

'Thought it might have been Mandeep, but now I'm not so sure.'

We stare as Tash and Sister Kevin lock lips on the flamingo, disappearing as they fall inside it.

Big Sue and Big Mand run towards us. 'Did you see what just happened?' Big Mand says, out of breath. 'Do you think he's proposed?'

'Looks like it. I guess we'll find out at midnight,' I say.

'You got the invitation?' Big Mand asks as we all exchange raised eyebrows.

'It's all very mysterious,' I say. 'And romantic.'

Liberty wanders over with Eddie. 'Enjoying the party?'

I am desperate to escape with Matteo and enjoy our honeymoon, but it feels too rude to slope away. I can feel Matteo tense next to me. 'Best birthday party ever, Eddie,' I gush.

'I mean, where else do you see human champagne fountains and powder paint fireworks exploding out of the DJ booth? It's awesome,' Liberty agrees, just as an explosion of silver streamers and ticker tape sprinkles down on us.

And it really is. It's a kaleidoscope of colour, noise and human sweat.

'Eddie needs to borrow Matteo for a moment,' she says. 'Something to do with business.'

I just have time to see Matteo being escorted away by Eddie. He looks back just long enough for me to catch a nervous look in his eye.

'Oh, did you receive an invite today?' Liberty says, as though she's just remembered.

I nod.

'Me too. Strange. I suppose we'll just have to go.'

'Erm, where's Eddie taking Matteo?' I say to Liberty, but she's already moved on to dancing with Cherry, who looks like she is making up for days of lost time. She has a cocktail in each hand, held up high while she gyrates to the music that is pumping out. They are magnets to a swarm of men in skimpy thongs.

'They certainly know how to get an all-over tan here,' says Ged, sidling up to me. 'Where's your new hubby gone?' He takes in my disappointed expression. 'Not work again? Seriously? This is getting ridiculous.'

I am starting to agree with him.

'I'm sure he'll come straight back,' he backtracks. 'He adores you.'

'It's almost time for the birthday firework display and light show!' yells Liberty. 'Come on. Then we need to get changed for this chapel thing at midnight.'

'Well, Liam and I need at least an hour to chill first. Will we all meet at the love sign and go together?' he says, before dashing off.

'I guess so,' I say, losing everyone in the crowd. Suddenly, I'm no longer in the mood to dance.

30

After a Disney-style fireworks display, the whole place is ablaze with twinkling lights and the party is showing no signs of slowing down, even though it's very late. I've taken myself off to Ged's cabana because it's empty and I need to message Luke to tell him that his life is no longer in danger and that it never was and that he should carry on with his life as planned because it was all simply a horrendous case of mistaken identity. I'm sure he'll see the funny side eventually. I've just pressed send when Cherry, a veritable sweaty mess, grabs my arm. 'I'm going to go get ready. I've only got half an hour to get changed.'

I check the time. 'Where is everyone?'

'God knows,' she says. 'Can you remember what floor we are on?'

'I'll come with you. Hopefully, Matteo will be in the room.' I haven't had any messages, and I haven't messaged him because I don't want him to think I'm clingy, now that we are married. We battle through the crowds. There must be at least three thousand people here. Bumping up against each other, grinding away, arms flung around shoulders, swaying this way and that, two-stepping on tables as the DJ creates different moods with a selection of brilliant tunes. We reach the patio area, and the emptiness of the lift is a nice relief.

As we make our way along the corridors, Cherry clings to my arm. 'This has been a life-changing trip.'

'It certainly has.'

'I've realised how much I love my family,' says Cherry unexpectedly as we walk along.

Must have been when she gambled their house away and won it back a few minutes later.

'I've also realised how much I love my friends,' she says, stopping to look at me. 'Thank you, Connie.'

We share a moment of deep emotional connection. I've seen every side of her over the last few days. Some of the sides were not pretty.

Cherry's soft expression is short-lived. 'Don't you dare tell anyone I said that. And by the way...' She rummages in her bag and pulls out a wad of notes. 'That's to pay off your credit card.'

'Are you sure?'

'Of course.' She gives me one of those rare smiles that reaches her eyes, and she bleeps the key card against her door to unlock it.

'I love you, too, my friend.' As soon as the words leave my mouth, a visceral feeling sweeps over me. It feels awkward in a way. As though the words have been stuck inside me, gathering dust. That's when I remember why.

* * *

As I continue along towards my room, I realise that I haven't spoken those words since my mother died. I told her that I loved her, and she basically died in my arms. I've never been able to say those words since.

I need to tell Matteo that I love him. I speed up and rush into the room, half expecting Matteo to be there. Instead, I get a text from him. It says he is running late and will meet me at the love sign. A wave of disappointment floods through me.

Where is my husband?

I check the time. I will jump in the shower, make sure I smell divine and quickly throw on some clothes. As I'm putting the finishing touches to my barely-there make-up and dragging a brush through my hair, there's a knock on the door.

Cherry is standing outside. 'I can't find anyone. So, I thought we might as well go together, seeing as...' She stops speaking. 'Connie, you look gorgeous, pet. Absolutely gorgeous.'

I immediately blush at the compliment. I've only had time to do a flick of mascara and throw on a knee-length summer dress I found at the bottom of the suitcase.

'Here, let me finish your hair for you.'

By hair, Cherry means a full face and an updo. She spends ten minutes swishing brushes over my face, fiddling with my eyebrows and talking about her children as she takes clips from between her lips and digs them into my scalp.

'The oldest one insists on a French plait every day for nursery. Even though I've told her she doesn't have the right face shape for it.' She chuckles to herself. 'But being a mother is nice, I suppose.' Cherry has a peaceful, faraway look on her face as she lifts and backcombs strands of my hair. 'I'm going to try and spend more time with them when I get back.' She sprays a whole can of hairspray over me. 'There you go. It'll take a hurricane to budge that.'

Cherry has transformed me into an elegant version of myself. She has given me a gentle smoky eye, full plum-coloured lips in matte and lashings of mascara. Tendrils of hair frame my face while my thick hair has been swept up into a stylish knot.

'I'm afraid the hair has upped the game dress-wise,' she says, inspecting her handiwork. She marches over to the wardrobe and yanks the door open. 'Oh. My. God. What's this?' she says, pulling it from the hanger. 'Put it on immediately.'

'It's my wedding night underwear,' I say, my voice tinged with regret. 'He didn't even get to see me in it properly.'

'Well, he will tonight.' Cherry flicks through the few clothes I have hanging up and grimaces before settling on a floral blue shift dress and flings it over to me. 'That'll have to do.'

I slide into my wedding underwear easily. I'm not even sure I've eaten today. The shift dress hangs off me too.

'Come on,' she says. 'We don't want to be late, or Tash will never forgive us.'

'I can't believe they're getting married,' I say, feeling genuinely excited for them. 'I hope she knows what she's doing.'

Cherry stops in the doorway to raise an eyebrow at me.

Hah! Fair enough.

A small burst of laughter escapes my lips. 'Point taken.'

We scurry down the corridors, busy with people. Considering it is almost midnight, most of them look like they are just beginning their evenings rather than going to bed. As we get out of the lift, Cherry checks her phone. 'Shite. We're late. They've gone without us.'

'Oh, no!'

'Not to worry,' she says. 'We'll jump in a cab.'

'But Matteo is meeting me at the love sign.'

I can't miss another opportunity to be with him. I'm supposed to be flying back home tomorrow and I've barely seen him. Tears prick my eyes.

'He's gone with the others. They've said to hurry up,' Cherry booms, half dragging me outside. Luckily, there's a taxi waiting at the entrance and Cherry wastes no time.

'Take us to The Little White Wedding Chapel. The one where all the celebrities get married,' Cherry says. 'Typical of Tash to want to get married there. She'll be hoping for a passing Kardashian.'

'I'm so happy for her,' I say as Cherry squeezes my hand.

'Yeah, me too. I hope Sister Kevin appreciates all that she is. I hope they end up as happy as you and Matteo seem to be.'

At the mention of his name, my heart swells. There's a fluttering in my stomach as a feeling of emptiness grips me. 'Did Matteo definitely say he went on ahead with the others? Because it seems a bit out of character.'

'Why do you sound so nervous? You guys are happy, right?'

'Yes. Yes, we are. It's just...'

Cherry squeezes my hand, her expression full of empathy.

'It's just I haven't had the chance to tell him I love him. With all of the chaos on our wedding day, then Birdie stealing him away, then Eddie and the party... I've had no time to tell him how I really feel.'

Cherry smiles at me. 'Then tell him now.'

It's a few seconds before I realise we have arrived at the chapel. I lean over to pay but the driver says, 'It's prepaid, ma'am.'

'Okay, well, thank you.'

We clamber out to find Liberty is waiting in the vestibule. 'Hurry,' she says, waving us in. 'You're late. Everyone is inside.'

'Is Tash here?' I ask.

'Yes, she's inside.'

'Inside? At the altar already?'

She shakes her head.

'Then who's getting married?' I ask.

Liberty smiles and hands me a big bag. 'You are.'

Oh, my word.

Liberty and Cherry unzip the bag and carefully unfold my pristine wedding dress. While Liberty yanks my baggy shift dress from my body, Cherry is pinning flowers and a tiara in my hair.

'You all knew?'

'Uh-huh,' Cherry mumbles, her mouth full of clips.

'But the invite? None of us knew who it was for.' My mind is spinning. 'Unless... Matteo organised... while I was busy... and you all pretended...'

'Yes, Sherlock.' Cherry spins me round to do the back of my hair. 'We all deserve Oscars. Now, hold still.'

They were all in on it. All of them. No wonder

they were so keen to get me here. I draw in deep breaths as the magnitude of what is happening unfolds. I feel incredibly blessed to be surrounded by such amazing people. I love them. I absolutely, totally and completely love them.

'Okay, Mrs Grande. It's time for you to renew your wedding vows.' Liberty and Cherry help ease me into my wedding dress, smoothing it down and deftly buttoning up the back. They step back to admire their handiwork. 'Stunning. Simply stunning.'

Cherry roots around in her bag and pulls out an iPad. She fiddles with it while I stand in a daze. 'Just one more thing. Smile for the camera.'

'Is this really happening?' I ask. 'Oh my God, Dad!' I squeal as his lovely, kind face appears on the screen. I can tell he has been crying. His voice is croaky and his eyes are puffy. It immediately sets me off.

'No,' warns Cherry. 'All the happy tears can wait until after the ceremony. See you in there.' She leans over, says, 'Hi, Mr C,' to my dad, and gives me a kiss on the cheek. She disappears through a heavy wooden door.

'What's going on?' I ask him.

He chuckles. 'I could ask you the same thing.'

'I'm so sorry I'm doing this without you,' I gush. 'It all happened by accident.'

'Hey, hey. Connie, love, Matteo has explained everything. I'm very happy for you.'

'You've spoken to Matteo?'

This is getting more bizarre by the second. They've never even met. I've never even mentioned him.

My dad smiles. 'I really like him.'

An overwhelming feeling of gratitude floods my body. I feel my shoulders drop as the tension eases from me.

'You look beautiful, darling. Your mother would be so proud of you. And I can't wait to meet your new husband in real life. She would have loved him. I think you'll both be very happy together.'

'I can't believe you're not disappointed in me.'

His eyes fill with tears. 'How could I be? Look at you. Bursting with joy. You're full of life and love and adventure. Your mother would have totally approved. In fact, I'm sure she's with you right now, giving you her blessing.'

'I love you, Dad.'

'I love you too, sweetheart. See you soon.'

After he ends the call, Liberty takes the iPad from me. 'Ready?'

I take in a deep, calming breath. 'Ready.'

The doors sweep open, thanks to Ged and Liam. I take in the chapel, adorned with swathes of white fabric, green and white flowers tumbling from the huge arch, which stretches over a golden table, laden with an open Bible and a golden vase overflowing with the same beautiful flowers. It is floor-to-ceiling white, only the stained-glass windows either side adding a splash of colour. My best friends take an arm each as Liberty scuttles to the top of the aisle. They are dressed in white suits with matching flowers in the buttonholes.

How is this possible?

'May we?' says Ged, tenderly. Liam has already broken the seal and has tears flooding down his face. Ged hands him a tissue while I give him a hug. Liam sniffs up his tears.

'You better not cry like this when it's my turn,' Liam says, dabbing at his eyes with a wonky smile.

I let out a giggle. 'I won't. I promise.'

We all know that this is a huge lie.

The music tinkles out across the room. This time it is a classical piece. A beautiful haunting melody.

Oh, my God.

I stop to catch my breath.

This is my mother's song. My dad must have told Matteo.

My hand flies to my locket.

Deep breaths.

Deep breaths.

I blink slowly to clear away the tears and lock eyes with the person responsible. The wonderful, thoughtful, caring man that I accidentally married on a gondola two days ago.

I love him.

I absolutely love him.

I'm not sure my soul can take this much happiness. And as I walk towards him, a feeling of weightlessness envelops me as my friends gush excitedly for me. I make a quick mental note to find out why they were all hiding in Macy's. Mine is not the only love story unfolding here, I think, as I take in their happy faces.

Matteo stands a few feet away, his glossy hair just the right kind of messy. He fills out his white tux perfectly as I sweep my gaze the length of him. He has a dangerous twinkle in his eye and does a cheeky flex of his bicep just to keep things real.

He literally takes my breath away, smiling in a way that leaves me in no doubt whatsoever.

I am walking towards the greatest adventure of my life.

'Hi,' I whisper as he takes my hand and gives it a gentle squeeze.

'You okay?' he mouths. 'You want to do this?'

I have never wanted to do anything more in my entire life. This is me being reckless, courageous, fearless and vulnerable, all at the same time, and it feels overwhelmingly worth it.

I look deeply into his eyes and pull him to me. 'I love you,' I whisper in his ear. 'I will always love you.'

He stares back in mock horror. 'Are you saying we should have hired a Dolly Parton instead?' He nods towards our Elvis officiator. A different Elvis, one that comes with the church rather than the one that comes with gondolas. 'Because I think it might be too late.'

I giggle. 'Let me rephrase that then.' I look deeply into Matteo's gorgeous dark brown eyes. 'You are always on my mind. Always have been from the moment we met and always will be.'

There's a group 'aaaah' as I briefly curtsy to my lovely friends (because I've nailed it) before turning back to face my husband. I can't see how he'll top that.

'And I really can't help' – Matteo takes a deep inhale, his eyes twinkling with mischief – 'falling in love with you... Big Guy.'

* * *

MORE FROM JO LYONS

Love Ahoy, the next laugh-out-loud, feel-good read from Jo Lyons, is available to order now here: https://mybook.to/LoveAhoyBackAd

ACKNOWLEDGEMENTS

Enormous thanks to my wonderfully talented editor Francesca Best for her brilliant energy, support and advice. Thanks to the entire Boldwood team for welcoming me into the family and working so tirelessly and enthusiastically to get my books out in the world. Special thanks to copy editor Jennifer Kay Davies and proofreader Ross Dickinson for helping get it in shape and the clever Alex Allden for making the cover look fabulous.

A MASSIVE thank you to my friends Jemma and Harald who recently got married in Las Vegas and shared their happy (and enviably bonkers) experience with me over a few glasses of wine (yes, I may have plied them with some booze to get to the nitty-gritty) and also the fabulous Local Ladies – Marina Baja walking group in Albir for all their Vegas confessions!

Huge thanks as always to my wonderfully supportive family, cousins and aunties who buy my books and to all my fabulous, funny friends who inspire me with their stories over many a night out. I couldn't do any of this without my writing tribe (you know who you are) who encourage and support me every step of the way.

And lastly, thanks to my lovely readers who buy the books, leave the most joyful and amazing reviews (which I read and shed a happy tear or do a little dance) and recommend them to their friends. I am truly grateful.

ABOUT THE AUTHOR

Jo Lyons is the bestselling author of uplifting, laugh-out-loud, warm-hearted romantic comedies, and was shortlisted for the prestigious Comedy Women in Print Awards in 2021. She spent years working abroad in sunny destinations like Turkey, Spain and the south of France at a vineyard (trying her best not to drink them out of business).

Download your exclusive bonus content from Jo Lyons here:

Visit Jo's website: www.jolyonsauthor.com

Follow Jo on social media here:

- facebook.com/Jo-Lyons-Author
- x.com/JoLyons
- instagram.com/hinnywhowrites
- goodreads.com/jolyons
- tiktok.com/@jo_lyons_author
- bsky.app/profile/jolyons.bsky.social

ALSO BY JO LYONS

Standalone Novels

A Billionaire for Christmas

The Girls Series

Girls Just Want to Have Sun

Girls Gone Rogue

Girls Take Vegas

Boldwood

Boldwood Books is an award-winning fiction publishing company seeking out the best stories from around the world.

Find out more at www.boldwoodbooks.com

Join our reader community for brilliant books, competitions and offers!

Follow us
@BoldwoodBooks
@TheBoldBookClub

Sign up to our weekly deals newsletter

https://bit.ly/BoldwoodBNewsletter